LONGARM TURNED OVER, INSTANTLY AWAKE . . .

The cabin was as black as pitch, but even so, as his eyes peered up through the darkness, he became aware of her tall, naked form. She ran her finger swiftly over his face, and a moment later she was kissing him, softly at first, her lips parting his with a gentleness that was close to a caress.

Then swiftly, she slid in beside him and he felt the warmth of her long limbs next to his . . .

*Also in the LONGARM series
from Jove*

LONGARM
LONGARM ON THE BORDER
LONGARM AND THE AVENGING ANGELS
LONGARM AND THE WENDIGO
LONGARM IN THE INDIAN NATION
LONGARM AND THE LOGGERS
LONGARM AND THE HIGHGRADERS
LONGARM AND THE NESTERS
LONGARM AND THE HATCHET MEN
LONGARM AND THE MOLLY MAGUIRES
LONGARM AND THE TEXAS RANGERS
LONGARM IN LINCOLN COUNTY
LONGARM IN THE SAND HILLS
LONGARM IN LEADVILLE
LONGARM ON THE DEVIL'S TRAIL
LONGARM AND THE MOUNTIES
LONGARM AND THE BANDIT QUEEN
LONGARM ON THE YELLOWSTONE
LONGARM IN THE FOUR CORNERS
LONGARM AT ROBBER'S ROOST
LONGARM AND THE SHEEPHERDERS
LONGARM AND THE GHOST DANCERS
LONGARM AND THE TOWN TAMER

→◆→ TABOR EVANS ◆←

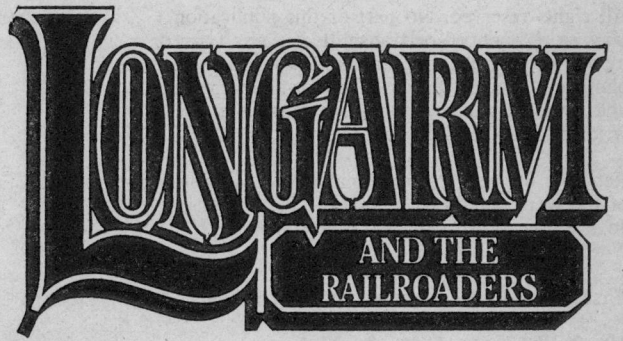

LONGARM AND THE RAILROADERS

A JOVE BOOK

Copyright © 1980 by Jove Publications, Inc.

All rights reserved. No part of this publication
may be reproduced or transmitted in any form or
by any means, electronic or mechanical, including
photocopy, recording, or any information storage
and retrieval system, without permission in
writing from the publisher.

Requests for permission to make copies of any part
of the work should be mailed to: Permissions,
Jove Publications, Inc., 200 Madison Avenue,
New York, NY 10016

First Jove edition published September 1980

10 9 8 7 6 5 4 3 2 1

Printed in the United States of America

Jove books are published by Jove Publications, Inc.,
200 Madison Avenue, New York, NY 10016

Chapter 1

Longarm stopped suddenly and turned.

Was that someone ducking back into a doorway? He squinted for a moment through the early-morning light, then shrugged and continued on. He had spent most of the previous evening in a smoke-filled room at the Windsor, cursing his cards. Fortunately, a generous and warm-hearted widow woman of his acquaintance had rescued him from his folly. Now it was the bright beginning of a new day, and he was heading for a greasy spoon he frequented on the corner of Seventh and Larimer.

Dressed in a brown tweed frock coat and pants under a snuff-brown Stetson, he loomed spookily in the dim street. He was a big man, better than six feet tall, but he moved with the silent ease of a giant cat, his strides eating up the ground faster than most men could manage at a trot. His lean, raw-boned features had been cured to a deep brown by the elements. If it were not for the gunmetal blue of his wide-set eyes and the tobacco-leaf color of his close-cropped hair, he could easily have been mistaken for an unusually tall Indian.

He reached the small restaurant and went in. The beanery was not empty. A scraggly fellow was seated on a stool in the corner. He glanced nervously up as

Longarm found himself a stool and sat down. Longarm nodded silently at the man, who promptly went back to his mug of coffee. The fellow was dressed in tattered buckskins, and Longarm could smell his sweaty fragrance from where he sat. The cook appeared from the kitchen and Longarm ordered beer and chili.

As the hot dish was placed before him, Longarm reached for the red-pepper shaker and covered his beans with the powdered fire. Soon his powerful jaws were enthusiastically masticating the chili, while his forehead broke out in tiny beads of sweat. He looked fiercely intent as he chewed thoughtfully for a while, then doused the fire with heroic gulps of beer. As he dried his drooping John L. Sullivan mustache with a swipe from the back of his hand, he belched contentedly.

The hairy fellow in the buckskins glanced over at him warily. When Longarm went back to the chili, the man relaxed some, then pushed himself a little bit back from the counter. The place was empty except for the two of them. After serving Longarm, the cook, as was his custom, had retreated back into the kitchen. The cook knew Longarm casually, but the man did not seem able to get used to the hard, sometimes mean stare from Longarm's gunmetal eyes.

Someone pushed open the beanery's door and stepped in. The man in the buckskins slid back off his stool and turned to face Longarm, whose big left hand had already slipped under the hot bowl of chili. He hurled the bowl and caught the fellow's bewhiskered face dead center; then he whirled to face the newcomer. He was a beanpole of a man with wild hair and crazed eyes. In his right hand he held a big Navy Colt.

Moving swiftly away from the counter, Longarm reached across his belt buckle and drew his double-action .44. The tall one's Navy Colt thundered. Longarm felt a stroke of air across his cheek, as light as a woman's kiss. Behind him, the scraggly fellow grunted in pain as the errant slug sent him crashing back into the wall. Crouching low, Longarm fired up at the beanpole. The round plucked away the right side of the man's face. As he staggered back against the doorjamb, he kept hold of the big Colt and fired blindly down at Longarm. But Longarm was already crabbing sideways. As the round slammed into the wooden floor at Longarm's feet, he fired up at his attacker a second time, catching him just below the belt. The man folded silently over his gun and collapsed facedown onto the floor.

Longarm spun.

The bewhiskered man was sitting on the floor, his back resting against the wall, his face smeared with scalding chili. Through bits of meat and beans, his eyes stared wildly at Longarm. There was a mean-looking belly gun in his fist. The fellow squeezed off a shot. The slug missed Longarm and splintered a section of the doorjamb. Longarm fired point-blank at the chili-smeared face. The round transformed the face into something raw and dark. The man's gleaming eyes winked out. As his belly gun dropped from his lifeless fingers, his body sagged slowly to one side.

Longarm stood up. The cook had vanished from the kitchen. Glancing through the serving window, Longarm saw an open door leading out onto the back alley. Wearily, he dropped his weapon back into his waxed, heat-hardened holster. Absently, he patted the double-barreled .44 derringer that rode snugly in the right-hand pocket of his vest. He hadn't needed it this time; the bowl of chili had served in its stead. But it was always nice to know he had that surprise ready in an emergency. In his other vest pocket he carried his Ingersoll watch, a gold-washed chain draped across his vest front, connecting it to the derringer. As the sound of pounding footsteps neared the still-open door of the beanery, he pulled out his watch and consulted it.

A little after seven. His two would-be assassins had

been out early. Longarm shook his head and dropped the watch back into his vest pocket. It was his own fault. He had been entirely too regular in his habits of late. This was the fifth morning in a row that he had come to this beanery for his breakfast. He figured it would be a good idea for him to seek out some other, less convenient place to fill his gut in the future.

A uniformed member of the Denver Police Department burst into the place and nearly fell over the sprawled body lying athwart the entrance. The copper's face was vaguely familiar. He pulled up abruptly and lowered his billy club.

"Jesus, Mary, and Joseph," the copper swore, almost reverently, as he looked down at the two men. "What a pitiful sight this early in the morning!" He glanced at Longarm and shook his head sadly. He was a large man in his forties, with a round, florid face. "It's you, is it, Longarm? I might have known. What can you tell me about these poor devils?"

"You know me, do you?"

"The whole Denver force knows you—and we're all glad you're on *our* side. These two unhappy souls were after you, were they?" As the copper said this, he bent for a quick examination of the dead man at his feet. Straightening, he looked across at the other one, but seemed in no hurry to inspect him more closely.

Without warning, three passersby crowded into the restaurant. The one in front, a Chinese, was pushed by those behind him over the crumpled body in the doorway. He almost stumbled into the copper's arms.

"Get out!" the copper cried, waving his nightstick menacingly and shoving all of them back out through the doorway. "You damned bloody heathen!"

He swung the door shut and turned again to Longarm. "Would you be knowing who they were, Longarm?"

"That long drink of water near you was stealing horses in Arizona some time ago. They called him Long Tom Luke."

"A horse thief, by God!"

"That's what he was, constable—among other things."

"But he wasn't stealing horses in here, now was he?"

"No, he wasn't," Longarm acknowledged grimly. "I stopped Long Tom in mid-career, you might say. The last time I clapped eyes on him, he was leaving the courtroom on his way to Yuma, with a mean look in his eye. Guess he busted out and came looking for me, first thing."

"And he found you, looks like. You're a lucky man, Longarm."

"Maybe so. Caught a glimpse of him in the hotel lobby last night. I wasn't sure it was him, though, not until I spotted him tailing me not too long ago. His partner over there was waiting in here for me. One look at him and I knew what was up. He had that stink a man gives off when he's fixing to kill someone."

"You're going to have to come with me, Longarm. We'll have to get your complete statement."

Longarm had expected it. With a sigh, he went back to the counter and finished his beer. Feeling a little better, he nodded to the man. "Sure thing, constable."

A little past ten that morning, still hungry and needing a shave, Longarm entered the Federal Building at the foot of Capitol Hill, climbed to the second floor, then pushed open a door marked UNITED STATES MARSHAL, FIRST DISTRICT COURT OF COLORADO. Nodding to a somewhat startled, pimple-faced clerk looking up from his typewriting machine, he made his way to an inner door and pushed on into Marshal Billy Vail's office.

To his surprise, Vail was overjoyed to see him—despite the fact that Longarm was more than two hours late. "My God!" Vail cried, pushing himself to his feet. "You're all right!"

"Sure, I'm all right. And I got all my teeth, too.

What's the problem? Can't a man be late once in a while?"

Vail slumped back into his chair, obviously relieved. Mopping his brow with a handkerchief, he reached into a desk drawer and pulled out a bottle of whiskey. Slapping it down on the desk, he placed two glasses beside it and began to pour.

"Celebration?" Longarm asked, amused at his chief's evident relief to see him whole.

"You're a lucky man, Longarm," Vail pronounced solemnly, as he handed a glass of whiskey across the desk.

"I know," Longarm admitted, taking the drink.

"No, you don't," Vail insisted. "Do you know where Wallace is right now?"

"Where?"

"At your rooming house, camped outside your door. He's been there all night. Where in tarnation *were* you last night? We been trying to get hold of you since eight o'clock."

"Why?"

Vail took a hefty belt of the whiskey, his eyes narrowing. "Ever hear of a jasper calls himself Long Tom Luke?"

"Yup. A horse thief I collared once."

"That's the one. Well, I got a telegram earlier this week from the warden at Yuma. He said Tom Luke and a buddy of his broke out a week ago. Said he thought they might be after you. Then, late yesterday, a town marshal telegraphed me, said someone spotted the two of them on a stage heading for Denver earlier in the week. Those two are in Denver right now, Longarm. A real mean pair, from what I hear, and they're looking for you."

"So you sent Wallace to warn me. I appreciate that, Billy, but—"

"Now let me finish, Longarm. I got a plan to get you out of this—an assignment just west of here. And if I were you, I wouldn't waste any time getting to it. Those two jaspers killed a guard escaping from Yuma."

"Well, first I should tell you—"

"Just listen, will you? We don't have time to sit here and palaver." He gulped down the rest of his whiskey. "You heard about Colonel Mackenzie?"

Longarm nodded. He had heard quite a bit about this tough little Indian fighter. Colonel Mackenzie had the Indians scared skinny. His tactics had defeated every tribe he campaigned against, and unlike Custer, he seldom lost a man. When a tribe got out of hand, Mackenzie made a beeline for their main camp, with his flanks guarded by sharpshooters. He'd strike while the warriors were out raiding, then round up the women and children, burn the tribe's belongings, shoot their ponies, and frog-march his prisoners to the nearest reservation. If the warriors wanted to see their squaws and children again, they were free to come in, unarmed, and make a treaty. Most of them did. The rest of the tribe he would go after with Gatling guns and fieldpieces, scorning cavalry charges as futile and good only for headlines.

"What's Mackenzie up to now?" Longarm asked.

"He's ordered the Horse Utes to those Utah reservations. So far, it looks like the tribes are moving out. But there's trouble in Horse Ute country. A railroad is being built there, and the railroad's subcontractors have reported to the Bureau of Indian Affairs that Indians have been raiding their stocks and robbing their supplies. Mackenzie says there ain't supposed to be any Horse Utes left in those mountains, but he has vowed to go in there and roust them out if he's proven wrong. And he'll do it, too."

"That could get messy," Longarm agreed.

The pudgy chief marshal mopped his bald head with a rumpled handkerchief, and nodded in agreement. It was a shame to see how much lard the chief was carrying around, Longarm reflected. Marshal Vail was a sad example of what could happen to a man who let himself be corraled by a desk job.

"I don't think it is the Utes, Billy," Longarm said. "If Mackenzie told them redskins to move out, likely as not, they did."

"Maybe. But the bureau wants you to go find out. If there *are* any Utes still operating out there, maybe you can prevent a fight. The bureau figures if any white man can get near a Ute and come back with his scalp still attached, that man's you. But what you say may be true enough. There's more than one outfit battling to build a railroad through that country."

Longarm took out a cheroot and bit off its tip. "So my job is to find out what kind of Indians are messing up the building of this here railroad. Is that it?"

"You can handle it, Longarm. Besides, Denver is not a very safe place for you right now." Vail smiled bleakly. "You don't want to let those two escaped convicts blow you clear into next week, do you?"

"Nope," Longarm admitted, striking a sulfur match on his thumbnail and lighting his cheroot. "But I'm not one bit worried about that, chief."

"Well, maybe you should be," Vail retorted, thrusting a file folder at Longarm. "Anyway, read what's in this report. There's some maps and letters and a telegram from the railroad's engineer. Ogilvy's his name. It might do you some good to look through it." As Longarm took the folder, Vail got up. "I'll send my clerk to your place, Longarm. We'll have Wallace pack your bags and bring them in here. Meanwhile, I'll see to your train tickets."

"That's sure decent of you, Billy," Longarm said, getting to his feet. "But I can pack my own bags."

"Sure you can," Vail agreed, resting his hand warmly on Longarm's shoulder. "But I wouldn't think of it. I don't want to lose one of my best men. Now you stay right in here and look through that file. We'll have you out of Denver in no time at all. And with those two escaped killers none the wiser."

"Guess you're really looking hard for those two jaspers, right, Billy?"

"Those two have been in town for close onto three days, I'm figuring. That means they've had plenty of time to stake you out and lay for you."

Longarm could not keep the smile off his face any longer. "Would you like to know where I think you might find them, Billy?"

"Why, damn your eyes!" Vail said, his eyes narrowing. "What're you trying to tell me?"

"Only what I been trying to tell you since I first walked in here."

"You know where they are?"

Longarm chewed at a corner of his mustache, and his smile became wolfish.

"*Where*, damn it!" Vail pressed.

"Try the city morgue."

"The *morgue?*" Vail's face purpled, causing his bushy black eyebrows to stand out starkly.

"That's where they were headed last time I looked, Billy."

For a moment Longarm thought Vail would burst. Then, slowly, the steam eased out of his boiler. He took a deep breath and shook his head. "Oh my," he said, chuckling softly, as he turned around and headed back to his desk. "I should've known. I just should've. All right, Longarm, tell me how you did it—and when you finish, I'll let *you* tell Wallace. He's been outside your door all night, waiting for you to get back so he could warn you. He volunteered, Longarm, and as far as I know, he's still there."

Longarm chuckled. "Asleep, more'n likely."

And Longarm was right. When he reached his room not much later, he found Wallace slumped in a wooden chair beside the door, his head leaning back against the wall, his mouth open, snoring. It was an awesome sound the man was making, but Longarm doubted that it would have been enough to protect him from Long Tom Luke's big Navy Colt.

Still, Longarm realized as he approached the deputy and shook him gently, it was the thought that counted.

The country west of Denver lifted spectacularly as it climbed toward the Continental Divide. Looking out through the window of his train, Longarm saw a series of peaks, twisting canyons, and creeks that boiled silently through narrow defiles far, far below the spidery trestles over which the coaches clacked. The land was high. It was raw. It was dangerous. As the train snaked higher and higher into the Rockies, it followed three-foot-wide tracks, clinging to cuts only inches wider than the coaches themselves. It wasn't long before Longarm decided he would feel a little more relaxed if he smoked his cheroot while not looking out the window.

Leaving the train at Leadville, Longarm rented a powerful black from the town's livery and rode north toward Redcliff, the temporary headquarters of the Rio Grande Western, where he hoped to find the line's engineer, Ogilvy. His journey took him past grotesque masses of red stone that looked as if they had been frozen in the midst of some supernatural catastrophe. Longarm made it a point not to camp too close in under their looming, intimidating presence.

When Longarm rode at last into Redcliff, he needed a bath, a shave, and food on a platter—not necessarily in that order. He left his mount in the town's livery stable, and when he saw the restaurant across the street from it, he decided the bath would just have to wait.

He had finished his meal and was on his third cup of coffee. He leaned back and noticed suddenly how empty the place had become. The restaurant had been reasonably crowded when he entered. Perhaps he should have taken that bath first. Glancing around, he saw the obese waitress who had served him standing close by a window, peering out into the street. At the same moment Longarm became aware of a rising crescendo of sound from outside the restaurant. It was a crowd sound. An angry crowd.

Longarm pushed himself away from his table and hurried to the door. Opening it, he looked out. A mob was surging around a corner and coming toward him. It had the look, the sound, the smell of a lynch mob. Longarm looked back at the waitress.

"What's going on?"

"They's goin' to hang them two train robbers, the ones they found tryin' to stop the payroll train!" Her small, mean little eyes gleamed in her bread-dough face.

"Train robbers?"

She nodded. "Ben Ogilvy caught 'em waitin' for the train in the draw. They just been tried in Wally Stanton's saloon. Now they're gonna be strung up, looks like." She looked as if she could taste what was coming. And liked it.

Ben Ogilvy. That would be the chief engineer of the Rio Grande Western, the man he had come to Redcliff to see. Longarm pulled his Stetson down snugly and started from the restaurant.

"Hey, mister!" the waitress called sharply. "You ain't goin' nowheres till you pay for your meal!"

Longarm turned around impatiently. "How much?" he asked her.

She considered for a moment, her eyes greedy. "Seventy-five cents."

Astounded at the outrageous sum, but in too much of a hurry to argue, Longarm dug into his pockets for the change and tossed it to her.

The mob had reached the stable by the time Longarm caught up to it. The narrow street was solid with shouting, happy spectators. The show was about to begin. The two train robbers, their faces pasty with terror, were being roughly herded under a beam that projected out from the stable's loft. A rope snaked up and over the beam.

"Hold it!" Longarm shouted, flashing his badge at the fellow who was obviously in charge. "My name is Custis Long. I'm a deputy U.S. marshal. What the hell do you think you're doing here?"

Annoyed, the fellow frowned angrily about him. "Hey! Look at this! We got ourselves a federal lawman! He wants to know what the hell we're doin'!"

The crowd roared angrily and surged closer. "Show him!" someone at the rear cried. At once, a ragged chorus seconded that suggestion.

"Hang the two sons of bitches!" cried one loudmouth.

The fellow in charge turned to Longarm. "There's your answer, Marshal. We're hanging these men after a fair trial. You'd do well to stand aside. This is true Western justice!"

"Just who the hell are you, mister?"

"I'm Ben Ogilvy. I work for the Rio Grande Western."

"I've come a ways to see you, but after listening to that bullshit about Western justice, I'm wondering why."

"Now listen here, Marshal. These men demand action, and they've charged me to see to it."

The engineer was a tall, slim fellow with sandy hair and mustache and clear blue eyes. He had on a heavy sheepskin jacket and thick denim pants tucked into high boots, and wore his wide-brimmed hat with the brim turned down. He was so youthfully eager for this job of hangman that he would not understand what he had done until he glanced up a moment from now and saw his handiwork. Longarm was determined to save him from that moment, and to rescue the two alleged robbers from "Western justice."

"I'm taking these men from you, Ogilvy. These two

men will have to be bound over for the grand jury and tried in a circuit court. *That's* justice, Western or otherwise."

"We're not going to wait that long, mister!" shouted someone striding through the mob toward Longarm.

The tall lawman turned to face this newcomer. The fellow looked like an Eastern executive visiting the frontier. He was wearing a suit of black corduroy, with a heavy gold watch chain looped across his vest. A dapper string tie was knotted at the neck of his white shirt, and a straw boater was perched jauntily on his head. Curling from beneath the hat were strands of light brown hair that matched the neatly trimmed Vandyke gracing his chin. He looked like a genial Mephistopheles.

"And who might you be?" Longarm asked wearily.

"Walter Stanton," the fellow replied. "I own The Miner's Hole just around the corner. You're welcome to enjoy its pleasures as soon as you let our crude but effective justice take its course."

"I can't allow that."

"This man's a deputy U.S. marshal," Ogilvy told the newcomer.

Stanton frowned unhappily at Longarm. "But we've already had a trial, Marshal. Why in tarnation do you want to protect these men? Ben here found them crouched beside the tracks they had blocked this morning. They were armed. And not ten minutes ago they admitted they were planning to stop and rob the line's payroll train."

"I don't want to protect *them*," Longarm explained patiently. "It's the fellows like you and this tenderfoot Ogilvy I'm trying to protect. You've got a queer notion of Western justice. You hang these men, and you'll likely hang soon after."

"You mean you'll take us in?"

Longarm smiled coldly. "That's right, since you two seem to be the masters of ceremonies around here."

Ogilvy appeared to sag. He turned to Stanton. "Hell," he said, "maybe this lawman is right, at that."

"Hey!" someone in the crowd yelled. "Let's go! String 'em up!"

More cries followed. A general uproar ensued as the crowd began to surge still closer. The two would-be train robbers began to cower visibly. Having heard what Longarm had told Ogilvy and Stanton, they made an effort to move closer to him. Stanton turned to face the crowd and held up both hands for silence. The shouting gradually died as the sullen crowd waited to hear what the saloon owner had to say.

"This here's a deputy U.S. marshal!" Stanton told the mob. "He says we can't hang these two! He says it ain't legal!"

"Hang him too!" someone shouted.

Shouts of agreement followed that suggestion. The crowd edged yet closer. The faces nearest to Longarm were distorted with rage and the lust for blood. They had come to witness a hanging, and were not about to be cheated of this entertainment by a lone lawman. Longarm saw beads of sweat standing out on the two wretches' foreheads as they made a feeble effort to crowd themselves still closer to the tall deputy. But the nooses had already been dropped over their heads and both men had their hands tied securely behind their backs.

The shouting from the crowd grew more vicious. The angry faces surged even closer. Longarm found himself debating the wisdom of unholstering his Colt. Perhaps a warning shot over their heads would settle them down. But it was the sound of pounding hooves that stopped the crowd. Glancing down the street, Longarm saw a rider lashing his lathered mount toward them. As the man rode, he was shouting something.

"It's O'Leary!" someone cried.

The crowd broke toward the oncoming rider. As the horseman reached the mob's outer fringes, he flung himself from his exhausted horse and pushed through the crowd toward Ogilvy, his eyes wild.

"Ogilvy!" he cried. "They've got Molly!"

"What do you mean, Mike?" demanded the tall engineer. "*Who's* got her?"

"The other two train robbers! They were already on the train!"

The sensational news passed swiftly through the crowd. The mob broke up into excited, jabbering groups, then crowded about O'Leary as the man told his story. It seemed that as soon as the two confederates of the men now waiting to be hung had learned that their plan to rob the payroll car had gone awry, they had hijacked the train and were now holding Molly as a hostage to ensure their safe passage. Molly—and this Longarm found difficult to believe—was not only O'Leary's daughter; she had been in the baggage car, guarding the payroll.

"We can still reach the train and stop it at Shoshone Pass," Mike told Ogilvy, as he finished up. "But if they get by us there, we'll never catch them!"

Ogilvy nodded. "Let's go, then!"

The engineer called out to four or five men in the crowd. These worthies immediately hurried off with Ogilvy and O'Leary, while the rest of the lynch mob, its remaining members talking excitedly among themselves, headed for the nearest saloon.

Longarm turned to Stanton. "I don't understand much of this," he told the saloon owner. "What in blazes is a woman doing guarding a payroll?"

Stanton smiled ruefully. "That was Molly's idea, Marshal. Once that crazy girl gets a notion, there's not much any of us can do to shake it loose. And that includes poor Mike. She's just as stubborn as her father, and that's a fact." He shook his head in wonderment. "Of course, maybe that's a good thing. O'Leary's the man who's building us a railroad. No one but a pair as stubborn as those two O'Learys would even try to build a railroad through this high country. And we need that line."

Mike O'Leary and Ogilvy, plus the five riders they had enlisted, were mounted on fresh horses by this time and were now riding out of town. Longarm watched them gallop out for a moment, then turned back to Stanton.

"I've got a job for you," he told the man. "I'm deputizing you to take care of these two prisoners. You'll be responsible for their safety. Anything happens to them, I'm coming after you. Personally."

"Hell, Marshal! We don't even have a jail in this town. Where do you propose I keep them?"

"You don't have a jail?"

"Nor a town marshal."

Longarm shook his head. "You mean this is the first trouble you've ever had in this here town?"

"I mean nothing of the sort. We have never needed a jail before this, because we had swifter remedies. Hot lead, a boot in the ass on a few occasions, and once in a while a quick rope took care of any troublemakers."

" 'Western justice,' huh?"

"You may scoff. But that is precisely what it is."

"Well, not this time," Longarm commented grimly. "Use a back room of that saloon of yours, and assign a couple of men to stand guard."

"My saloon?"

"That's right. It just might make you and the rest of the town fathers elect a town marshal and then build a jail. Most civilized communities have them, you know. It's the price of civilization, you might say."

"Civilization!" the man spat. "A tuxedo on a Barbary ape!"

"Maybe we'll argue that point someday over a glass of Maryland rye, Stanton, but right now I'm holding you responsible for the safety of these two men."

Glancing at them as he spoke, Longarm noticed their sallow faces and shadowed eyes. He thought he caught a malignant gleam in both pairs of eyes and felt a cold chill run up his spine.

"You know what, Marshal?" Stanton said.

Longarm waited.

"If those other two train robbers do any harm to Molly O'Leary, it'll take a lot more than a single deputy U.S. marshal to keep these two here from swinging."

"I've already thought of that," Longarm replied. "That's why I reckon I'd better go along to see what I can do to keep that from happening. But right now, Stanton, I'd purely appreciate it if you'd hustle these two sorry-looking blackguards out of sight."

As Stanton turned to the two would-be train robbers, Longarm cut through the remaining few onlookers, on his way to the livery. He needed a fresh mount if he was going to overtake Mike O'Leary and his gang before they reached Shoshone Pass. Maybe he could keep them from making matters worse—not only for those two men Longarm had just saved from the rope, but also for a very stubborn young lady they called Molly.

Chapter 2

Longarm caught up to the riders well outside of town. When he pulled up beside O'Leary and beckoned to him to hold up, he could see that the distraught man did not take kindly to his plea.

"Damn it!" the man cried, as he sawed back on his reins. "Who the hell asked you to butt in?"

Longarm smiled and nudged his hat back off his forehead. He understood the man's desperation and took no offense. "I'm just interested in helping out, that's all," he said easily. "You say your daughter is a hostage inside the baggage car?"

"Yes, damn it! That's what I said!"

"Is the entire train running, or just the engine and the baggage car?"

"The engine and baggage car."

"How are you going to stop the train?"

"What the hell . . . ?" O'Leary looked around at Ogilvy. "Now just who *is* this fellow?"

"He's a deputy U.S. marshal," Ogilvy told him.

O'Leary looked back at Longarm. "Molly's in the baggage car with one of them. The other bank robber is up with the engineer and the fireman. We'll slow the train down with some ties, damn it! Then we'll board her and take those two!"

"That sounds pretty dangerous."

"Dangerous?"

"To your daughter. To Molly."

"I know what I'm doing, mister! And Molly knows how to take care of herself in an emergency. Now let's stop all this fool palaver. We've got to block them tracks!"

With that, O'Leary clapped spurs to his mount and bolted down the trail ahead of them. Ogilvy and the others spurred swiftly after him, Longarm following. As he rode ahead, Ogilvy glanced back at Longarm as if to say there was little any of them could do to hold O'Leary back or change his plans.

The ride to Shoshone Pass gave Longarm still one more taste of this rugged land's almost impassable terrain. They thundered through narrow, twisting canyons, forded swift streams with the water tugging at Longarm's heels, then scrambled up steep slopes, the detritus and shale treacherous under their horses' scrambling hooves. How this engineer, Ogilvy, could build a railroad through such land was a wonder to Longarm.

At last the eight riders pulled up on a ridge overlooking Shoshone Pass. Ogilvy had constructed a long trestle to lift the tracks smoothly through the pass. There was a point where the freshly laid tracks ran close in under an overhanging shelf of rock, Longarm noticed. O'Leary, however, was pointing to a spot on the track well before the trestle, where the tracks passed close by a canyon wall.

"We can block the tracks down there!" O'Leary cried. "Let's go!"

The men clattered off, O'Leary well in front. But as soon as they disappeared beyond the ridge, Longarm pulled up and changed his direction, heading toward the pass and the rocky overhang he had noticed. He rode as far as he could, then dismounted, untied a coil of rope from his saddle, and began to angle down the slope toward the pass directly below him.

He was a few hundred feet above the ledge when he heard a dim cry from the narrow trail far below him and saw the others riding frantically toward the tracks. They were strung out in a line. As Longarm watched, the train emerged from the canyon. It was moving at top speed. Great black plumes of smoke were belching from its conical stack. Longarm heard shots and saw a few of the riders firing fruitlessly at the oncoming train. There was answering fire from the baggage car and from the engine. One of the riders toppled from his horse. And then the little train had thundered past them, lifting onto the trestle, heading toward Longarm.

He scrambled on down the slope, found himself about ten feet above the ledge, and jumped. He landed hard and rolled forward onto his hands and knees, almost losing the rope. He scrambled back up onto his feet and glanced over the ledge. The train was thundering up the long trestle, its pounding engine causing the walls of rock on both sides of Longarm to echo powerfully. He poised himself carefully and waited for the engine to pass under him. He closed his eyes to protect them from the smoke and cinders, then opened them to glimpse the tender passing beneath him. When he saw the coupling, he stepped off the ledge and dropped to the top of the baggage car, his knees bent slightly to cushion the shock of his landing.

The narrow wooden catwalk snapped under his weight. He felt himself begin to pitch sideways off the swaying roof, and threw himself down and clung to the walkway. As the train rocked through the pass, he pulled himself to a sitting position. He had lost his hat, but not the rope. He glanced past the tender at the engine. So far, the single outlaw in the engineer's cab had not seen him.

Swiftly, he looped the rope around the chimney venting the baggage car's stove, and flung himself out over the side. His heels scraped against the car's siding. He dug his fingers into the rope, then flexed his knees powerfully and pushed himself away from the car. Heels first, he swung back to it and crashed through one of the narrow windows.

Releasing the rope, he landed on his hands and knees on the floor of the baggage car. He skidded over the shards of glass and fragments of wood from the window frame. A girl was screaming from a corner at the other end of the car. Longarm reached across his belly for his Colt. A cannon went off behind him and a blast of heat seared his cheek. He flung himself around and fired up at a dark figure crouched over him.

The fellow did not go down. Longarm squeezed off two more shots. Each round slammed into the wavering body. Crabbing sideways, Longarm saw the man's slight frame buck convulsively with each slug's impact—then crumple like an empty potato sack. The screaming girl was suddenly silent. Longarm straightened up and glanced at her. She was still huddled in the corner of the car, but she had stuck her fist into her mouth. Eyes wide, she straightened slowly.

"You . . . you killed him," she said, her fist dropping from her mouth.

"Reckon so, ma'am."

"Who are you?"

"Custis Long," he told her. "And I guess you'd be Molly."

"Yes," she said, her voice hushed.

Longarm bent beside the fallen train robber. He was lying facedown, a large Walker Colt in his gnarled fist. He stank of sweat and death. Longarm looked up at Molly, who was moving cautiously closer, her wide eyes still on the fallen man.

"Better not come any closer," Longarm told her, standing up and holstering his Colt. "It don't smell so good and it don't look very pretty."

She looked at him and halted. "He heard you up there and was waiting. He was right behind you when he shot. How did he miss you?"

"I was lucky. And he was a mite nervous."

She looked at him with something approaching awe. "Yes," she said softly. "I suppose that's it."

Molly O'Leary was dressed in a man's red-checked cotton shirt and Levi's, with her pants legs stuffed into the tops of her high boots. She wore no hat, and her thick auburn hair was cut short enough to keep it from reaching her shoulders. Her face was a pale oval out of which peered wide, luminous brown eyes. Her nose was a pert button, her lips full, her chin round and dimpled. She could not have been more than twenty, and her already mature breasts swelled provocatively against the buttons of her shirt.

She saw the way he looked at her, and blushed. Longarm frowned, aware that it would do him no good to apologize for the direction of his thoughts, so clearly mirrored in his appraisal of her. He would just have to ignore it and tend to the business at hand.

"One down," he told her, "one more to go."

She nodded, looking toward the engine.

"That one out there is the worst of the two," she told Longarm. "This one you killed made him stay out there with the engineer." She moistened her lips nervously and glanced quickly away from Longarm. "He did it to prevent that other one from mauling me." She shuddered. "He is an animal."

Longarm did not comment. He walked to the door leading from the baggage car to the tender. As he pulled it open, he turned to Molly. "Stay back here, Molly. I'll handle this."

Longarm stepped out onto the narrow platform that swayed over the coupling and pulled the door shut behind him. The tender was piled high with freshly cut wood. He pulled himself up onto the uneven pile and began to clamber carefully over the load toward the engineer's cab. Careful not to dislodge any of the logs and alert his quarry, Longarm eventually found himself peering over a fragrant chunk of pine at the backs of the three men in the cab.

The engineer was sitting with his hand on the throttle. Across from him was the fireman, resting momentarily. Behind both of them stood the remaining train robber, his sixgun out and trained on both men. There was no talking among them. The chuffing of the small but powerful engine and the pounding of its flanged wheels on the narrow track created too much of a racket for any kind of conversation. Longarm decided to keep his Colt holstered. With the way the engine was swaying, he did not want to risk a shot. There was too great a likelihood that he might hit either the fireman or the engineer.

He pulled himself into a crouch and was about to jump down into the cab when the engineer leaned over and yelled something to the fireman, who instantly yanked open the firebox's door and turned to pull down some fresh wood. At sight of Longarm, he froze. Noticing the fireman's hesitation, the gunman spun swiftly, caught sight of Longarm, and fired from his hip.

The round missed. Longarm ducked back and lost his footing on the shifting pile of wood. He was reaching for his holstered Colt when he saw Molly. Leaning past him, she flung a heavy piece of firewood at the gunman. There was a dim cry, followed by a metallic clatter. Longarm looked down and saw the fellow down on one knee, holding onto his shattered right wrist, his gun spinning into a corner. Longarm jumped down beside the gunman just as the man regained his feet and spun frantically away toward the tender.

He was too fast for Longarm—and for his own good.

Sweeping around a curve, the train rocked abruptly. The centrifugal force caught at the train robber. He tried to grab the handrail, but was already in space. Screaming, he dropped out of sight. Longarm leaned out of the cab and saw the gunman's limp body bouncing out of sight beyond a ridge far below. The train swept around another sharp bend and Longarm pulled himself back into the cab and motioned to the engineer to slow down. At once the engineer nodded and began pulling levers.

Longarm glanced back at Molly. She was still on her knees atop the firewood, a wide-eyed, frightened look on her face as she looked down at Longarm. He smiled at her. For the first time, Longarm realized, Molly O'Leary was becoming aware of the kind of chance she had just taken.

"Scared?" he called out to her.

She nodded. The color began to return to her face. He reached up and helped her down beside him. The train was slowing, the wheels screeching on the rails, the chuffing of the small engine increasing to an almost deafening pitch.

"Thanks," Longarm told Molly, his mouth close to her ear. "I'm right glad you didn't stay back in that baggage car like I told you. He had the drop on me."

"I hated him so much!" she yelled above the roar of escaping steam. "I wanted to see him get it!"

She leaned close against Longarm as the train came finally to a shuddering, bone-rattling stop, her arm tightening about his waist.

Colonel Ranald Mackenzie pushed his chair back and got to his feet, lifting his glass of wine as he did so and smiling down the table at Longarm. The colonel was a slim man, fine-boned. He wore no beard, only sparse sideburns. The smile that now lit his face was a bleak one, but Longarm had no doubt it was genuine.

"Ladies and gentlemen, a toast," he proclaimed in his sharp, clear voice.

At once, all present reached for their glasses, only recently filled by the two hustling servants hired by Molly and her father for this occasion. They saw at once the colonel's intent and, looking in Longarm's direction, got to their feet also.

"To Deputy U.S. Marshal Custis Long!" Mackenzie intoned, his voice ringing in the spacious dining room. "A brave man, who singlehandedly prevented the hanging of two would-be train robbers, then went on to save our lovely hostess from their benighted companions in crime. And this too, singlehandedly. My compliments, Longarm!"

The colonel drank his wine as did the others, all of them smiling broadly at the discomfited lawman. Longarm could not be sure, but he was almost certain that his face had gone darkly red. He nodded swiftly about the table, started to mumble something in reply, then thought better of it and grabbed for his own drink.

Obviously sensing Longarm's embarrassment, Molly stayed on her feet when the rest of her dinner guests sat down. Her dark eyes agleam, she addressed them: "Perhaps now would be a good time for our guests to adjourn to the parlor. The men may smoke all they want in there, and the women may smoke also, if they've a mind to."

"Really!" laughed a buxon lady sitting beside her husband.

The sound of chairs scraping on the floor filled the room. Above the hubbub of sudden, animated conversation, Longarm heard his name called quietly. He looked over the heads of the guests and saw Colonel Mackenzie beckoning to him. Longarm nodded, strode through the crush, and joined the colonel in the parlor.

"I am sure I am responsible for that blush, Longarm," the colonel said. "I beg your pardon. But I felt that toast was in order."

"Maybe," said Longarm. "But I hope that's the last time it happens to me." As he spoke, he handed the colonel a cheroot, then lit himself one.

Longarm could not help noticing Mackenzie's left hand. It was more a claw than a hand, and the diminutive army colonel kept it tucked casually behind his back as he smoked. Longarm knew little about the man's hand beyond the fact that the wound which had crippled it was only one of six wounds the colonel had received in the War before his twenty-fifth birthday. Because of the maiming, his Indian foes had long since taken to calling the colonel Bad Hand.

"I think the trouble you have been sent here to clean up is not the work of Ute Indians," Colonel Mackenzie said. "My men and I have scoured the mountains around here. The Utes have cleared out, as I suggested to them earlier." The man's smile was barely perceptible.

"Got any suspicions, Colonel?" Longarm asked.

"White Indians. Spoilers. Hardcases. Perhaps Otto Pears is bending a few rules in his haste to get to Eagle Pass before Mike O'Leary and his Rio Grande Western. They look friendly enough right now, I admit. But that is one fierce rivalry."

Longarm followed Mackenzie's glance and picked out the short, stocky Otto Pears and his equally large wife. The man had her furnished with the very best, however. She resembled a porcine Christmas tree, with all the jewels and necklaces he had hung on her. Her hair was done up in tight, blonde curls, and she had slightly rouged cupid's-bow lips. Her name was Mabel, and as Longarm glanced at her, she caught his eye and her face lit up like a railroad fusee.

"Oh oh," said Mackenzie, as he saw the woman drag her husband through the crush on her way toward them.

Longarm took a deep drag on his cheroot and readied himself for the worst. This was what he got for staring. As Mabel and Otto Pears pulled up in front of them, Longarm bent himself slightly at the waist and smiled at the woman. Mackenzie was just as gallant, as he straightened to his full five feet nine and inclined his head slightly toward Mabel Pears.

"I just told Otto we simply *had* to chat with our two heroes!" she trilled.

"Thank you, ma'am," said Mackenzie. "That is very kind of you."

"Not at all, not at all," said Otto Pears. He smiled benignly at both of them and seemed to extend his huge belly out an inch more at least. His face was ruddy, his mustache and sidewhiskers white. Though he smiled often and was smiling now, his eyes, small and somewhat beady, remained cold. "I am especially interested in how you managed to get the Utes out of here without a full-scale war!"

"Yes, Colonel!" cried Mabel, eyes glittering. "Just how did you do it?"

The colonel looked uncomfortably at the woman for a moment, then waved his cheroot negligently. "I told them to leave," he said. "They saw the futility of arguing with me, and left."

"You make it sound so simple," said Otto Pears, laughing.

The colonel shrugged. He was not enjoying the conversation and Longarm wished there were something he could do to rescue the man, but Mrs. Pears was relentless.

"It wasn't that simple, Colonel, was it?" she insisted. "You must tell me how you did it! I want all the details."

By that time Mabel Pears' strident voice had carried far enough to bring the rest of the dinner guests flocking around. Mackenzie's face went cold, his eyes flinty, as he composed his reply. Puffing a couple of times on his cheroot, he then removed it from his mouth and looked bleakly at the well-powdered woman.

"As I said, Mrs. Pears," he began, his voice low, ominous. "I simply rode into the Ute camp and advised the chieftains they would have to leave Colorado or fight me. When they began to argue this among themselves, I told them they would have ten minutes and no longer to make up their minds. This astonished them, but in that time twenty of the principal Ute leaders told me they would leave Colorado."

"And what would you have done if they had not agreed to leave?" the woman persisted.

"We would have fought them, ma'am."

Mabel Pears' eyes were glittering more brightly now, it seemed to Longarm, than the diamonds resting on her full bosom. "Details, Colonel. Please!"

"Shall I tell you the details of our attack on Dull Knife's camp, Mrs. Pears?"

The woman nodded eagerly as the rest of the guests moved still closer, so as not to miss a word. Longarm could see the anger just below Mackenzie's civil tone, and knew that the man was prepared to let loose both barrels.

"We attacked at dawn, my troopers and our allied Shoshone braves. We killed about fifty of the hostiles, the Shoshones lifting scalps with great dexterity and sometimes without waiting to club their victims to death first. The snow was soon ribboned with blood as we set about destroying Dull Knife's camp. The Shoshones were particularly inspired that morning, ma'am, because they found necklaces among the Cheyenne lodges."

"Necklaces?" the woman asked, her voice considerably subdued.

"Yes. Necklaces that were made from Shoshone fingers and from the severed hands of Shoshone children. In one case they found the entire right arm and hand of a Shoshone woman had been fashioned into a necklace, as well. It was not a very light or very handsome bit of jewelry, you must admit, but it seemed to arouse the blood of my Shoshone allies quite considerably."

The Pears woman uttered a tiny cry and took a small step backward, but Mackenzie continued his account relentlessly: "You might say the sight of these Cheyenne artifacts sort of inspired our men. When the Shoshones and my troopers got through, the camp was a shambles, the Indians' provisions destroyed along with their horses, and Dull Knife's people scattered about the cruel, winter wilderness. Finally the survivors—deprived of food, clothing, horses, and armament—gave up the fight and straggled in to surrender to my men. Unfortunately, not a few of the young Indian babes had frozen to death by this time, and in a few cases my men had to forcibly take from the Cheyenne women their tiny, lifeless burdens."

At last Colonel Mackenzie's somber voice went silent. Toward the end of his story, Mabel Pears' face had grown steadily ashen. At mention of the frozen babes, she had closed her eyes. Now, one dimpled hand held up to her mouth, she took a hesitant step backward.

"Thank you, Colonel," she said in a tight, unsteady voice. "Most gruesome, I must say."

"Yes," Mackenzie said coldly. "War is very gruesome—when you get to the details."

Somewhat unsettled by Mackenzie's manner, Mabel Pears and the rest of the guests drifted away, and Longarm was glad to see them go. Mackenzie put his cheroot back into his mouth and chewed on it angrily.

"Who's that fellow?" Longarm asked the colonel in order to change the subject. He indicated a tall, buckskin-clad figure sipping wine with a smaller companion. "I didn't get his name when Molly introduced us earlier."

"That's Ty Flynn," Mackenzie replied. "He's the subcontractor who blew the whistle on the Utes. He insisted it was the Indians who were stealing his stock and running off with his wagons. And if Ty Flynn does not get his operation straightened out soon, Mike O'Leary's line won't be able to beat Otto Pears' Denver & Rocky Mountain to Eagle Pass. It would be all over for O'Leary then. Eagle Pass is the only way through the mountains. And the first line to reach it, has it."

Longarm shook his head in wonderment. "So O'Leary invites Otto Pears and his wife to his home for dinner. Just like they were the best of friends."

"Hell," Mackenzie said with a laugh, "they are! Those two were penniless prospectors not so long ago—before they struck it rich and decided to become railroad magnates. Where do you think Pears got that wife of his?"

"From a straw-mattress crib somewhere in these mountains," Longarm guessed, with a wry smile.

Mackenzie smiled coldly in return, and nodded. "A house in Leadville, it was. She was the madam, and ran a tight ship, the way I heard it."

"Who's the smaller fellow standing next to Ty Flynn?" Longarm asked.

"His partner. Name's Tramp Butterfield. The two have been together for years. They know this country and should have beeen able to provide O'Leary with all the ballast and ties and firewood he needed. Someone *is* sabotaging their operation, only it isn't the Utes."

"You think it's Pears?"

The colonel took the cheroot from his mouth and smiled at Longarm. "That's for you to find out, isn't it, Longarm?"

Gloomily, Longarm nodded. It was a tangle, sure enough. If it wasn't Ute renegades—and Longarm was more than willing to take Mackenzie's assessment on that point—it would have to be white renegades bent on stopping O'Leary's Rio Grande Western. And that pointed the finger directly at Otto Pears, the only man who would stand to gain if O'Leary's line was stopped.

And yet, as Longarm glanced across the room at the rotund Pears and his loud, brazen wife, who were now joking with O'Leary and a few other guests, he found it difficult to imagine such a fellow as part of a conspiracy. Difficult, but not impossible. As Longarm had long since come to realize, all was fair in love and war—and building railroads.

Molly, free of her apron, her hair freshly combed back, appeared in the doorway. She waved to her father, but when she caught sight of Longarm standing alongside the colonel, she hurried toward him, her scrubbed face beaming.

"Ah, Longarm!" she cried, as soon as she reached him, "I want you to know I heartily endorse Colonel Mackenzie's generous toast. I can still see you crashing through that baggage car window. You scared me half to death!"

Longarm smiled down at Molly. "And I can still see you, Molly, heaving a piece of firewood at that train robber. I think the colonel should have included you in that toast."

"Yes, Molly," said Mackenzie, smiling and bowing slightly toward her. "Perhaps I should have, at that."

Molly's face went scarlet. "If you had," she gasped, "I would have *died!*"

"Molly," Longarm asked, "do you suspicion that robbery try yesterday was part of the conspiracy to halt your father's line?"

Molly thought for a moment, considering the question carefully. Then she looked up at Longarm, her eyes bright with sudden insight. "Of course!" she cried. "The men were going to strike if we didn't pay them yesterday—and many were threatening to walk off the job altogether. And that's the first time they ever threatened to do anything of the kind, even though we've been late before with the payroll. The men never seemed to worry before. They knew I'd bring them the money."

"But this time was different."

"Yes. Very. This time they seemed to know something was up."

"This time," said Mackenzie, "they seemed to know there was going to be a robbery."

"Yes," agreed Molly. "I'm sure of it now. They knew!"

Longarm frowned. "First thing in the morning, I'd like to jaw some with those two train robbers we've got holed up in Stanton's saloon. Might be surprising what they could tell us." He turned to Mackenzie. "What are your plans, Colonel?"

"There's been some talk of renegade Utes on the Wyoming border. Probably just some hysterical nester who doesn't know a renegade Ute from a pine tree, but I have orders to investigate." The colonel turned to Molly. "Longarm has just reminded me that I have a long day in the saddle ahead of me, Molly. Would you extend my compliments to your father and accept my thanks for a splendid meal? I must be off."

"Of course, Colonel."

Gallantly, Colonel Mackenzie swept up Molly's hand and brushed it with his lips, after which he strode from the room. Watching him walk out, Longarm could not help noticing that the slim officer seemed to be moving with some difficulty. Longarm glanced at Molly.

"Is there anything wrong with the colonel? He walks like he's in pain."

Molly nodded, sighing. "It is only when he gets tired that it becomes so noticeable, Longarm. It is the many wounds he carries around with him, I am told. And it is a fact that he can no longer ride more than twenty-five to thirty miles without suffering considerable pain. But the man drives himself without stint, nevertheless, and refuses to baby himself. My father says he is an able and remarkable soldier, Longarm. But I am afraid he will not live to a ripe old age. Not if he stays in the army."

"He'll stay in the army," Longarm said. "It's his life."

"Yes," Molly agreed, and looked up at him. "I have been anxious to speak with you all night," she said, her face growing scarlet at the audacity of this admission.

Longarm smiled. "You wanted to talk to me, did you?" Longarm said gallantly. "Well, I've been wanting to talk to you as well, Molly. Thank you for this opportunity."

Molly laughed, delighted. "Thank *you*, Longarm. I declare, I am somewhat embarrassed at my own boldness, but now you do make it easy for me."

Before they could say anything further, there was a sudden commotion in the parlor doorway. Longarm turned and saw Wally Stanton burst into the parlor. When Stanton glimpsed Longarm, he headed quickly across the room toward him, a red-faced Mike O'Leary hot on his heels.

"Now listen here, Stanton," O'Leary cried. "You weren't invited!"

Ignoring O'Leary, Stanton halted before Longarm, a sardonic smile on his lean face. "Marshal, I did not ask you for the privilege of taking care of those two would-be train robbers—at my expense—now did I?"

"No, you didn't."

"Well, those two son of bitches are gone! They broke out of my back room less than an hour ago."

"Sorry to hear that, Stanton."

"I am too, Marshal. But not for the reason you might think."

"Oh?"

"They didn't go meekly. No sir, they didn't. They killed one of my girls who was bringing them food, and then gunned down—in cold blood—the barkeep that's been with me for five years. He was a good and true friend, and now I'm holding you responsible for his death and for the death of that girl. Had you let justice take its natural course yesterday, those two killers would be dead now, and the barkeep and that girl would still be alive."

Longarm could not see any point in commenting.

He could understand Stanton's anger, and it was difficult for him not to share it. Though the two men he had saved from the noose the day before had appeared pathetic and thoroughly cowed, apparently Longarm had misjudged them grievously—and had unwittingly brought tragedy to a couple of innocent bystanders as a result.

"I am going after them first thing in the morning," Stanton told Longarm. "I have come here to tell you that when I find them—and find them I will—I shall *not* bring them back for your justice. I will hang them on the spot!"

Stanton turned to leave.

"Stanton!" Longarm called after the man, his voice harsh.

The saloon owner halted and turned back around to face Longarm. The crowded room was hushed; all eyes were now on Longarm.

"I'll be going with you, Stanton," Longarm told the man. "We'll find those two killers together. Then maybe we'll see which kind of justice will prevail, yours or mine."

Stanton whirled and brushed through the crowd of guests. For a moment there was a tense silence, then pandemonium erupted as everyone started to talk at once. This sensational incident had done much to enliven the dinner party.

Longarm turned to Molly. "I reckon the party is over for me now," Longarm told her with a rueful smile. "And it looks like I've got me a long ride tomorrow."

She reached out and took his arm, pulling him closer. "Will I see you before you leave, Longarm?"

"Why, I'd never presume to guess the intentions of Molly O'Leary," he told her.

Gently, he disengaged her hand from his sleeve and went to take his leave of his host and the other guests.

Chapter 3

Well before the first chill rays of the morning sun broke over Redcliff, Longarm was out of bed and attending to his morning toilet, the room's single kerosene lamp burning low. He did not have a toothbrush, so he plucked his bottle of Maryland rye off the dresser, pulled the cork with his teeth, took a healthy slug, and sloshed the rye around in his mouth for a minute, then tipped his head back, gargled softly, and swallowed the rye. Then he poured tepid water from a pitcher into a basin on a nearby stand, and spiked it with some more rye. Unfolding a washcloth, he dropped it into the mixture and began rubbing himself down thoroughly from hairline to shins.

The bedsprings behind him squeaked and Longarm heard Molly's low laughter. "Now what kind of a bath is that, Longarm?"

He glanced back at her. "Thought you were asleep. Its name ain't very polite; it's called a whore's bath. Now close your eyes until I'm decent."

"I'd rather not," she said, sitting up in the bed and propping her back against the brass bedstead, tightening her arms about her drawn-up knees. "I'd just as soon watch."

"Suit yourself," Longarm replied, glaring at her in

what he thought might be an intimidating frown. But his well-trimmed, drooping longhorn mustache added a comical touch to the frown, and Molly just laughed at him, delighted.

"You can bet I *will* suit myself, you big old grouch."

With a shrug, Longarm reached for his tight, knit-cotton longjohns, sat his naked rump on the bed, and proceeded to wrestle them on. He was reaching for his brown tweed trousers when Molly yanked them out of his grasp and threw them across the room. He spun about to face her and she flung her arms about his neck and kissed him. When he tried to extricate himself from her grasp, she pulled him back down on the bed, climbed atop him, and sat imperiously on his chest, as naked as a plucked chicken, but considerably more seductive.

"Ain't you had enough, girl?" Longarm asked, grinning up at her.

"That depends."

"On what?"

"On whether or not you really have to go after those two train robbers with Stanton. Let him go. Let him hang them. Stay here and find out who's robbing my father's subcontractor. If it isn't those Indians, it's got to be Pears or someone working for him."

"Like who?"

"Like Jack Lynch, the Pinkerton who's in charge of that gang of men Pears calls his rangers."

"Rangers?"

"That's what he calls them."

"And you think he might be behind the raids on Ty Flynn's men?"

"Yes."

"Do you have any proof?"

"No."

"If I catch those two train robbers and prevent Stanton from killing them, they might give me all the proof I need. You remember? We decided earlier that that train robbery was more than likely designed to get your father's men to quit the tracks—to make them stage a walkout. I figure those two robbers might sing quite a tune next time I clap my hands on their necks."

"Oh. That's why you're going with Stanton."

"That's why."

"Then I guess you'll be gone for a while?"

Longarm shrugged. "That depends."

Molly leaned forward suddenly, her incredibly white breasts brushing his shoulders, and kissed him on the lips, working his mouth open. The kiss was designed to inflame him. It did. She pulled back and smiled down at him.

"Let's say goodbye now, then, as nicely as we can. I want you to think about me while you're riding over those trails. I don't want you to forget Molly O'Leary."

"That ain't likely, ma'am," he said, reaching up and pulling her down upon him, his lips finding hers.

His tongue was probing hungrily between her lips when she laughed and pulled herself quickly back. With surprising ease, she rolled him over onto his side, her hand thrusting boldly between his thighs. In a moment her fingers had released the buttons of his longjohns and she freed his erection. Laughing delightedly, she grasped him with a strength that almost caused him to cry out. He hugged her to him and she buried her face in the thick hair of his chest. Impatiently, he unbuttoned his longjohns completely. She began nibbling with her fine white teeth on one of his nipples, while her hand continued to close, viselike, around his erection.

Longarm was astonished. This was a different girl entirely from the quiet, cuddly kitten he had enjoyed when first she had joined him earlier that same night. But he was not complaining.

With a deep, guttural mutter of delight, he took hold of her firm buttocks and pulled her hard against him. She gasped and let go his erection. Swiftly, he rolled over onto her and probed swiftly into her warm softness. She cried out and thrust herself against him, wrapping her legs about his waist. He plunged deeply into her and gasped in pleasure. No longer the quiet, submissive maiden, Molly began turning her head rapidly from side to side, her eyes shut tight, swearing in a steady stream with a fluency that amazed him.

He lost all sense of time. The mindless rhythm of his thrusting achieved a life of its own. Soon he was hovering, with a kind of maddened frustration, on the edge of his orgasm. Then, suddenly, with a grim, wild plunge, he drove into her, driving her buttocks down hard on the bed, grinding her into it.

He felt her shudder convulsively under him. She let out a startled cry that was almost a wail of terror. The sound of it frightened him for a moment, but then shockwaves of desire swept through him and his muscles grew taut as he began to pulse completely out of control. The two of them clung together on the bed, entwined, as progressively more violent climaxes convulsed them. They grew tenaciously into each other, and became one flesh, one twisting, moaning entity. . . .

Resting his head on his palm, Longarm was smiling down into Molly's still-dazed eyes, listening to her explanation.

"You have no idea," she said, "what it has been like. I wanted to know what it was all about, so I allowed myself to be taken by this man. But he was as innocent as I was, and it was a sorry experience for both of us." She laughed softly. "So I concluded there was nothing in the experience for me to hanker after, and promptly did my best not to think about it." She stopped talking then, and lifted her face and kissed him on the lips. "Until, that is, you came along. Last night, when I saw you standing there alongside Colonel Mackenzie, I decided I ought to give it another try."

"And this time?"

She smiled warmly up at him. "I began to get some inkling of what it might be like."

"Just an inkling?"

"And then I fell asleep in your arms, and dreamt. It was a lovely dream, Longarm, and when I woke up and saw you standing there in the light of the lamp, washing your lean body with rye whiskey, I knew I was getting close."

She closed her eyes and leaned back, a happy smile on her face.

"You got close, all right," he said.

"Yes," she replied. "And then I went right on over. Now I know what the poets and songwriters have been singing about. Only they'll have to go some to equal it, I'm thinking."

Longarm smiled at Molly. "And that's what I'm thinking too."

She opened her eyes and looked at him. "Are you horrified at me?" she asked suddenly, alarm showing in her eyes.

"Horrified? Why?"

"I swore so! And I screamed. I'm sure someone must have heard us."

"If you'll forgive me for saying so, Molly, I've heard lots worse than that from women. It's something that just pops out, seems like, when the fever takes over, if you know what I mean."

She leaned back, relieved. "I know what you mean."

Longarm sat up and began buttoning his longjohns. Then he got up to retrieve the pants Molly had hurled across the room. As he wrestled on the britches, Molly sat up in the bed and watched him. She was still watching him a few moments later when, fully dressed, he took his snuff-brown Stetson from its nail on the wall, positioned it carefully on his head, dead-center and tilted slightly forward, cavalry-style, and walked back to the bed to gaze down at Molly's sweet nakedness.

"I'm leaving now, Molly. Are you sure you're going to be able to explain your absence to your father?"

"I'm sure."

"I'm glad you gave it another try."

"I am too. You be careful, hear? I don't much trust that Stanton. He's a philosopher, I hear tell. I never could abide a man who uses words too big for plain folks to understand."

"I'll be careful."

He bent, then, and kissed her softly on her lips, touched his hatbrim to her, and left the room. Before he closed the door behind him, he glanced back in at her. There was a contented smile on her face and it looked as if she were going back to sleep. He closed the door softly and moved lightly down the stairs.

Longarm let his big black gelding pick its way down the slope toward Stanton's midday camp. Stanton appeared not at all startled at the lawman's approach, as he continued messing with the coffeepot, aiming to set it firmly down on the glowing coals of his campfire. Entering the camp, Longarm reined up a few feet from Stanton.

"That coffee smells good, Stanton."

"That it does. Light and we'll both have us some pretty soon."

Longarm swung down and tied the black, half-hitching the reins carefully to the branch of a small willow. Then he hunkered down on his heels and tipped his Stetson back on his head.

"See you got your hat back all right," Stanton remarked, reaching for the pot.

After Longarm had stopped the train, he had insisted that the engineer back up until he found his hat. Only then would he allow the train's engineer to go back for the body. Word of his eccentric concern for his battered Stetson had evidently spread.

"That's right," Longarm said. "It's a little the worse

for wear, but it's a hat I'm used to, so I'd hate to lose it."

"I understand perfectly. Had a wife like that once. A little the worse for wear, she was. But I missed her something awful."

Longarm chuckled. "Can't say I ever heard a wife compared to a hat before, but I reckon you'd know more about that than I would."

Stanton handed Longarm a tin cup of steaming coffee. "Guess I would at that, Marshal, if you've never tied the knot."

"Never have," Longarm admitted as he took the coffee. "And you can call me Longarm."

"Call me Wally, then."

The saloon owner made good coffee. The top of Longarm's scalp lifted just a mite as he sipped it, a sure sign of good coffee that hasn't been boiled all the way to China and back. Longarm shifted his weight and sat back on the ground, resting his shoulders against a low boulder. Crossing his long legs before him, he studied Wally Stanton.

The man still resembled an Eastern executive eloped from Wall Street. His black corduroy suit, white shirt, and string tie were a bit dusty now, but the heavy gold watch chain still reached across his vest, and his straw hat remained canted at the same jaunty angle. For the first time, however, Longarm noted gray hairs mingling with the golden curls that stuck out from under the hat's brim, and streaks of gray in the fellow's neatly trimmed Vandyke beard. Stanton was a strange bird, all right, and it seemed more than a little odd to Longarm that he should have allowed himself to be bullied into tracking those two killers by this man—and that now the two of them should be companions in the hunt.

"You sure you don't want to go back to that saloon of yours, Stanton?" Longarm inquired. "Now that you've prodded me into chasing after these two?"

"You don't think I can handle my end, is that it, Longarm?"

"From what you told me last night, Wally," Longarm said as gently as he could, "I figure those two jaspers are as mean as rattlesnake juice. Tracking them won't be easy, and then there's always the chance we'll catch up to them."

Stanton smiled and finished his coffee. "Yes, there's always that chance, isn't there?"

"And besides, I'd about decided to go after them myself—once I figured they might know something about this here trouble O'Leary's been having with his supplies."

"That so?"

"It is."

"Well, it doesn't have to make any difference to me."

"You want them."

"That's right. I want them."

"To hang."

"That's what I told you before, isn't it?"

Longarm untangled his feet and stood up. Tossing the remains of his coffee into the fire, he headed for his horse.

"You sure are hell-bent to hang those two gents, and that's a fact." He reached for the reins and began to untie them from the willow sapling.

"And you know why that is," Stanton replied, his voice tight.

"You told me in front of a crowd, as I remember. That don't mean I have to believe it."

"No, I guess it doesn't. But that doesn't mean I have to care what you believe."

Longarm vaulted into his saddle and smiled amiably down at Stanton. "Well now, I reckon that's also a fact. I suspicion we'll just have to wait and see how this all turns out," he drawled. "Should prove mighty interesting."

"That it should," Stanton agreed.

Astride his horse, Longarm waited while Stanton broke camp.

Later that same afternoon, they reached the crest of a ridge to find a narrow valley stretched ahead of them. Longarm pulled up sharply. "Can you see them?" he asked Stanton softly.

Stanton nodded, his eyes fixed intently on the distances before them.

On a knoll well down the valley, Longarm saw movement again. He squinted and saw, briefly, two dark specks moving over the crest of the knoll. And then the two riders were gone.

"How far off are they?" Stanton asked.

"Five, six miles."

"Let's go, then!"

Longarm halted him with an upraised hand. "No point getting our bowels in an uproar. Won't do us a bit of good to kill the horses. I don't know about yours, but this black under me has already covered near thirty miles today."

"So what do we do?"

"Stop palavering and keep going and hope those sons of bitches slow down or have an accident."

That didn't satisfy Stanton, but he said nothing more as they went on down the slope at a walk.

They were halfway across the valley when Longarm glanced sidewise at his companion. "How long you been out West, Wally?"

"Five years now."

"Gold fever?"

"Lost my wife," Stanton replied matter-of-factly. "She had the consumption. It made me sick of the East, so I lit out for the wide-open spaces." He looked suddenly about him at the peaks that hemmed in the lush valley. "And that's what this land is, for sure—wide open."

"You like it?"

"Well enough. But I found out it doesn't matter where you go. Sickness, disease, and death move right along with you. Some call it civilization."

Longarm chuckled. "Never heard anyone put it that way before. But I reckon you're right."

"I'm right, damn it! Wish I weren't."

"You're angry too, ain't you?"

"You might say that."

"And you want to hang all the bad ones, all by yourself. The law acts too slow, you think. Justice should be swift and merciless."

"Of course. That's the way it is in nature. The Law of Tooth and Claw. Survival of the fittest."

"Seems like I've heard that before somewhere, back in Denver. Overheard some professor types in a hotel lobby, talking up a storm. Place was like to lift up off the ground, what with all that hot air being generated."

"It is not hot air, I assure you, Longarm. It is a fact. Charles Darwin has proven it in his book, *The Origin of Species*."

"You sound like a professor yourself," Longarm commented.

"A man doesn't have to be a member of a faculty in order to read, Longarm. Books can be purchased by anyone who has the price. I read widely. But I don't suppose you're much of a reader."

"Oh, I've been known to read a mite in my day, mostly when I'm in Denver with nothing much on my mind. But most of the time I have to read other things than books."

Stanton glanced swiftly at Longarm. His eyebrows rising a notch, he said, "Yes, I suppose you do. You'd have to, in your line of work."

"Survival of the fittest, you said. I reckon that means the devil take the unfit."

"Of course. The devil. Or nature."

"I don't get you."

"Nature, acting without rancor, with cold, ruthless precision, simply weeds out the unfit to allow the strong to survive. Only the strong *deserve* to survive. Otherwise the species will decline."

"Of course, you figure yourself among the strong, the ones with the right to survive."

"Precisely."

"What about your wife, Wally? Did she deserve to be weeded out by nature?"

The man stiffened slightly, and his face went hard. "No, she didn't deserve to die, as you say, Longarm. But it was nature's edict, not mine. She was weak, she was sick. Therefore she could not survive. And that is the way it has to be. I do not like it. But that makes no difference. Nature has no conscience. It can't allow itself that luxury."

"Hell, who says having a conscience is a luxury? I figure it's a necessity."

"For man, yes. For nature, no."

" 'The Law of Tooth and Claw,' eh?"

"Precisely."

"You sure can talk up a storm, Wally. And I don't mind that. It's purely interesting. But I hope you don't let all that book-learning get in the way of your thinking."

"On the contrary, Longarm. It will allow me to think more clearly, more decisively. It clears the mind of indecision, rubs away the cobwebs of confusion."

"You ain't confused," Longarm said, turning his head to regard Stanton squarely.

"No, I am not."

"You know what's right and what's wrong."

"Of course."

"And this here Darwin has given you all the answers."

"Not all of them, but a great many."

"Well, that's right nice," Longarm said, turning back again and fixing his gaze dead ahead. "Maybe I ought to read the fellow. I sure as hell know what the law is, but I never was too sure about right and wrong. Things get mighty confusing for me at times."

"So you just follow the law blindly."

"I'm a lawman."

Stanton shook his head. "You are an intelligent man, Longarm. But you have allowed yourself to be hoodwinked. The laws of man mean nothing. It is the laws of nature that must be respected."

"I see."

"I am afraid you don't."

Longarm chuckled. "Why, sure I do, Wally. You know what the laws of nature are, and that's the law you're going to follow, without no never-mind about man's laws. You're just like those two jaspers we're trailing. Only you figure you're stronger than they are. And that's why you're going to hang them."

Stanton frowned.

"There's only one thing, Wally."

"What's that?"

"Suppose they're stronger than you are?"

"They are vermin."

"That's right. Vermin with sixguns. Ain't very natural, sixguns. But they sure do make a big difference out here in the wide open. Or ain't you noticed?"

Stanton did not reply.

Beyond the valley they hit a wide flatland covered with shale and loose rock, where they promptly lost the fugitives' trail. Longarm and Stanton were forced to circle the entire flat in order to pick up their sign, but by that time glowering clouds had rolled in over the peaks to the north and were flowing swiftly across the clear blue vault above them, and Longarm realized that a mountain cloudburst was on its way.

Longarm pulled his black to a halt, dismounted, and started to untie his blanket roll. "Better get out your slicker, Wally."

Wally glanced nervously skyward. "Didn't bring it."

The rain came in a sudden, leaden rush, pounding down upon them hard and cold. The trail ahead of them was almost immediately transformed into a sea of mud. An hour or so later, with the rain still pounding down relentlessly, they pulled up on a ridge and looked down upon a miserable huddle of buildings close in under a stand of timber. Running before the buildings was the narrow, raging torrent of a mountain stream, swollen dangerously now as a result of the cloudburst.

Through the sweeping curtain of rain, Longarm studied the homestead. The soil this high up, Longarm realized, was thin, the grass precariously rooted, the growing season short, the winters brutal. All of this, the nester's place accurately reflected.

The farmhouse itself was a mean log cabin, ringed with pinyon stumps. Its roof was of sod squares and its ridgepole sagged. The privy sat crookedly behind the cabin on an uneven slope of ground, the hole dug half-heartedly out of the stony soil. Littering the front yard was a tangle of rusted farm implements, a rotting mattress, a wheelless buggy, and an overturned grindstone. Only the tall pole barn seemed the result of a solid effort on the homesteader's part.

Longarm glanced at his sodden companion. Stanton was soaked to the skin, his dark suit plastered to his narrow frame, his straw hat scrunched well down over his forehead, a steady rivulet of water pouring off the brim.

"Stay sharp, Wally," Longarm warned. "They could be holed up in there."

"Yes," the man replied bitterly. "It looks like the kind of rat's nest they would pick."

As they rode up to the stream, then carefully forded the narrow torrent, a large, ragged-looking collie left the protection of the barn to bark at them. Ignoring the dog, the two men pulled up in front of the homesteader's cabin.

The door opened and the homesteader peered out through the rain at them. He said nothing to Longarm and Stanton as he glared at the barking dog, then spoke sharply to it. The dog slunk miserably through the downpour, back into the barn. The homesteader's wife, a swollen, lank-haired creature, lurked in the gloom of the doorway just behind her husband.

The homesteader carried what looked like an ancient Hawken. Before approaching the homestead, Longarm had affixed his badge to the front of his slicker, and now he held his arms out to his sides and indicated the badge with a downward motion of his chin. "Afternoon, pilgrim," he said. "I'm a deputy U.S. marshal, and this man's riding with me."

The homesteader lowered the huge-bored weapon, and Longarm nodded to the woman in the doorway.

"Howdy, ma'am."

She muttered something to her husband and vanished promptly from sight.

"We're looking for a couple of men might've ridden through here just before this rain," said Longarm to the homesteader.

"Yup. The Possum Boys."

Longarm glanced at Stanton. "That's them," Stanton confirmed. "Dick and Lou Poser. That's what they call 'em, the Possum Boys."

"Which way were they heading?" Longarm asked.

"They was off to Eagle."

"Much obliged."

"You're welcome to light and rest a spell." The homesteader's sharp eyes looked Stanton over alertly. "And maybe dry off some."

Longarm considered this for a moment as the nester met his gaze sourly. The fellow's sunken cheeks and cadaverous frame bore mute testimony to his success in this region. He didn't look like much of a threat, at that. And this poor fool sitting his horse beside Longarm was nearly drowned. "Much obliged, mister," Longarm said finally.

"See to your hoss, then. I'll see my woman sets two other places at the table."

He turned and went back inside.

Longarm glanced at Stanton. He was not looking forward to the cabin's interior or the supper that had been offered. But it was a poor sort of man who let himself turn down any hospitality on the trail, and Stanton would likely turn into a puddle if they didn't both get out of this.

"Thanks, Longarm," said Stanton, dismounting slowly. "Maybe we should keep on after those two, but I sure do hanker after a dry place."

Longarm nodded, swung stiffly out of his saddle, and led his horse into the barn, Stanton trudging soddenly after him.

The interior of the cabin was dank, and lit only by a single coal-oil lamp hung from a rafter. After Longarm stepped out of his slicker and hung it on a hook by the door, he found he was almost accustomed to the smell, though his stomach threatened to rebel continuously. A glance in Stanton's direction showed that the man's face had grown almost green from the effects of the small cabin's rancid interior. The smell was compounded of coal oil, unwashed bodies, and swill—all of it caught up in a close, fetid cloud that hung like an unspoken curse in the air of the place.

A huge pot was simmering on the stove, tended by a young woman with long, stringy blond hair. As she stirred the thick, meaty broth, she glanced nervously over her shoulder at Longarm and Stanton. Her second glance brought her a heavy-handed cuff on the side of the head from her mother, and the girl almost lost her hand in the roiling stew.

"Keep your eye on what you're doin', girl!" the

woman snarled, then went back to setting the plank table.

The homesteader leaned his Hawken against the wall and sat down at the table, beckoning to Longarm and Stanton to join him. As the girl served them a moment later, Longarm made no effort to ask what kind of meat was in the stew. He could see potatoes and root vegetables swimming in the thick broth, and when he started eating, he was pleasantly surprised. The stew was hearty enough to warm his insides clear down to his bootheels.

The meal was a silent one. The homesteader spoke in half-intelligible grunts to his wife, who silently passed him what he required. The girl ate swiftly, her lean, pale face low over her dish, her eyes kept resolutely straight ahead. Her manner was that of one who expects the whip momentarily. Longarm caught Stanton glancing occasionally at the girl, his eyes concerned.

The girl was the first to finish, and she did not take seconds. She got to her feet and, as soon as her father gave her a sign, began clearing the table. When it was cleared, the homesteader chuckled suddenly and lifted a jug of moonshine up onto the table.

"Name's Matt Swinnerton," he told them, as he passed the jug across the table to Longarm. "This here's my wife, Kate. And that young'un's her daughter. She ain't no kin of mine and is a bad sort. A soiled dove, she is—and anxious to get back to her trade."

Kate glared balefully at her husband, but said nothing. Longarm glanced at the girl. She seemed so busy with the dishes that she hadn't heard.

"What's the girl's name?" Stanton asked.

"You interested in buying her?" Kate asked sharply.

"I just asked what her name was, is all."

"Jenny."

The homesteader looked shrewdly at Stanton. "From the cut of your clothes, mister," he said, "I'd figure you could name a right nice price for Jenny. You're interested in her, too. I can tell."

"Jenny!" Kate called. "Get over here. Let this feller in the wet clothes have a look at you!"

Jenny dropped a dish into a wooden bucket, shoved the palms of her hands down along her filthy skirt, then pushed her hair back from her face and moved close to the table. She looked shyly at Stanton.

"Not interested," Stanton said heavily, reaching for the jug. "I don't buy people."

"She'd be right nice in the sack, mister," said the homesteader. "We been keepin' a sharp eye on her so she ain't got no disease."

"Ain't that right, Jenny?" the girl's mother demanded. "Ain't you clean?"

The girl nodded quickly, hopefully.

Stanton looked for help to Longarm. Longarm took the jug from him and lifted it to his lips. The smell reminded him of a mildewed silo. A moment later, as he blinked the tears from his eyes, he wondered if maybe he hadn't just swallowed a lighted kerosene lamp. "My friend here is not interested in Jenny," Longarm told the homesteader. "He's interested in the Law of Tooth and Claw. That means all he wants now is to get on after the Possum Boys."

"They killed a good friend of mine," Stanton explained. "Two good friends. I want to see them hung."

"Them Possum Boys is just hell-raisers, is all," Matt Swinnerton said heavily, as he took the jug from Longarm and passed it finally to his wife. "They's good friends to us poor homesteaders. Left us with some bills last time they passed by. And they was real nice to Jenny too. Paid good for that."

Jenny turned quickly and went back to the bucket of dishes she was rattling. Longarm could tell she was furious, but far too intimidated to raise a complaint. He looked back at the homesteader. "We'll pay well for a night's lodging. Maybe we could sleep in the barn overnight."

Swinnerton nodded. "There's plenty of hay out there. You're welcome to stay the night, but it'll cost you five bucks."

Stanton gasped.

"Pretty steep, ain't it?" Longarm inquired amiably.

"That's what them two fine Possum Boys left us," said Kate, lifting the jug a second time to her mouth. She took two long swallows, moistened her lips, then took a couple more.

Swinnerton saw the surprise on Stanton's face. "Kate don't get no chance to get at this jug less'n we got guests. Like now. She's just takin' advantage of the opportunity." Swinnerton looked at Longarm and winked broadly. "This here dude ain't been around much, has he? Seems like most things shock him."

"I've been out West now for five years, and I've seen plenty," Stanton said, his voice a little thick from the moonshine.

"Maybe," said Kate, smiling wolfishly at him. "Maybe you seen a lot, but it ain't been sinkin' in."

"He reads a lot," Longarm explained.

"No wonder!" Swinnerton exploded. "I never read a damn thing in my whole life, and I'm a damn sight the better for it! Kate here don't read neither, and it sure ain't slowed her down none."

"I can see that," Stanton said coldly.

They caught his drift and stiffened in anger. He felt himself too good for them, they realized, and it was almost more than they could abide. Longarm cut the sudden tension by getting to his feet, reaching into his pocket, peeling a five-dollar bill from his roll, and dropping it on the table.

"We'll stay the night," he told them. "And thanks for your hospitality. That was a fine meal."

Stanton got up also. "Yes," he said. "That was an excellent repast."

"My, ain't we fancy," spat Kate, reaching once again for the jug.

As Longarm lifted his slicker from the hook, he glanced at the girl. She was over at the stove now, clearing off the pots. He could not be completely sure, but he was almost certain he saw tears coursing down her cheeks.

He shrugged into his slicker and pushed out into the rain.

After both men had fixed up beds in adjoining stalls, Longarm paused before Stanton's stall and looked down at the man. He was naked, a saddle blanket wrapped around him, his clothes draped over both sides of the stall. They still looked pretty damp, and Longarm knew that the saloon owner was going to be dressing the next morning in icy, damp clothing.

"You almost got us killed in there," he told Stanton. "Those people are proud, no matter what you might think of them."

"Proud?"

"That's right. You think they're going to admit they're inferior to you just because they can't read?"

"But they live like pigs! They use their only daughter as a prostitute. Or, worse, they would willingly sell her to the next stranger who happens by."

"A girl don't have much chance out here to find a man. And maybe she'd be better off living with someone who was willing to give a good price for her."

Stanton shook his head in total negation. "No," he said. "It is barbaric. And do you know the worst part of it, Longarm? To see such lumps of deformity and disease, both in body and in mind, smitten with what you call *pride!* It is almost more than a man can bear! Yahoos! That's what they are! Yahoos!"

"That your own notion, Wally?"

"Have you ever read Jonathan Swift, Longarm?"

"Nope. Never have."

Stanton shook his head. "Well, maybe you shouldn't, then. It is too terrible what that man had to say. And now, here in this great, wide West, we have such examples as would have made even that man grow pale."

"You sound a mite finicky for a fellow who runs a saloon."

Stanton leaned forward intently. "Let me tell you something, Longarm. In my place the whiskey is not watered; it is the best imported variety. And the girls who sing and dance in my place are not required to do anything else. Furthermore, I have instructed them to sit with a man while he drinks and to comfort him if such is needed, but under no circumstances are they to cajole the customer into drinking more than he wishes. If he just wants to sit and talk, it is all right."

Longarm was impressed. "Sounds like a very fair arrangement."

"It is."

"How's business?"

"Excellent. I'm doing better than most of my competitors."

"I guess you would, at that."

"Survival of the fittest, Longarm. And the fittest is not always the most ruthless, the most rapacious—just the smartest."

"Guess you are that," Longarm admitted, straightening. "About some things, at any rate. Well, we better get us some shut-eye. We got us a long ride tomorrow. At least we got a pretty good notion where those two are headed. Eagle is less than a day's ride, but it is over pretty rough country."

"Are you sure we can trust Swinnerton to tell us the truth about the Possum Boys?"

Longarm snorted. "Hell, no. But I can't see a reason for them to lie to us. Don't seem like they owe the boys anything. We'll know for sure by morning."

"How will we know?"

"If they let us sleep through the night without murdering us."

Stanton gasped as Longarm, smiling, went to his stall and reclined on his bedroll. A moment later, his saddle serving as a pillow, he pulled his soogan's flap over him and closed his eyes, his Colt enclosed firmly in his right fist.

Chapter 4

A soft finger was resting on Longarm's lips. He opened his eyes to find Jenny's face inches from his, her long hair enclosing his face and head in a musky tent.

"Shush," she whispered softly, lifting back the soogan's flap and dropping her bony frame onto his. "I could tell you was different from that dude. He's all vinegar and book-learnin'. You're big and strong and warm, and I know you'll help Jenny. I just know it!"

When he tried to respond, her lips closed about his hungrily, her mouth working passionately. She might have been trying to devour him, face first. Her bony arms she flung passionately about his shoulders. He found his own arms reaching up to enclose her narrow back. But when she tried to move onto his growing erection, he moved sideways.

"I'm clean!" she whispered fiercely into his ear. "I washed all over, ever' bit of me. And I ain't got no social disease! You can take me! That's the God's truth!"

Again she wriggled onto him, this time closing about his member with a fierceness that astounded him. He had the momentary impression that she had it so securely that he was completely in her power. It almost panicked him. Almost. She flung herself back. He heard her pleased gasp as she leaned still farther back and worked herself down still farther onto him. Then she straightened and began to ride him, her head thrown back, her unruly hair flying out behind her.

Tightening his buttocks, Longarm found himself driving up to meet each thrust. Their pubic bones ground against each other. She was uttering tiny little choking sobs now, and he ran his hands up and down her skinny spine, feeling her bones riding under the tight, smooth skin. By this time her groans told him she was about to climax. He got a firm grip on her little buttocks and started pulling her down hard upon him. Her tempo increased. Longarm found himself stretching tightly under her, rising violently now to meet each thrust.

A tiny cry indicated her first climax. But she would not let him go. Despite the wetness, she still held him with that same force she had exhibited when first he had entered her. It delighted and dismayed him at the same time. She began rocking, then flung herself forward onto him. Her lips found his and she began to kiss him wildly, her tongue thrusting like something inspired as it probed deeply into his mouth. He felt himself growing even deeper within her, heard her cries of pleasure as she felt this, and realized that Jenny was all animal now; she was no longer that pathetic little drudge forced to stand beside a bucket of swill-laden dishes.

Aroused now fully, despite his sense of unease, he took charge and rolled swiftly over onto her, aware at once of her frailty as he pounded into her. She seemed not to notice his overwhelming strength, however, as she met each of his thrusts with one of her own, her head thrown back, her eyes shut tightly, her neck taut. She was growling now, the sound coming from deep within her throat. Abruptly, Longarm found he was no longer in control. Her eyes snapped open and she laughed. Then she grasped him even more tightly as they rushed into a long, shuddering, mutual orgasm.

At last she quieted under him. For a moment longer, Longarm allowed himself to lie upon her until he caught his breath, then he shifted his weight to his elbows and eased off her slim body.

"Will you take me with you?" she demanded hoarsely. "You see how I am! You see how I can pleasure you!"

"I'm afraid not, Jenny," he whispered. "You might get hurt. We're after two killers. The Possum Boys."

"I know them," she hissed. "They ain't nothin'! You goin' to take me with you?"

"Nope."

"But you see how they treat me!"

"I am sorry, Jenny."

"Then I won't tell you!"

"Tell me what, Jenny?"

He needn't have asked, for at that moment a shadow fell over them both. Longarm glanced up to see Swinnerton looming over them, a pitchfork raised high above his head, its tines gleaming dully in the dim light. Before the nester could bring the pitchfork down upon their naked torsos, a shot rang out. Swinnerton was slammed sideways. The pitchfork's tines caught in the side of the stall and the handle slammed on down, cracking Longarm smartly on the side of his head.

He shook off its effects, pulled his Colt out from under his saddle, and rose to his feet. He saw Stanton leaning over the side of his stall, a smoking revolver in his hand. Swinnerton was coiled on the straw-littered floor in front of the stalls, moaning softly and drawing his knees up to his chin. Longarm lifted his Colt, swung it toward the barn's entrance, and squeezed off a shot.

With a squeal of pain, Kate Swinnerton dropped the Hawken she was carrying and slumped in the open doorway.

"My God, Longarm," Stanton said. "You've killed the woman!"

"She was taking a bead on you, Wally. You left your rear exposed. Just like I did."

Jenny flung her shapeless dress over her head, then rushed over to the wounded woman. As she bent beside Kate, she glanced back at Longarm. "She's alive! You didn't kill her!"

"I'm glad of that," said Longarm. "Why don't you help her into the house, while I take a look at this one."

"No!" Jenny cried. "Finish her! She tried to kill you! Finish her for me!"

"That's enough, girl," Stanton said, his voice hushed. "Take your mother into the house."

With a snarling cry, Jenny snatched up the Hawken lying beside her fallen mother, jumped up, and pointed the barrel down at the still woman's head. She was breathing heavily, her shoulders rising and falling—an aroused tigress, ready to kill.

"Jenny!" Longarm snapped. "My Colt is aimed at you. I'll shoot you the way I shot your mother if you don't drop that rifle!"

Jenny glanced swiftly over her shoulder at Longarm, her eyes aflame with fury.

"I mean it, Jenny!"

She hesitated. In that instant, Stanton ducked over to her and snatched the rifle from her hands. The moment it was out of her grasp, Jenny slumped to her knees on the floor beside Kate and began to sob.

Stanton nudged her gently by the shoulders until she was back on her feet, then lifted Kate Swinnerton in his arms and started for the house. Jenny, sobbing now, started after him. Longarm dropped his Colt to his side and looked down at the nester. The man was still moving slowly, convulsively, a soft moan coming from him.

Longarm knelt on one knee beside him and attempted to roll him over. As he did so, his hand came in contact with what was left of his back. He wiped the warm blood on the straw at his feet, then stood up slowly.

By the time he was on his feet, Swinnerton was no longer moaning—and no longer breathing, either.

The few hours that remained before dawn, Jenny spent in tending to her mother's wound. The slug had grazed the fleshy part of Kate's neck without rupturing the jugular. It was a miracle of sorts. She had bled profusely, however, and was going to have a very sore neck for a long time to come.

Nevertheless, by morning's first light, Jenny had wrapped a bloody but tight bandage around her mother's neck and sat her up on a cot in the corner of the kitchen and given her the chore of peeling fresh potatoes for the breakfast that Jenny was preparing for Longarm and Stanton. Astonished, Longarm and Stanton had left the cabin to bury Swinnerton. They returned in time to see Jenny snatch the peeled potatoes from her mother's grasp and then demand that the wounded woman set the table. Longarm had kept his counsel earlier with some difficulty. But this new demand seemed a mite cruel.

"Now hold it right there, Jenny," he protested. "I don't think Kate's going to be able to stay on her feet, let alone set the table. She's lost a lot of blood, don't forget. We'll set the table ourselves."

"No you won't!" Jenny snapped.

Longarm looked at Stanton. Stanton returned his glance and shrugged.

When the two of them rode out a little later, Kate was at the sink, washing the dishes slowly and painfully, while Jenny stood in the doorway and waved goodbye to Longarm. Jenny had explained that her mother and Swinnerton had been paid handsomely by the Possum Boys to do what they could to delay any pursuers. Not only that, but the Possum Boys were kin to Swinnerton.

Cousins. Two good reasons for trying to kill Longarm and Stanton.

"You think Jenny will let her mother live much longer?" Stanton asked Longarm as they rode away from the cabin.

"She'll let her mother live as long as she can spend the time paying her back some. That's the way I figure it. Turnabout may be fair play, but it sure as hell can be cruel, looks like."

Stanton nodded thoughtfully. "Justice," he said after a while. "A cruel justice, but justice all the same."

"Maybe," said Longarm.

"You don't agree?"

"Do me a favor, will you, Wally?"

"Of course."

"No more palaver about justice. Let's just keep our eyes peeled and our weapons ready. A man's in trouble as soon as he starts thinking too much with his mouth open."

"Or when as he lets a young temptress disturb his sleep?"

Longarm glanced at Stanton. "I reckon you heard us going at it, huh?"

"Yes. But that wasn't what awakened me."

"No?"

"A most insatiable young lady," Stanton commented, a sly smile on his face. "She visited me first, you see."

Longarm winced, and rode on without comment.

A few hours before sundown that same day, they came upon the freshly laid tracks of O'Leary's Rio Grande Western and followed them into the newly created town of Eagle. The tracks sliced Main Street right down the middle, but no one appeared to mind.

On a hill overlooking Eagle, and flanked by prodigious mountainsides, sat the mine's shaft head and hoist works. Longarm glimpsed high-sided ore carts bringing the rough ore down to the new rail sidings alongside the still-unpainted train station, where open freight cars were waiting to accept the ore. It was plain to see that O'Leary's railroad was needed by this town's mine, and that as his line linked the other mining towns farther west on the other side of Eagle Pass, it could not help but be prosperous.

No wonder Otto Pears was competing so furiously with his old mining partner for the chance to serve these mines and the tough but prosperous little communities that sprang up with them.

All this Longarm took in at a glance, as he and Stanton rode down Main Street, looking for a livery stable —and hoping also for a glimpse of either one of the Possum Boys. The side streets running off Main Street were little more than narrow, pinched lanes; this, Longarm realized, was because there was so little level land in this rugged, nearly vertical country. Towering walls of rock loomed over Eagle on three sides. On the fourth side—the northeast quadrant—the mine's buildings, along with its huge pile of tailings in the rear, completed the town's encirclement.

The buildings were an unlovely mixture of the permanent and the transitory. There were small army tents and larger, more elaborate tents; rough, unpainted pine structures with traditional false fronts; and there were solid two- and three-story stone buildings that housed banks and elaborate, expensive hotels. Along the narrow wooden walks swarmed a crowd of mineworkers, carpenters, a heavy smattering of Chinese, well-dressed gentlemen—half of them gamblers, more than likely— and a generous complement of *nymphs du grade* employed by the numerous brothels that crowded close against the barbershops, restaurants, saloons, and gambling halls on both sides of the street.

At the end of Main Street, nestled in under a towering slab of rock that seemed to bend back over the town and crowd out the sky, they found a livery and dismounted. When Longarm inquired about a good hotel, he was given the name of the Eagle Arms, back up the street a few blocks. Longarm thanked the hostler, flipped him a coin, and started along the street with Stanton.

The town was booming, that was for damn sure. The mine was producing not only gold, but silver as well, and the air was filled with talk of other mines, just as profitable, opening up farther west. As they moved through the crush, Longarm's experienced eye picked out the oversized Negro bouncers, real plŭg-uglies that Longarm knew were quite dexterous with blackjacks, sheath knives, rabbit punches and groin kicks. The madams and girls that brushed past him were undoubtedly carrying jeweled derringers or tiny Smith & Wesson .22 revolvers—the famous "whore specials"—tucked into garters or worn as belt ornaments in beaded leather holsters. Longarm didn't blame any of the girls for this added precaution; he knew from experience how valuable those small but lethal surprises could be in a pinch. As he led Stanton into the Eagle Arms Hotel, he absently patted the derringer resting in his fob pocket.

After registering and stashing their gear in their second-floor room, the two men returned to the street. A short discussion had settled their plan. They would check out the saloons first, saying as little as possible so as not to arouse suspicion. If the Poser brothers were in Eagle, they would be eager to celebrate their recent escape from the law. Longarm's experience had taught him that men on the dodge were sometimes surprisingly indiscreet. It was not only the predictable company they kept; it was the way they blabbed. More often than not, everyone in town not only knew of their presence, but every detail, it seemed, of their crimes. If Longarm hadn't known better, he would long since have concluded that most outlaws were almost anxious to get caught.

The sixth saloon they entered that night was the most impressive of the lot. It was called The Sultan's Palace, and boasted a huge mahogany bar, behind which ran an equally long mirror with shelves of bottled liquor, imported wines as well as a fine assortment of whiskeys. Roulette wheels and faro tables crowded hard upon the bar, with the poker tables in the rear.

The place was densely packed, and it took some doing for Longarm and Stanton to push beyond the poker tables to the satin-draped parlor beyond. This place also was crowded, but not so densely. There was a smaller bar in the far corner, where four customers were quietly sipping their drinks, scantily clad girls hanging on their elbows. On a stand just under a lush, wall-length portrait of a nude woman reclining under a cottonwood, there glowed a mineral-oil lamp with a red bull's-eye shade. The faint odor of incense hung in the air. A curtained doorway led from the parlor.

Without going any farther, Longarm knew what he would find beyond the doorway: a dim corridor, and on each side curtained cubicles, perhaps no more than five feet wide, each crib containing a straw mattress, a rocking chair, a commode, and most certainly a young woman.

As Longarm approached the small bar with Stanton, a heavily rouged woman emerged from the hallway, plastered a smile on her round face, and came toward them. She was huge, her bosom more than ample, yet she carried herself as lightly as if she were still a slim young thing at the beginning of her profession.

"Evenin', gents," she said. "Jane Clyman's the name. Just call me Jane. Lookin' for company, are you! Well, you've sure come to the right place!" As the barkeep moved down the bar to serve them, she winked broadly at the man and said, "Tim, give these two gents the best we've got." She turned back to Longarm and Stanton and smiled broadly. "Your money ain't no good in here tonight. Everything's on the house."

"How come?" Longarm asked.

"You go on and order your poison, and I'll just join you over at that table in the corner, where it's quiet and a body can be heard."

As the madam headed for the table, Longarm ordered rye and Stanton ordered Scotch, and then the two of them carried their drinks over to the table and sat down. Jane Clyman beamed at them.

"Been waitin' for you to get here," she said. "Word is you two been makin' the rounds."

Longarm glanced at Stanton.

"That so?" Stanton said, sipping his Scotch.

Longarm, leaning back in his chair and fingering his mustache, said, "Guess you got something to tell us, Jane."

"You're lookin' for someone. You're the law. That right?"

Longarm answered for both of them. "I'm the law. Custis Long, deputy U.S. marshal. This here's my friend Wally Stanton. He owns a saloon in Redcliff."

Jane looked at Stanton speculatively. "I heard about you. Won't let your girls earn a little extra spendin' money on the side."

"You mean on their backs," corrected Stanton coldly. "They do what they want after hours. But it's their decision, not mine. I'm not a pimp. And my place is not a whorehouse."

The amusement in Jane Clyman's eyes faded swiftly. Her expression became bleak for a moment, then she forced herself to assume a more hearty aspect and looked back at Longarm.

"Who you lookin' for, Marshal?"

"Dick Poser and his brother, Lou. They been here?"

"Been and gone. Wore out three of my best girls, they did, and they weren't very nice about it, either."

"Where they headed?"

"Damned if I know."

"I'd like to talk to the girls they stayed with."

"Sure thing, but go easy on them, will you? They been through a lot, they have. Them Possum Boys is plumb mean."

"Where are the girls?"

Jane got to her feet. "I'll send them out."

"Thanks, Jane. Appreciate it."

"Anything for the law, especially the federal law. Don't want no trouble with the government."

As she hurried off and ducked beyond the curtain, Longarm glanced at Stanton. "You weren't very nice to her, Wally. One thing I never heard was a madam referring to her place of employment as a whorehouse."

"A whore's a whore, a whorehouse is a whorehouse."

"I ain't denying that, Wally. But you might make it tougher on us if you're not careful. Never saw a man so all-fired certain he knew the difference between right and wrong—less'n he was a preacher. You ever think of going into that line of work?"

"Of course not."

"Maybe you ought to consider it."

Before Stanton could reply, Longarm saw Jane Clyman hurrying back out through the curtained doorway, obviously agitated. Longarm rose to his feet as the huge woman stopped in front of their table.

"It's one of the girls," she told Longarm. "Daisy. She's not so good. And I can't find the other two. If you want to talk to Daisy, come with me."

Longarm followed the madam and Stanton out of the parlor, aware that the customers at the small bar were watching the three of them closely. As they hurried down the dim corridor, Longarm caught fleeting glimpses of pale women standing in the doorways of their cribs, their eyes lost in dark hollows, their faces gaunt. All of them wore long, pale robes as insubstantial as themselves. A few offered themselves listlessly, their words barely audible. Longarm heard no laughter. Passing one crib, he caught the rustle of straw and a tiny cry.

Then they were at the end of the hallway, and Jane came to a halt beside an open doorway. A single kerosene lamp with a lurid red shade hung on a nail beside the crib entrance. It was the only light as Longarm and Stanton entered the crib.

Daisy—her long, straight, flaxen hair spilling over her pathetic, child's bosom—could not have been more than seventeen years of age. She was crouched, weeping, in a corner of the crib, her skinny legs drawn up under her. On the straw mattress lay her crumpled shift and robe. But there was nothing erotic about her nakedness. The girl's shoulders and thighs were uncommonly thin and bony and covered with ugly, blotched, black and blue patches. One eye was completely closed, her face swollen grotesquely. Daisy's beating had been recent—and its obvious, thorough viciousness caused Stanton to gasp.

Longarm knelt on one knee beside the girl. "Who did this to you?" he asked Daisy softly, urgently.

Daisy focused her one good eye on Longarm, then glanced past him at Stanton, and then at the madam standing in the crib entrance. "No one," she said. "I done it myself. I fell down."

"That's all right, Daisy," the madam purred. "You can tell this man what happened. He's the law."

Hope flickered for a moment in the girl's eye. She tried to pull herself into a more presentable pose and only succeeded in making herself look even more pathetic. "*They* done it," she said, her words not very distinct. It was obviously painful for her to move her jaw, and she tried to speak without moving it.

"Who is *they*, Daisy?" Longarm persisted. "Who do you mean?"

"The Possum Boys."

"They still in town?"

She shook her head. "They left. They took Cherry and Faith."

"Why did they beat you?"

"I . . ." She glanced fearfully at Jane Clyman. Then her battered face became resolute. "I wouldn't do what they wanted. And I wouldn't go with them."

Jane Clyman spoke up then. "You mean they took Cherry and Faith?"

Daisy nodded. "They said they bought them. They bought me too, they said, but I wouldn't go."

"*Bought* them?" the madam demanded, moving swiftly into the crib and looming over the suddenly cringing girl. Her bulk shut off most of the light filtering in from the red lantern. "Who sold them, Daisy? Who was it?"

"I don't know!"

"What do you *mean*, you don't know? Of course you do! Was it Alfred? Was it?"

Daisy, still cringing, nodded. "Yes," she mumbled, her voice barely audible. "Yes, it was Alfred."

"Thought so!"

Jane Clyman turned to Longarm. "He's gone too! I knew he was up to something! I been losing too many girls lately, and he's been riding around in fancier and fancier carriages!"

"Who's Alfred?" Longarm asked her.

"One of the men . . . who work for me."

"One of your bouncers?"

She nodded. "A big blond Swede. I gave him everything!" She was livid at the news of this betrayal.

Longarm looked back down at Daisy. "Where did the Possum Boys take the girls, Daisy? Do you know that?"

"They're joinin' up with the Hardamen gang, they said. They're gonna cause trouble for Sam Chapman."

"Who's that?" Longarm asked.

Stanton spoke up. "He's O'Leary's construction foreman."

Longarm nodded and stood up. "Thank you, Daisy."

Jane Clyman pushed her sweaty bulk past Longarm then, and leaned threateningly over the girl. "You knew what Alfred was doin', didn't you!"

Daisy started to shake her head. Before she could finish, the madam slapped her so hard on the side of her face that the girl was sent sprawling awkwardly into another corner of the crib.

"Damn you!" the woman cried. "You tell me the truth!"

Before Longarm could protest the madam's action, Stanton reached past him, grabbed the madam by the shoulder, and flung her bodily back out through the crib's doorway. Longarm heard her powerful body crunch into the thin pine wall, causing the flimsy floor beneath him to shake. The lantern hanging on the nail swung violently. Stanton paid no attention to this, however, as he stepped past Longarm and, snatching Daisy's robe off the mattress, wrapped it swiftly around the girl. Then he lifted her frail form and carried her out of the crib and down the hallway, past the still-groggy madam, who was resting on her hands and knees, glaring after him like some fearsome, bloated beast.

Hanging back, Longarm saw the woman reach into her bosom. Her small Smith & Wesson .22 flashed in the lantern's lurid glow. Longarm yelled a warning to Stanton as he kicked out with his right foot and sent the weapon spinning from the madam's grasp. With a cry of rage, she rose on her massive legs and came at him. Her first furious rush sent Longarm stumbling backward into the crib.

He would rather have tangled with a grizzly. The weight of her body smashing onto his chest knocked the wind out of him momentarily. He was dimly aware of the woman pounding on his head and shoulders with her dimpled fists. He rolled out from under her awesome flesh, and was just in time to see a blond giant of a man stride into the crib, reach down, and lift the madam off the floor with an ease that was astounding.

"Alfred!" she screamed, proceeding to pound upon him furiously. "I'll kill you! You've been selling my girls!"

The Swede just laughed and, with her still in his arms, turned about and strode from the crib. She was sobbing with rage as he carried her out of sight down the dim hallway. Longarm snatched up his hat, snugged it down firmly, then strode shakily after Stanton.

He did not care what Alfred and the madam did to each other from this point on. All he could hope was that they would finally perish in their own hellish brew of greed and passion. The two obviously deserved each other.

Longarm caught up with Stanton at the door of the saloon. A town marshal was effectively blocking his exit, a crowd of red-faced, angry men encircling them.

"Kidnappin's against the law, mister," the town marshal was saying to Stanton as Longarm pushed himself through the crowd to the saloon owner's side.

"I ain't kidnapping this girl, damn you!" insisted the irate Stanton.

"Daisy belongs to Jane. That's who she's workin' for! You'll just have to bring her back to her crib. Ain't no way you're gonna have her all to yourself."

This assertion was greeted by howls of approving laughter, and the crowd moved closer, obviously ready at that moment to take Daisy from Stanton and restore her to her place of employment.

"Hold it!" Longarm snapped, taking out his wallet and flashing his badge at the town marshal. "This here girl's been assaulted, and me and my deputy here are taking her to a doctor! Now stand aside! All of you!"

At sight of the badge, the town marshal stepped back in surprise. Longarm nudged Stanton. The man moved forward, the girl's arms clasped tightly about his neck.

There was only a momentary hesitation from the crowd of men in front of Stanton, then the grim circle broke before him and he moved through the crush and out into the street, Longarms on his heels, the town marshal following behind him.

Stanton pulled up outside on the boardwalk and turned to Longarm. "I'm going to find a doctor," he told Longarm, then glanced past the lawman at the town marshal. "Where's the nearest physician, Marshal?"

"Down the street," the man said, pointing. "Above the barbershop."

Stanton nodded and set off.

Longarm stood where he was beside the town marshal and watched Stanton move off through the astonished townsmen. Shaking his head, Longarm turned with a sigh to the town marshal. "My name's Long, Custis Long, deputy U.S. marshal. You got a minute?"

"Sure."

Longarm led the way into a narrow restaurant, sat down at a small table by a window, and ordered coffee from the waitress. The town marshal did likewise, then looked across the table at Longarm.

"My name's Tom Wrightman, Long. I only been at this job a couple of weeks. So far I've broke a couple of heads and swabbed up too many buckets of puke. This sure ain't a job for a man who's got other and better talents."

Longarm grinned at the fellow. "That's true, I reckon."

Tom Wrightman was all bone and Adam's apple, with large, watery blue eyes, sandy hair, and what appeared to be a perpetually amazed look on his face. It was his light eyebrows that gave him this appearance. So light were they that it appeared he didn't have any. His mouth settled into a grim line and he shook his head. "I didn't know," he said, "that Daisy had been beat up on. Wonder who did it. You got any idea?"

"Either Dick or Lou Poser."

"Oh, them animals." He shuddered visibly and as the coffee was placed down in front of him, pulled it closer. "I should've known. They been in town raisin' hell since yesterday. I been tryin' to keep outa their way."

"They killed two people in Redcliff."

"That's what I heard. Some said they was boastin' about it, but I never heard nothin' official on it."

"It's official. Take my word for it."

"Reckon I will. What you want from me?"

"Just a little help. You saw them ride out, maybe?"

"Maybe."

Longarm drank his coffee. "What are they ridin', and how many were there?"

Tom Wrightman sighed. "One of the Hardamen boys was with them, and two of Jane's girls, looked like. The girls was dressed like men, Levi's and cotton shirts. They didn't act like they was unhappy at the prospect."

"What were they riding?"

"Dick was ridin' a big paint, and Lou was on a buckskin. Jason Hardamen was riding a bay. I don't know what the girls was ridin'."

"Which way were they headed?"

"West, through the gap toward Eagle Pass."

"How far have the Rio Grande Western tracks reached?"

"End-of-track?"

"That's right."

"Heard tell they're a good ten miles from Eagle Pass. They got some blasting to do yet, and a real mean cut to make."

"And the Poser brothers and Hardamen are heading in that direction?"

"Yes, Long. That's where they're headin', all right. You figure they got something bad planned for Chapman and his gang?"

"That's just what I figure."

The town marshal shrugged. "Well, that's out of my jurisdiction. All I got to worry about is Eagle. And that's more than enough."

From somewhere down the street, a shot rang out. There was the sound of many bootheels striking the boardwalk as men began to run, some to get closer to the action, others to escape the area. Wearily, Wrightman got to his feet and dropped a coin on the table for his coffee.

"See what I mean, Long? I got enough to keep me busy right here!"

Longarm smiled up at the man and nodded. "Reckon you have, at that."

Not long afterwards, Longarm found Stanton slumped in a chair just outside the doctor's inner office. Stanton looked up as Longarm entered. Longarm closed the door to the doctor's office, then turned and raised his eyebrows in query.

Stanton got to his feet. "She's hurt pretty bad, Longarm. The doc says she's got some broken ribs and a bruised kidney. He might have to pull some of her teeth too. Her jaw's a mess. He couldn't believe they just used fists on her. He swears they must have had a club of some kind."

"That's likely, I suppose."

"Animals," Stanton said. "They're animals."

"Yup."

"Is that all you can say?"

"What else *is* there to say? You called them animals. I think that's a mite unfair to the few animals I have known, but I reckon I know what you mean, all right. What's your play? You figuring on staying here in Eagle to take care of her?"

Stanton smiled. "You can't get rid of me that easy, Longarm. I want those two now more than ever. No. I'm leaving Daisy here under the doctor's care. He's got an empty room and a cot she can use. We can take after those coyotes as soon as you want."

Longarm nodded. "We'll leave first thing in the morning."

The inner door opened and the doctor appeared, his face filled with concern. As the doctor approached Stanton, Longarm told the saloon owner he'd meet him downstairs in front of the barbershop, and left.

Not until Longarm heard the sound at the window did he remind himself that the window was only a few feet above the hotel's porch roof. He eased the Colt from beneath his pillow. A shadow appeared behind the lace curtain. Next came a barely audible scraping sound as the sash was slowly, carefully lifted.

Stanton was still asleep beside Longarm. The man was most likely all wrapped up in a dream of himself aboard a fine white charger, righting all the world's wrongs in the name of Justice. Soundlessly, Longarm let himself down onto the floor behind the bed, his left hand on the brass bed frame, his right firmly clasped about the grips of his Colt. Lying flat on his back on the floor, he eased himself under the bed and, with his left hand, pushed himself all the way under the bed, clear to the other side.

There he waited.

Stanton's steady, light snoring seemed to reverberate in the small room. Longarm kept his eye on the window and saw the curtains thrust aside by the head and shoulders of a man he recognized instantly: Alfred, Jane Clyman's bouncer. The blond giant hesitated as he adjusted his vision to the room's darkness. Then, with surprising lightness for a man his size, he dropped from the windowsill into the room. Longarm saw the bright gleam of his gun barrel as he held his sixgun out before him.

Alfred moved cautiously across the floor. A floorboard squeaked and Stanton moved fitfully in his sleep and stopped snoring. The intruder froze in midstride. A moment later Stanton's snoring resumed, a bit louder and less regular now. After waiting awhile longer to make sure he had not awakened Stanton, Alfred moved closer to the bed. His giant frame seemed to fill the room as he loomed over the bed.

Longarm saw the barrel of Alfred's sixgun gleam once more as the bouncer extended it. He was taking careful aim at Stanton. Longarm heard the man cock his weapon.

"Down here, Alfred," Longarm said softly.

Even as he spoke, he fired up at the looming Swede. The man rocked back and his own revolver detonated, sending a round into the slops jar at the foot of the bed. It rang like a bell and a sudden stench blossomed in the room as the chamber pot exploded. But the man did not go down. Longarm fired up at him a second time. The big Swede twisted about completely and stumbled back toward the window.

In the small room, the reports were like cannon shots. The floor of the room seemed to heave under Longarm, and the walls hurled the detonations back at each other.

Alfred reached the window and fell forward over the sill, the curtains shrouding him. Longarm swung himself out from under the bed as Stanton, on his feet now, stood beside him, quivering like a bare branch in a winter wind. Longarm shoved him back down onto the bed.

"Stay down!" he commanded.

Then he moved cautiously toward the intruder. The fellow had already dropped his sixgun, and had flopped on his elbows over the windowsill and was trying to pull himself back out onto the roof. Longarm knew that both his rounds had found their target, that the giant before him had undoubtedly taken two .44 slugs at very close, certainly lethal, range. Longarm was surprised the man was still conscious.

"Jesus Christ!" the man cried, turning to look back at Longarm. "I'm gutshot!

"I didn't invite you in here. You tried to murder me. Get out! Now!"

"I can't! I'm dying!"

"If you don't get out, I'll blow your brains out, you son of a bitch! You tried to murder me in my sleep!"

"No! It was not you! It was that bastard who insulted Jane! It was him I was after!"

Longarm aimed a swift kick at the fellow's butt. His bare right foot took some punishment, but the fellow groaned painfully and flung himself out over the sill, taking a piece of the sash with him. He thudded down upon the roof. Longarm leaned out. The giant was rolling down the slight incline. Longarm saw the wounded man grab at the roof's gutter a moment before he vanished over the edge.

A terrible cry, a woman's cry, echoed in the street—then was abruptly broken off. Longarm turned back to Stanton, who had remained obediently on the bed. In the darkness he could barely see the man's pale, startled face.

The door of the room burst open.

Four or five of the hotel's guests were crowded in the open doorway. Stark naked, his Colt in his hand, Longarm spun to face them. The hotel manager and night desk clerk pushed through the crowd, saw Longarm, and pulled up abruptly.

The hotel manager was a small, round man wearing a long nightshirt. "What . . . what's going on in here?" he demanded nervously.

"We heard shots!" the desk clerk seconded. He was fully dressed and wore steel-rimmed spectacles and was still holding the paper he had been reading downstairs at the desk. His eyes were enormous behind the spectacles. All of them had their backs to the lamp on the wall behind them, so that their faces were in shadow while Longarm was exposed brilliantly in the harsh light.

A woman guest raised herself on tiptoe to see over the men, caught a glimpse of Longarm's naked torso, screamed, and vanished back down the hallway.

"You're damn right you heard shots," Longarm growled. "That big Swede works for Jane Clyman broke in here and tried to murder us in our sleep. I shot him and threw him back out the window. Get that town marshal Wrightman up here pronto!"

The hotel manager hesitated.

"Pronto!" Longarm thundered. "I'm tired and I don't want to stand here all night looking at you! Check on that Swede and get the marshal!"

Longarm's words finally sunk in. The hotel manager spun about and pushed his way back through the crush. Before the desk clerk could follow him, Longarm pointed his gun at the man.

"Hold it right there, mister!"

The desk clerk froze in his tracks. The guests in the doorway shrank fearfully back.

"My friend and I want a new room. This one stinks. And this time I want one with no roofs close in under the window. You got that?"

The clerk nodded quickly.

Longarm lowered his Colt. "All right then. Now get out of here. All of you!"

As the clerk scrambled out through the ranks of the alarmed guests, Longarm strode to the door and slammed it shut.

A little less than an hour later, settled in another room farther down the hallway, Longarm tucked his reloaded Colt under his pillow and reached for the lamp on the nightstand. The door opened and a haggard, still-upset Stanton entered wearily and closed the door.

"Well?" Longarm asked.

Stanton looked at Longarm with unabashed awe.

"Wrightman wasn't lying. That's what happened, all right. The woman must have been waiting for the Swede in the street under the window. When he rolled off, he must have struck her feet first, the doc said, crushing her chest. Said it took six men to haul them both off to the undertaker."

"All right. Turn off the lamp, will you? We got ourselves another long ride tomorrow to the end-of-track. Got to find that fellow Chapman."

As Stanton stripped for bed, Longarm began to chuckle. Stanton looked at him in surprise. "I don't see what's so funny," Stanton said. "That Swede almost blew my brains out. Just because I spoke plain to that devil of a woman."

"Well, ain't this what you been looking for?"

"I don't understand."

"Justice. Pure and simple. Two would-be killers dead together under our window. Case closed. No muss, no fuss."

Longarm rolled over, pulled the covers over his shoulder, and was soon asleep.

Chapter 5

Longarm and Stanton had been riding silently along for close to four hours when finally Stanton turned in his saddle and looked at Longarm.

"I've been doing some thinking, Longarm."

"Thought it was pretty quiet around here," Longarm replied, grinning at the man. "Fact is, I enjoyed it."

Stanton smiled back at Longarm. For a dude, Longarm realized, the man sat his horse pretty well. He was still dressed in his corduroy suit and straw hat, and the gold watch chain was still draped across his vest. But the white shirt was no longer very clean and the string tie hung limply. Even the Vandyke beard had become somewhat scraggly. Yet the man was hanging in rather well, Longarm realized, considering who he was—a saloon owner who maybe read too many books for his own good.

"I'm glad you enjoyed it, Longarm. What I've been thinking about is the way you slept like a babe last night—after that incredible slaughter in our room."

"I was tired, Wally. I'd been sleeping rather light up till then."

"I see. And all that action sort of wore you out."

"You might say that."

Stanton rode a bit farther in silence, obviously pondering Longarm's maddeningly laconic response. Then he shook his head. "Well, I don't mind admitting it. I was unable to sleep for the rest of the night. I just sat rigid beside you and stared up at the ceiling, thinking about what might have happened if you hadn't stopped that man when you did."

"Well, I stopped him. So that's that. No use in studying on it all that much."

With a frown, Stanton looked at Longarm. "Perhaps not, Longarm. I was also realizing how much I owe you as a result of that action. You saved my life."

"You saved mine a while back, I seem to recall. That nester was about to stick me with his pitchfork when you cut him down."

"Yes. And then you stopped his wife. Seems to me we've been pretty valuable to each other, at that." Stanton shook his head in wonder. "Makes me wonder how either of us ever got along without the other."

Longarm smiled. "You got a point there, Wally."

Stanton guided his horse around a boulder, then kneed it closer to Longarm again on the other side. The trail was pretty steep at this point, and for a while the two men rode with considerable care, easing their mounts by leaning forward in their stirrups occasionally. At last, reaching a crest and finding a more level trail stretching ahead of them, Stanton cleared his throat, evidently anxious to finish the point he had been trying to make earlier. Longarm waited patiently, but with little enthusiasm. Stanton was a man, he realized, who just didn't know how to read silence; he had to spell everything out, it seemed.

"What I meant was," Stanton resumed, "if one or the other of us wasn't on hand these past few days, the other wouldn't have survived. One of us would be dead now."

"Yup," Longarm said. "Reckon that's right."

"Doesn't that strike you as odd?"

"Why should it?"

"Surely you don't consider that nester or his wife—or that bouncer who worked for Jane Clyman—to be more fit than either of us."

"Never said I did."

Stanton shook his head. "I just don't understand it."

"Seems pretty clear to me," Longarm said reluctantly, since he never liked to point out the obvious to anyone else. It seemed to him that if a jasper couldn't figure a thing for himself, it never did much good to take him by the hand and lead him to the proper conclusion; it just never seemed to do the other fellow any good that way.

"How so, Longarm? It surely isn't clear to me."

Longarm sighed. "Ever hear of cooperation, Wally? People working together? Like, say, a deputy and a U.S. marshal? What's the name of that fellow wrote that book again?"

"Darwin. Charles Darwin."

"Didn't he mention anywhere how things work a mite better when there's cooperation? Ain't that what helps survival? It sure helped us, and that's a fact."

Stanton smiled at Longarm. "Why, yes. I believe it did. Made us the fittest."

"Well, then."

Still smiling, Stanton shook his head in wonder. "I suppose that was obvious. Don't know why I didn't think of it."

"I don't know either."

They rode a considerable distance in silence, and Longarm was beginning to relax when Stanton cleared his throat again. Longarm took a deep breath and braced himself. Next time, he promised himself, he'd not make this kind of a mistake. He worked better alone, without a talking machine to contend with.

"I'm thinking of Daisy now," Stanton said, his voice troubled. "She's certainly not capable of protecting herself alone. And she has been hurt very badly, used most cruelly. I suppose I should just shrug my shoulders and say since she's too weak to live on her own, let her die."

Longarm stirred himself reluctantly. "That's what your friend Darwin would say."

"I know, Longarm. But I couldn't do that. That would be terrible."

"Yep. I suppose it would. But a lot of women end up like that. And die out here in the wide West with no one to take notice. Happens every day. That fellow Darwin would probably say things were working just fine."

Stanton shuddered. "Well, all of a sudden I don't think so. I left some money with that doctor. And as soon as I get back there, I'll do what I can for Daisy. Find out where she came from and take her home, if she'll go. She needs someone to help her, and it looks like I'm elected."

Longarm looked shrewdly at the saloon owner. In spite of himself, he was impressed by the fellow's concern for the young prostitute. Longarm knew the man was not interested in the girl for personal reasons. The man was square in that regard. He just wanted to help a fellow human being in trouble.

Again, reluctantly, Longarm stirred himself to make a point. "Guess you realize how much some people take to folks that want to reform them. Or look after them."

Stanton laughed. "Indeed I do, Longarm. Indeed I do. It's a chance I guess I will just have to take."

Longarm nodded and looked back at the trail. He hoped the saloon owner would say no more about it. They had already just about talked the tails off their horses. To Longarm's immense relief, Stanton rode the rest of the way that morning without any more palaver.

Longarm had been following a route suggested to him by the town marshal. A little before noon, it brought him within sight of the tracks. A mile or so farther on, Longarm found himself within sight of the end-of-track.

As the two of them, riding alongside the newly laid tracks, neared the tightly organized, circus-like activity, a horse and rider broke away from the workmen and headed down the track toward them.

As the rider got closer, Longarm recognized him from Tom Wrightman's description as Sam Chapman, O'Leary's construction foreman. Chapman pulled up as soon as he was within ten yards or so, and tipped his head alertly. He obviously wanted to know who Longarm and his companion were and what they were doing riding into his camp. Longarm pulled up also.

"Name's Custis Long," he told Chapman, taking out his wallet and showing the man his badge. "This here's my deputy, Wally Stanton. I'm a deputy U.S. marshal, come to investigate the trouble you been having."

"How far you come from?"

"Denver."

"That so?" The fellow was obviously impressed. He turned his horse. "Well, come along then. I'll fill you in."

As Longarm rode beside the foreman, he got a chance to look him over. Sam Chapman was not what Longarm had expected to find. After all, he was boss of close to five hundred mule skinners, disillusioned miners, adventurers, newly arrived immigrants, runaway sons from Eastern families, fed-up farmers, gamblers, and problem drinkers—not to mention the so-called Celestials: Chinese brought in by the Central Pacific years before, who still found employment building railroads.

It was a motley, troublesome crew this man had to direct, and the intimidating terrain over which he had to fling this narrow-gauge track could not have made overseeing such a conglomeration of humanity any easier. Yet Chapman had the youthful appearance of a twelve-year-old, and could not have been taller than five feet four.

But he was heavily muscled and tough in appearance

with a thick, curly beard that reminded Longarm of some Russian sailors he had glimpsed once in San Francisco. His eyes were piercing, revealing an inner resolve that belied his small stature. A large, ivory-handled Colt was stuck in his belt and he rode beside Longarm with a stiff, unrelaxed back and a combative look, as his eyes swept over the men laying track.

"How many men do you have?" Longarm asked, as they rode on past the gangs of workers to a camp set up on a small bluff within sight of the track.

"Four hundred and eighty, all told. About half of them are tracklayers. The rest are graders and teamsters, herdsmen and cooks."

The three men dismounted. A Chinese lad trotted up swiftly and took their horses from them. Chapman led them to a fire smoldering outside a cooktent.

"I'll see to some coffee," he told them and, knocking on the tent pole, stuck his head into the cooktent and said something to the cooks inside.

A moment later the three men were sitting on canvas camp chairs sipping hot coffee thick with cream as Chapman gave them a terse account of the trouble he'd been having. So far, it turned out, there had been few attacks on the tracklaying crews themselves. Most of the trouble he had been having concerned the subcontractor, Ty Flynn. Ty and his partner had been unable to keep the supplies coming at the rate they were needed if the Rio Grande Western was to reach Eagle Pass before the Denver & Rocky Mountain crews.

"How much trouble are *they* having with Indians?" Longarm asked.

Chapman gave him a sharp, appreciative look. "None whatsoever, as far as I can tell. None whatsoever."

"You feel that is significant, do you?" asked Stanton.

"Don't you?" Chapman snapped.

"It's not Indians," Longarm said, "not according to Colonel Mackenzie."

"I didn't think it was," Chapman replied. "But Ty was the one whose men were being attacked, so I didn't feel I had the right to contradict him."

"You think it might be hired guns?" Longarm inquired.

"Of course."

"Hired by whom?" Stanton asked.

Chapman snorted. "Isn't that obvious? Otto Pears, of course."

"We got no proof of that," Longarm pointed out.

"That's why you're here, I presume," said Chapman. "To secure that proof."

Longarm smiled. That was not entirely why they were here. The Bureau of Indian Affairs had a part in giving him this assignment; but it did not matter. And perhaps Chapman was correct. If Otto Pears was behind the trouble Ty and his partner were having, it was up to Longarm to find that out for a fact.

"You've got quite a few Chinese working for you," Stanton observed. "Are they really as good as everyone says?"

"That they are," Chapman said enthusiastically, "and maybe a little better. When I was working for the Central Pacific some years back, we had some fine Cornish lads drilling rock for us. Then the Chinese came on and pretty soon the Cornish boys came to me and said they wouldn't even try to compete with the heathen. It didn't make all that much difference to me. All it meant was we went a bit faster, that's all." He chuckled. " 'Crocker's pets' is what we called them. I won't tell you what the Christians called them. But they got the job done, whatever job it was, and right now they're blasting a cut for us."

"Where?" Longarm asked.

"A few miles farther along."

"West?"

"That's right."

"Look there," Longarm said, pointing.

Chapman followed Longarm's finger and saw what the tall lawman had been studying for almost a minute or so—a lone Chinaman, his queue almost straight out behind him as he ran, drawing slowly, steadily closer.

Chapman jumped to his feet. "Trouble," he said. "Those Celestials never leave a job unless there's trouble. And I think I recognize that one. He's a section boss with the men working the cut. Let's get our horses and meet him!"

As the three men hastily mounted up and spurred their horses toward the oncoming figure, they saw the small fellow stumble and pick himself up, hardly missing a stride in the process. Galloping closer, Chapman waved to the fellow and shouted his name.

"Li Wang!" he cried. "Hold up!"

The Chinaman stopped and, swaying slightly from exhaustion, waited for the riders to reach him. Chapman flung himself from his horse as soon as he got close enough to Li Wang, and hurried up to him.

"What is it, Li? Indians?"

Li Wang nodded, his oriental eyes wide.

By this time the tracklayers, graders, and ballast haulers had left their work area and were crowding around the Celestial, as eager as Chapman to find out what was wrong. The little man stood with his curious, dishpan-shaped hat still held onto his head by a thin chin strap, his blue cotton pants torn from countless brushes with nettles and sharp rock, his yellow, shiny face grave, his delicate hands now hidden in his outsized sleeves.

"Bad trouble," Li Wang intoned, shaking his head in despair. "Indians shoot Chinaman in basket. Others cut ropes. Chinese workers drop to river far below. Drown. Terrible trouble!"

"Take care of him!" Chapman cried to a burly Irish foreman who had just shouldered his way through the encircling workers. "He's run better than three miles. And be gentle with him, Pat! You hear?"

Grudgingly, the man nodded and, placing a big hand on Li Wang's seemingly frail shoulder, led him away through the excited crowd.

"And the rest of you get back to work!" Chapman barked, as he remounted his horse.

Cutting away from the tracks, with Chapman in the lead, they rode up a graded, winding trail that commanded a seemingly endless sweep of dense forest and rugged mountain peaks. Clattering through stands of graceful tamaracks and gigantic pines and firs, they reached a peak that commanded an impressive view of the roadbed far below. Down they charged toward it, sweeping past the gangs of frightened, huddled graders. The massive granite rock face, up the side of which the Chinese were blasting a roadbed, was now less than a quarter of a mile ahead of them.

The Eagle River gorge cut a narrow swath through the mountain barrier, and it was far above the gorge that the Chinese were working. Galloping closer, Longarm glanced up to see the wicker baskets that held the Chinese powder monkeys hanging still against the granite wall. And as he swept even closer, he could make out the slumped figures of a few of the Chinese, their limbs hanging, their heads tipped forward over the edge of the baskets. A few ropes were whipping in the wind, the baskets that had once dangled from them having long since disappeared in the swift river far below.

The three riders pulled up before they reached the gorge. Obviously, Chapman intended to dismount and discuss their approach, since they had no idea what the situation was by that time. But as Longarm started to dismount, he heard a distant cry followed by what might have been a rifle shot. Glancing up, he saw a tiny, blue-clad figure peel out of a basket high above. Twisting slightly, the Chinaman dropped out of sight beyond a projecting shelf of rock.

Chapman swore, and Longarm heard Stanton's gasp. They knew what the situation was now.

"Them Indians, or whatever! They're still up there, still firing on my men!" Chapman cried.

"Is there a quick way up to that ridge?" Longarm asked.

"That trail over there," Chapman said, pointing. "On the other side of them pines. There's another trail farther down. I'll go that way. Cut them off!"

Longarm turned his black about and galloped toward the pines, with Stanton following close after him. They found the trail easily and began climbing. The ascent was steep, the going treacherous. Loose shale and wet gravel caused the horses to slip to their knees on more than one occasion. But their hearts were good and they kept going, though both mounts were dangerously close to foundering by the time they neared the summit.

Cutting around a boulder, Longarm drew on his black's last ounce of endurance as he lifted it to a lope and swept along a narrow cleft that appeared to lead to the ridge, still maddeningly distant. Without warning, Stanton—who had managed to keep abreast of Longarm—dove out of his saddle, grabbed the lawman's left arm, and dragged him off his horse. A second later Longarm felt his hat tugged violently back off his head and heard a buzz, as though an angry hornet had sped past his ear. It was only after the two men were lying facedown on the trail that Longarm heard the two shots, dim and muffled by distance. Beside him on the ground, Stanton was shaking his head groggily. Longarm stared at the ridge. A rifleman was silhouetted against the sky for a fraction of a second. And then he was gone.

Longarm reached back for his hat. There was a clean bullet hole in the brim. He swore and put it back on, then crabbed over to his horse where it stood cropping the ground a few feet in front of him. He snaked his

Winchester from its saddle scabbard, then darted off the trail and ducked low behind a nest of boulders.

"He'll think I'm hit!" Longarm called back to Stanton. "Ride on without me! There's no one up there now. But don't be careless. Soon's you see another rifleman, take cover. I'll work around behind them."

Stanton nodded, snatched his horse's reins, mounted up, and rode on down the trail, heading toward the ridge. Longarm watched him ride, noting with satisfaction how warily he proceeded, then moved swiftly off into the rocks.

Just before he reached a flat leading to the ridge, he heard a sudden explosion of galloping hooves echoing off the rocks. Ducking back into cover, he saw the Possum Boys and three other men riding from the ridge almost directly at him. Longarm was well hidden by a clump of juniper as he watched. The riders were strung out in a ragged line as they cut around the huge boulders strewn over the flat. At times one or two of the riders disappeared completely behind an outcrop.

As the five riders thundered closer, Longarm smiled grimly and levered a cartridge into the chamber of his Winchester.

The Possum Boys were out of sight behind a nearby boulder, but the other three riders were crossing an open space. Longarm tracked the first rider, then squeezed the trigger gently. The rider grasped at his saddle horn with both hands, then pitched forward in a headlong dive. The rider behind him cut his horse sharply to avoid the downed man as Longarm levered again, tracked the rider carefully, and triggered the Winchester once more. Hit in the chest, this second rider fell with desperate cunning into a tangle of brush and rocks.

Longarm paid no further attention to him. The third rider swept his horse brutally about and galloped back the way he had come. Longarm waited for the Possum Boys to reappear when he heard them pull up. Then came the clatter of their hooves as they changed direction, keeping the rocks between them and Longarm's position. Longarm raced from cover and just managed to get off a single, fruitless round before the Possum Boys vanished from sight on the far side of the ridge.

He turned and trotted toward the two riders he had shot from their mounts.

The first downed rider was dead; the other one was sitting up with his back against a rock, holding his left shoulder. As Longarm approached, the man forgot about his shoulder, snatched his revolver up off the ground, and snapped off a shot. The round went wild. Longarm stopped, aimed briefly, fired. The man crumpled forward, rolled into a small depression, and came to rest against a gnarled pinyon.

Lowering the Winchester, Longarm heard rifle fire from the direction of the ridge. Keeping his head down, he started toward it. The firing stopped abruptly. Longarm held up, then ducked behind some nearby rocks. He listened for a long minute, then started up again.

A moment later he saw Stanton and Chapman, both men aboard their horses, driving an unhappy, bedraggled "Indian" before them on foot. It was the same rider Longarm had sent back. Now that he was closer, Longarm could see how the man had darkened his face with berry juice. There was even a ragged feather stuck in a headband.

"You get the Poser brothers?" Stanton called out as Longarm got closer.

"We heard shots," Chapman said. "Figured you'd pick them up."

Longarm waited until he had reached the two men and their sullen captive before he replied. Looking up at the still-mounted Stanton, he said, "I got two more 'Indians.' But the Possum Boys got away."

"Damn!" said Stanton.

"Well," Chapman said, "can't be helped. At least we

got this one. Let's take him back down to end-of-track. I'm sure the Celestials will be purely happy to see one of the 'Indians' that's been shooting them out of their baskets."

"Jesus!" cried the captive. "You ain't gonna let them heathen loose on a white man, are you?"

Longarm turned toward the man. He did not like what he saw. Not one bit. He kept seeing in his mind's eye those slack figures hanging in their wicker baskets against the side of the mountain, and then that pitifully small figure twisting slowly to his death on the rocks far below.

"What's your name, mister?" he barked.

"Name's Tip Wills," the fellow replied, pulling his sinewy six-foot frame to its full height.

"Who're those others?"

"You think I'll tell you that, you're crazy."

Longarm shrugged and looked back up at Chapman. "There's two others behind me on the trail," he said. "Both dead. I figure we might as well leave them for the vultures. First time in their lives, maybe, they'll serve a good purpose. But this one I want kept safe, Chapman, no matter how anxious those Celestials might be to even the score."

Chapman nodded. "I suppose you got your reasons."

"I have. I want this fellow to tell me—and by and by he will—who's behind this Indian masquerade."

"Mount on up behind me then," Chapman said, "and we'll take you to your horse."

Longarm nodded. As he took Chapman's arm and boosted himself onto the cantle behind the foreman, he saw Stanton looking at him closely.

"You know which way the Possum Boys went, Longarm?"

"North," Longarm told him. "That way," he continued, pointing beyond the ridge. "We'll get after them first thing tomorrow."

This seemed to satisfy Stanton. He smiled, leaned

back in his saddle, and nudged his horse forward. Chapman followed, Tip Wills stumbling anxiously along just ahead of them. Chapman urged his horse into a faster pace and the hapless Wills fell into a ragged trot. Chapman obviously took some satisfaction from seeing the man struggle. Like Longarm, maybe, he was remembering those powder monkeys hanging dead in their baskets.

And the trouble was that the three of them would not be the only ones to have that awful vision before them. The Chinese would be remembering also.

Longarm shook his head. It was not going to be an easy matter to keep Tip Wills safe from the Celestials, especially since he was not entirely confident that he could count on either Chapman or Stanton for their help in this. They sure wouldn't be overly anxious to help save such an animal.

Hell, Longarm realized, saving Wills from the justified vengeance of the infuriated Chinese didn't fill *him* with any enthusiasm either. But damn it! He had a job to do.

Chapter 6

Chapman had allowed the work crews to quit early, and the camp had quieted down by now. The hysteria and red-eyed fury of the past hour seemed to have run its course. Tip Wills was safely incarcerated in an equipment shack that had been set up alongside the right-of-way just above the camp. And two burly roustabouts had been selected by Longarm to guard the shack and the terrified prisoner within.

Now Longarm was walking alongside Chapman as the small but forceful construction foreman showed him the crowded quarters of his Chinese powder monkeys. The man was obviously pleased with them and anxious to share his enthusiasm with Longarm.

Chapman pulled up. "Look there," he said, his voice like that of a proud parent. "Now ain't that something?"

Longarm was indeed fascinated.

As the Chinese coolies trooped into camp, every man jack shed his work clothes and stepped naked into line behind the tents. The Chinese cooks, Longarm saw, had set out rows of whiskey kegs—one for each man, it appeared. As Longarm watched, the cooks filled each keg with steaming water, after which a naked coolie would step into the steaming bath. Behind the kegs, the cooks had stacked neat piles of towels and clean clothes. As soon as the workers had soaped, rinsed themselves, and stepped out of their baths, they appeared to dab themselves with water of some kind; then they dressed in the clean clothes and moved off to the cooktent. The rule was obvious: no bath, no dinner.

As Longarm watched this remarkable performance, he asked Chapman what that water was that they doused on themselves after their bath.

Chapman chuckled. "Flower water."

Longarm shook his head. He had had occasion to be impressed by these people before. But this instinct for cleanliness, this order—contrary as it was to all the vocal hysteria directed at the Chinese—was most instructive.

Chapman turned then and directed Longarm's steps back to his own tent overlooking the camp. As they walked, Chapman told Longarm how the Chinese had become so competent at blasting tunnels through rock or cutting trails out of the sides of mountains, no matter how precipitous. It had begun, he said, during the Central Pacific's magnificent run through the Rockies on its way to Promontory Point in Utah.

Surveys had confirmed a route to Dutch Flat from Colfax, fifty-five miles from Sacramento, that wound up the vertiginous face of the American River gorge for close to twelve miles. It was the most logical route, but it meant blasting into ledges that rose a plumb quarter-mile above the riverbed. There were no trails, not even a goat path. The workers called the giant cliff "Cape Horn." The white gangs were made up of steeplejacks, ex-sailors—anyone who would not be afraid to dangle over that blue-black gulf hour after hour in bos'n's chairs while they hand-chipped holes, tamped in the blasting powder, fixed and lighted the fuses, and then shouted for the men on top to haul them away from the dangerous blasts.

"But things didn't go very well," said Chapman, as the two men sat down on canvas chairs outside his tent. "We lost quite a few men, you see, and that scared off the rest. It got so anyone with steeplejack experience or any sailors we might have signed on simply wouldn't own up to having such experience."

Longarm took out two cheroots, handed one to Chapman, then struck a sulfur match and lit his own. "What were the problems?"

"The fuses were sometimes too short," Chapman said. "Other times the workmen at the top were busy arguing or sleeping, and delayed too long in pulling up the poor devils after they set the charges. And a lot of the poor blighters didn't know how to handle the blasting powder. To put the icing on the cake, the Central Pacific was manufacturing its own nitroglycerin, and the stuff was not that stable, if you take my meaning."

Longarm nodded.

Chapman went on then to tell what happened.

A Chinese foreman stepped up to one of the officials of the Central Pacific one evening, bobbed his hat, waited for permission to speak, then explained that his countrymen were skilled at such work as was now going on over their heads on Cape Horn. This little fellow explained that his ancestors had built massive fortresses in the Yangtze gorges, and had carved and laid the stones for the Great Wall. Why not allow a Chinese crew to work on the massive wall of granite that loomed above them at that moment?

When the official shrugged and gave his consent, the Chinese promptly sent for reeds to be brought up from San Francisco, and in a matter of days baskets had been woven from these reeds. They were waist-high and round. The eyelets woven into the top were located in the proper orientation to the Four Winds and painted with symbols that were intended to keep off the Evil

Eye. Ropes ran from the eyelets to a central cable. Each basket was then assigned a hauling crew, which would be stationed on the top of the precipice.

Of course, the white crews watching all this activity sneered in disbelief. Until that time, whenever they had seen the Celestials, they were swarming over the hillsides like a disturbed ant colony, shoveling, wheeling, carting, dumping earth—as they worked on the grades and filled ravines. It seemed to be work for which they were eminently suited. But this was a prodigious and daring enterprise they were now tackling, and none of the white crews believed for a minute that these little people with their dull, moony eyes staring out from under their immense basketlike hats could possibly have the stomach for such an undertaking.

Of course, they were wrong. For one thing, the Chinese needed little if any instructions in handling the gunpowder and other explosives. After all, gunpowder was a Chinese invention. Every little Celestial knew how to set off firecrackers on New Year's and other feast days and holidays. They knew the possibilities inherent in the stuff and could fashion a handful of the gritty gray dust into lightning bolts.

All through the fall and winter of that year, the wicker baskets bobbed like tiny gray kites against the skyline. The hand drills chattered. Powder blasts puffed flame. By spring the little men had blasted a trail up the face of Cape Horn so wide that four men could walk abreast.

Chapman, finished, leaned back in his chair and puffed on his cheroot, his eyes squinting thoughtfully as he peered into the past.

"You were there, weren't you?" Longarm prompted. "Seems to me you mentioned it before."

"That I was," the fellow said, shaking his head in wonderment at it. "That I was. In fact, I was one of those sailors who preferred not to take a chance in a bos'n's chair."

"The Chinese were able to do the job, then, without casualties."

"I didn't say that."

"No, you didn't."

"We never kept track, you understand. But more than once a rope—or the sides of a wicker basket—would give way. And no matter how careful some of them were, that new nitroglycerin was treacherous stuff." He looked at Longarm. "Have you ever heard the phrase, 'not a Chinaman's chance'?"

Longarm nodded.

"Sometimes I think that's where it came from. Every gully trestle, every blasted cliff and tunnel from Colfax to Truckee, was a headstone for their unknown dead. And right now they're risking their lives again for the Rio Grande Western and Mike O'Leary."

Chapman turned to face Longarm, a sudden scowl on his wide face.

"It's bad enough they have to face the ordinary terrors and accidents of their jobs, Longarm—and the hatred of other workers and politicians anxious for office—but to have to be shot like ducks in a barrel by unwashed white men of the caliber of that Tip Wells is enough to make a decent man sick."

"He'll be prosecuted, I guarantee you," said Longarm. "But we've got to find out just who is behind him."

"Hell! That ain't any problem! You know who it is —who it *has* to be."

"Otto Pears."

"Of course. Pears and Jack Lynch."

"I've already heard of Lynch, I believe."

Chapman nodded grimly. "He's got himself an army of freebooters that are terrorizing Ty Flynn's men. Do you know why I *really* stopped work early tonight?"

Longarm did not reply; he knew Chapman would answer his own question.

"Because we're running out of ballast, ties, and bridge timbers, that's why. Better than a third of Ty

Flynn's men have been killed or run off by Lynch. You say it wasn't Indians, and the capture of Tip Wells tends to prove that. So it has to be Lynch's men. After all, who else stands to profit if we can't reach Eagle Pass before Otto?"

"Why not send an advance party to the pass?"

"Hell, Longarm, I'm way ahead of you. I've got a party of graders and blasters working there already. They've been there for a week now. Trouble is, now they're out of supplies too."

"But not out of ammunition."

Chapman grinned. "That's right, not out of ammunition. They are prepared to hold Eagle Pass, come what may. But the thing is, we've got to back them up with track. If the tracks of the Denver & Rocky Mountain reach the pass before we do, it will be all over for Mike O'Leary."

"All over but the shooting."

"Yes. I'm afraid that's right, Longarm."

"You said earlier that my job was to prove whether it was Otto Pears or someone else behind these attacks. You can see now why I want to make sure we keep this fellow Wills alive."

Grudgingly, Chapman nodded.

"He's in that bitty shed now," Longarm went on, "listening to the sounds of the camp outside. I'd expect him to be mighty nervous about now, especially every time he hears the voices of them Chinese as they maybe pass by his shed."

Chapman chuckled and puffed appreciatively on his cheroot. "Guess maybe he is, at that."

"By the time I speak to him a little later tonight, I'm sure he'll give us whatever information we need."

"Let us hope so, my friend," said Chapman.

Longarm frowned. He was looking beyond the right-of-way at the dim outline of the shack where Wills had been imprisoned. Everything was quiet about the small building. No crowds of angry Chinese were visible, trying to get past the guards. There weren't any curious crowds of white workers, either. Indeed, the shack seemed deserted. Squinting through the swiftly gathering dusk, Longarm got to his feet and peered through the gloom, searching in vain for sight of either of the two guards that had been placed outside the small prison.

"What is it, Longarm?" Chapman inquired, getting to his feet also.

"I ain't sure," Longarm told him.

Between the spot where they were now standing and the far bank, atop which the shack sat, was the white worker's camp. There were a few tents—about ten, all told—most of them saloons or whorehouses. But sitting on the tracks were the white workers' chief living quarters. Only they were strange living quarters, for a fact.

Longarm had glimpsed their like on earlier assignments: triple-decker bunkhouses on wheels, living quarters that rolled along the newly laid tracks, keeping up with the men, filled to the brim with bunks, smoking stoves, smelly kerosene lamps, small tables for poker, and lice—a real Hell on Wheels, as they had come to be called. Two cars necessary to the laying of track had been placed just before the rolling bunkhouses; one contained a feed store and saddler's shop, the other a carpenter shop and wash house. At the rear came the long dining car that served at least two hundred men comfortably, and after that, finally, the kitchen, with a telegraph office crowded into a rear corner of it.

There were no such elaborate accommodations for the Chinese. In order to minimize the inevitable friction that arose between the two groups, the Celestials were kept well apart from the Terrestrials. Besides, the Chinese were perfectly content to crowd together in tents along the right-of-way, and they had their own cooks to prepare their somewhat exotic meals. The

Celestials' diet was a strange one, as every white worker—content to subsist on an unvarying fare of boiled beef and potatoes, beans, bread, butter, and coffee—was quick to point out. The Chinese consumed an amazing variety of fish—including oysters, cuttlefish, and abalone meat—along with an equally astonishing variety of oriental fruits and vegetables, bamboo shoots, seaweed, and mushrooms.

It was a good thing, therefore, that the two races kept their distance, at least during their leisure hours. It was precisely this fact, however, that troubled Longarm at the moment. For the Chinese and white workers were *not* apart now. Instead, they were huddled *together* on this side of those triple-decker bunkhouses. Furthermore, both of their campsites were empty of life. Not a soul stirred.

Stanton! Where the hell was Stanton?

Tossing his cheroot into the gathering darkness, Longarm started down the slope toward the bunkhouses.

"Be right back," he told Chapman over his shoulder. "I've got a funny feeling, and I think Stanton's the answer to it. I'm going to find that dude now."

"Now wait a minute, Longarm! Why don't you just stay up here with me?"

Longarm pulled up and spun around to face Chapman. "Damn it!" he cried. "You're in on this with Stanton!"

"I don't know what you're talking about, Longarm."

"The hell you don't!"

Longarm spun about then, and ran down the slope. As he neared the mass of workers crowded on the near side of the bunkhouses, he saw they were covering their heads with hats or coats or pieces of canvas or whatever was handy, while those who had clambered to the top of the bunkhouse cars were shading their eyes carefully as they peered at the isolated shack on the rise above the camp. Reaching the bunkhouses, he stared around at the averted faces, the hunched bodies, and tried to find Stanton.

"Stanton!" he cried. "Where are you?"

But there was no response. A few of the workers called to him to get down, but the rest seemed too intent on keeping low to pay any attention to him. By that time, of course, Longarm had a pretty good idea what was going on—and what was about to happen.

He darted around the nearest bunkhouse, crossed with one leaping stride the narrow three-foot gauge of the tracks, cut between the empty tents, reached the slope beneath the shack, and began to scramble up it. He thought he heard someone laboring behind him, but he was too intent on reaching the shack to pay it much mind. His booted foot slipped on the soft gravel of the slope and he went down. He felt a hand on his shoulder, shook it off, and kept going.

When he reached the top of the slope, he saw that his worst fears were realized. The shack was less than fifty feet from him, and there was no sign of either of the roustabouts he had assigned to guard Wills. He heard someone scrambling up behind him. It was probably Chapman, he knew, trying to stop him.

But he paid no heed and began to run toward the shack. Something heavy struck him in the back of his legs, and then he felt two solid arms wrapping about his knees. He pitched forward, cursing furiously. He twisted around and found himself grappling with Stanton. The man was surprisingly strong as he struck down at Longarm with his fist, catching the lawman on the point of his chin and stunning him. Longarm felt himself being slung over Stanton's shoulder. Stanton had some difficulty in turning and staggered a bit under Longarm's weight, but kept going doggedly.

They had reached the lip of the embankment and Stanton was letting Longarm down so he could negotiate the steep grade when it happened.

The first thing Longarm felt was an immense shock

wave—as though an invisible force were trying to lift him and carry him off. Hard after it came a booming roar that pounded on his ears with almost physical force. An instant later the thunderous explosion was echoing far out on the hills and mountains surrounding them as Longarm was flung helplessly back down the embankment, Stanton tumbling alongside him. Longarm felt something hard slamming up at his face and the sudden pain that followed. Lights exploded deep inside his skull, and he felt no more.

Li Wang was tending him in Chapman's tent. Longarm, looking past the Chinaman, saw Chapman standing in the entrance, his hand on the tent pole, one of Longarm's cheroots glowing in his mouth. Beside him stood Stanton, a worried look on his face.

When Li Wang saw Longarm open his eyes, he stepped back, pleased. He turned quickly to Chapman.

"Longarm, he awake now. Him all light!"

Chapman and Stanton hurried into the tent to look warily down at Longarm. Longarm put a hand up to his forehead and felt the cold compress. It seemed as if his forehead had grown somewhat in size, and he was having difficulty in focusing his eyes. He also had the granddaddy of all headaches.

"How do you feel, Longarm?" Stanton asked nervously.

"You two son of bitches," Longarm croaked. "You blew that poor bastard to kingdom come."

"You bet your ass we did," said Chapman. "This was the first time them Chinese and the other workers agreed on anything. It was a pretty thing to see such cooperation between them. Don't believe I'll see the like during my lifetime."

Grimly, Stanton said, "It was only justice, Longarm. Relatives of the Chinese that were killed set off the fuse."

"Justice, hell!" Longarm protested. "It was foolishness! Wills would have told me anything I wanted to know, he was that scared. Now I've got nothing to go on, except for a cold trail left by the Poser brothers."

"You know all you need to know," said Chapman, his back suddenly straight, his dark eyes glowing with angry certitude. "Otto Pears and his hired assassins, Jack Lynch and the rest of his Pinkertons—they're the ones that hired Wills and the Poser brothers."

Longarm shook his head wearily. "It's too messy this way, nibbling away at your supplies, hiring white-trash outlaws to dress up like Indians. There's just something about it I can't rightly buy, that's all. And Wills was my best hope of finding out. Hell, if it *is* Pears behind all your trouble, like you think, wouldn't it have been nice to hear Wills say so, and then have him testify in a court of law?"

Doggedly, the little bearded man shook his head. "Maybe," he said. "Maybe. But we're going to beat Pears and his men to Eagle Pass, no matter what. We don't need Wills' testimony to stop that overstuffed crook."

Longarm sighed and leaned back on his pillow. The slight excitement engendered by the argument had weakened him surprisingly. He closed his eyes, aware of a sudden, overwhelming drowsiness, and felt himself beginning to drift off. But he didn't want to. He wanted to open his eyes, to say something more to Wally Stanton. But he couldn't remember what it was, and his eyelids were as heavy as anvils. . . .

The tent was bright from the overhead sun. The glare caused him to close his eyes quickly, then open them again more cautiously. He squinted around him and felt of his chin, and was astonished at the length of the stubble he found there. Passing his hand quickly over his face, he found to his dismay that his cheeks seemed to have sunk, that his cheekbones stuck out gauntly.

He reached down and flung the blankets off his

body, noting, as he did so, his long, almost skeletal fingers. As soon as he sat up, his head began to spin. He rested it forward in his hands. He felt old and incredibly tired. Was this how Rip Van Winkle felt when he awoke after twenty years? Longarm wondered. His body felt unclean, greasy. There was a rancid, unpleasant odor hanging about him; it came from his filthy longjohns, mostly. He wanted a bath badly, and with this thought galvanizing him into action, he got shakily to his feet and lurched toward the tent flap.

He would have gone down if he had not reached out and grabbed the tent pole. After a moment, he poked himself out of the tent. The fresh air was a relief. With the glare of the tent behind him, his eyes seemed more functional. He stood there, searching for the camp, and to his surprise he realized that the tracks had progressed almost to the limits of the valley—the work camp, corrals, tents, and bunkhouse trains having gone right along with it.

Everything had moved on except Sam Chapman's tent—and Longarm.

"Ha! Mr. Long!"

Longarm turned his head to see Li Wang approaching from the rear of the tent, a bundle of firewood in his arms. He was heading for a cooktent just behind Chapman's quarters. At sight of Longarm, however, the coolie dropped the bundle of firewood and hurried to Longarm's side.

"You awake now! That fine!"

Longarm reached out for the small man and let his right hand close about his narrow shoulder. It held up sturdily under his weight. "Need a bath, Li," Longarm said. "And some food. How the hell long have I been in there?"

As Li Wang guided the tottering Longarm toward the cooktent, he said, "You been sick long time. Talk much. Act crazy in the head! You all light now?"

"I'm fine, damn it. Just tell me how long I've been out!"

"Week is all. Maybe some longer."

Longarm nodded wearily. That was about what it felt like. His feet were a little sturdier by the time he reached the cooktent. "Like to stay outside for a bit longer, Li," Longarm said, swaying slightly.

Li Wang nodded quickly and darted into the tent, to return a moment later with a folding chair. He placed it down in front of the tent and Longarm collapsed into it. He took a deep breath, aware that perhaps it would be best if he ate first, then had that bath.

"Food, Li Wang," he told the coolie. "I could eat a full-grown grizzly about now—either that or one small Chinaman. You get my meaning?"

"You wait," Li Wang cried. "I have stew."

A moment later Li Wang brought a folding table out of the tent, set it up in front of Longarm, then placed a bowl of stew in front of him. Longarm caught sight of dark chunks of beef swimming in it, and the tips of boiled potatoes. Snatching the spoon out of Li Wang's hands, Longarm devoured all of it.

Strength was flowing back into his limbs by the time he had consumed his third bowl, and with great satisfaction he leaned back as Li Wang, without being instructed to do so, placed a steaming cup of black coffee on the table before him.

Sipping the coffee, Longarm realized there was only one thing more he required. He had been trying to break the filthy habit for ages, but now was not the time to begin. "My cheroots," he told Li Wang. "You'll find them in my coat pocket. Bring me one, will you?"

"Cheroots?" the coolie asked, frowning.

"Cigars. Small cigars."

"Oh . . . !"

Li Wang disappeared into Chapman's tent and returned promptly with a handful of Longarm's cheroots.

Longarm selected one, offered one to Li Wang, then leaned back as Li Wang returned from the cooktent with a match and lit Longarm's cheroot and his own.

"Pull up a chair, Li Wang," Longarm said. "I got some questions."

Li Wang was busy puffing. He was inhaling a great deal, but it didn't seem to hurt him, though his eyes did appear to be growing larger. He mumbled something unintelligible in response to Longarm's comment, and continued to puff away furiously on the cheroot.

"Where's Wally Stanton?" Longarm asked.

Li Wang frowned at him, then coughed. He had been too busy smoking the cheroot to catch the question.

"Stanton!" Longarm said again, louder. "Where is he? The man I rode in with."

Li Wang's eyes lit up then. He got up and hurried into Chapman's tent. When he returned to Longarm, he handed him an envelope with his name on the outside, then darted suddenly behind the tent.

As Longarm ripped open the envelope, he heard Li Wang heaving up his guts. He smiled to himself. Maybe this would teach Li Wang not to smoke, and the poor son of a bitch would not have to fight the habit for the rest of his life. Then Longarm began to read.

Longarm:

I hung around for three days, hoping you would come to your senses. But you sure must have got a tough whack on the head. I figure it is my fault, so I don't feel so good about your being hurt. But there isn't anything I can do hanging around here, watching you.

I still need to get the Poser brothers, and I'll be back to get them as soon as I can. But I am worried about that poor girl, Daisy, so I am riding back to Eagle to make sure that the doctor is taking good care of her. You'll be all right. Chapman has told Li Wang to leave his work crew and tend you.

Anyway, I'll be back as soon as I see how Daisy is doing, and we can get after those Posers. I guess I am sorry now that we blew up Wills. I just never thought you'd get hurt. Chapman said he would be able to keep you with him until the shed blew.

Get better soon, Longarm—and I suppose if you're reading this, you already are!

Wally.

Longarm chuckled as he folded the letter and placed it back into the envelope. What came through in the letter was the voice of a man who was sincerely concerned about him—and not a little worried about what he might have done to a friend. As a result, the letter warmed Longarm even as it impressed him. This fellow Stanton knew how to spell and string words together so they made sense. He was no dummy, that was for sure.

The letter also provided Longarm with an opportunity for which he had been waiting since first he pulled up in front of Wally Stanton's campfire.

Longarm shouted for Li Wang. He was ready for that bath now. And then he would dress and get back on his horse where he belonged. There was no sense in losing any more time in taking after the Possum Boys, and a man alone could track a hell of a lot faster than two could—especially if one of them liked to talk.

And Stanton, as sure as God made little green apples, liked to talk.

Li Wang appeared, looking somewhat green around the gills. Longarm laughed outright at the man's watery eyes and shaky appearance, then told him what he wanted. As Li Wang scurried off to find one of the kegs the Chinese used for bathing, Longarm got up and swiftly peeled off his stinking underwear and stood naked in the hot sunlight. He was anxious now to be on the trail once more, and this time alone.

Chapter 7

Late the next afternoon, Longarm—freshly shaven and feeling uncommonly light in the saddle—rode into the cool shade of a twisting, rock-strewn gully. Halfway through, rounding one of the gully's serpentine bends, he found himself staring into the bewhiskered face of an ancient prospector. The old man was peering down at him from a rock shelf that extended out over the trail.

Longarm pulled up quickly.

The apparition's only weapon seemed to be the long-handled shovel he was brandishing, blade first, well out in front of him. His hat's brim had been ripped from the crown; his torn cotton undershirt was yellow with sweat and grime. The fellow appeared half-crazed. Whether this was from simple loneliness or from fear, Longarm had no way of knowing; so he sat his black gelding quietly and was careful not to make any sudden moves.

He had been following the only trail the Possum Boys could have taken from that ridge, considering their direction. He was hoping now that this solitary denizen of the mountains might have seen them go by —or better yet, might know where they were heading.

"You can put down that shovel," Longarm told him

casually. "I'm just passing through and I was wondering if maybe you could help me." Longarm smiled then, in an effort to settle the fellow down some.

"You don't need no help passin' through," the prospector growled, his voice old and raspy. But as he spoke he straightened up a little, and his eyes lost some of their madness.

"I'm a lawman," Longarm explained, "looking for some bad sorts you might've seen ride on through here a time back. I'd appreciate your help."

The fellow lowered his shovel and stood up a little more. "Lawman, are you?" he repeated warily. "Let's see your badge."

Longarm reached slowly into his coat pocket and brought out his wallet and flipped it open, displaying the badge. The fellow straightened completely and leaned on his shovel. His tattered trousers were held up by a piece of rope tied about his waist, and one of his shoes had broken through at the toe, which was as black as the soil on which the prospector stood. The fellow scratched his long gray beard as Longarm put away his wallet.

"My name's George Kilmer. They calls me Crazy Kilmer, but I ain't crazy." He grinned then, and Longarm caught a glimpse of worn yellow teeth. "I'm persistent. I know what's out here and I aim to find it. What fellers you lookin' for, anyways?"

Longarm quickly described the horses he knew the Poser brothers were riding, and did his best to describe the brothers as well. He did not mention the girls, Faith and Cherry, who might still be accompanying them.

The old man's face darkened as Longarm spoke, and when he had finished, the fellow tipped his head. "Would them fellers have any womenfolks along?"

"Might be."

"How many?"

"Two of them. I believe their names are Cherry and Faith."

"That's the bunch, all right. I sure remember that gang. Yes, I do! Follow me and I'll lead you to my camp. We can set a spell while we talk."

With surprising agility, the old prospector jumped down from the shelf and swiftly led the way through the boulder-strewn gully. Once through it, he turned sharply, climbed a steep trail to a ledge, and led Longarm toward a sod-and-brush shack that had been constructed beneath an overhanging shelf of black rock. Dismounting, Longarm took the time to loosen the cinch on his black while Kilmer poked the campfire back to life and filled a blue enamel coffeepot with water and coffee. The water he got from a wooden bucket sitting near the edge of the ledge, alongside a spring that was oozing through a vein in the rock.

As Longarm sat down crosslegged by the fire, he took out a cheroot, handed it to the old man, then took out one for himself, bit off the end, and leaned his supple frame close enough to the fire to light the cigar. Sitting back, he nudged his hat back off his forehead and waited while Kilmer lit his cheroot with a burning twig. The fellow puffed happily on the cheroot for a while before turning his attention back to Longarm.

"Yep, I remember that party. And I do sure hope you find them. The women, especially. They weren't nice. No, sir. They weren't nice at all."

"How so?"

"They laughed too much—and at the wrong things. Cackled like hens, they did. Everything them boys did, they thought was funny. No matter how cruel—pointless." The fellow paused and shook his head as he remembered.

Longarm smoked his cheroot and said nothing, content to let Kilmer set the pace.

"There was more than them two brothers and the girls."

"How many?"

"One more, a feller called himself Hardamen. Jason Hardamen. He was as bad as them girls and almost as bad as them brothers." Again Kilmer shook his head. "They was mean as grizzlies, Marshal. Meaner, since a grizzly maybe has a good enough reason for taking after a body."

"What did they do?"

"Tortured me is what they did."

"Why?"

"For the pure devil enjoyment of it, that's why. Wouldn't believe it to look at them. Meek as pie they was when they rode up. Polite, even. But they're pure devil right to the bone marrow, and that's the truth."

"Where were they heading?"

"You mean after they robbed me of my supplies and kicked me until I was too weak to cry out?"

"That's right."

"Heard them talk about a place they had in Butte Canyon."

"How far is that?"

"You sure want a lot of information for this here cheroot, don't you?"

"I have another."

"Yes. You give it to me and I'll save it. Don't often come across them out here."

Longarm took out another cheroot and handed it to Kilmer. The fellow took it, got up, and went into his sod shack. He returned a moment later with two tin cups, and bent over the coffeepot. It was sending out a delicious aroma by this time, and Longarm felt his stomach knot hungrily.

Kilmer poured the coffee for them and handed Longarm his cup. "Ain't got no fixin's," he said without apology, as he sat back down beside Longarm, his bony legs folded under him. The smell of the cheroots and the rich aroma from the steaming coffeepot helped mask the man's strong, rancid stench. Except for skunk,

Longarm didn't know an animal whose smell wasn't pleasant, in a way. But there was nothing ever pleasant about the smell of an unwashed human.

"Butte Canyon," Kilmer began, sipping his hot coffee carefully, "is a two, maybe three days' ride, due west of here. Best way to go is through Pine Valley, where that teamster and his clan live. His name's Tatum. You can't miss the place. He's got mules and wagons all over the place. But he don't keep his animals the way a man should. He is a mean, slipshod excuse for a man, and that's a fact."

"You don't like him."

"Nope. Don't like him or his women." Kilmer glanced at Longarm. "Don't like most humanfolk. Never did see one I could trust further than I could throw a polecat."

"Maybe you ain't been looking in the right places, old man."

"Ain't no right place for a human—not on this here globe, leastways. We don't have no use, 'cept to stink up the place. Buzzards make more sense than a man does."

"What are you doing out here then, Kilmer?"

"Doin' what most fellers do—tearin' up the landscape. Diggin' and diggin', hoping to strike it rich. And I will too."

"How long you been out here?"

"Too long."

"How come you stick it out, then?"

Kilmer looked craftily at Longarm, and that hint of madness Longarm had caught earlier reappeared in the old man's eyes. He leaned forward, so close that Longarm's head spun from the stench. "I found me a chunk of gold as big as your fist—a float, it was, off the mother lode itself."

"When was this?"

The light died in the man's eyes. He frowned as he tried to recall just how long ago he had come upon the float. "Eight, maybe ten years ago, I'd say. When I found the first one, that is. I found the second one higher up, and this chunk was bigger. It proved out at two hundred dollars a ton!" Again the light returned to his eyes. "I'm gettin' closer to that lode. I can tell. I been workin' uphill, pannin' all the way, and I been findin' color most ever' time. It's out here!" He looked quickly about him. "I'll find it!"

"The mother lode."

"Yes! The mother lode."

Longarm nodded. He could understand why a search over so many years for a prize that fabulous would taint a man with madness. It would be the madness in the end, and only the madness, that would keep him going.

And those Poser brothers had stolen from, and beaten this crazy old codger while their women looked on and cackled. Shaking his head, Longarm tossed the dregs of his coffee into the fire and stood up.

"Thanks, Kilmer," he said, "for the information and the coffee."

"Now, you don't need to rush off," the fellow protested, scrambling to his feet with remarkable agility considering his condition and age. "You won't get anywhere before full dark. Camp here with me and get an early start in the mornin'. Been a long time since I slept near another human. A man gets lonely."

"Even for a fellow human?"

"Long as he ain't mean," Kilmer replied, glancing warily at Longarm.

"I'll go see to my horse," Longarm told him.

Longarm groaned inwardly as he saw who it was looming over him. Kilmer's gaunt frame managed to block out the bright moon, and quiet though he had been in his approach, it was the stink of the old man that had alerted Longarm, dragging him from his deep sleep. His right hand closed tightly about the grips of his Colt as he braced himself.

The old man paused a moment. Was he about to repent of his nefarious intentions? Longarm held his breath and continued to gaze up at the frozen stick of a man through his partially closed eyelids. Then he saw the man lean back, the broad blade of a bowie knife gleaming in the moonlight as Kilmer raised it high above his head. Before he could bring the weapon down, Longarm rolled out of his soogan.

Startled into immobility by Longarm's unexpected move, the prospector could only gasp as Longarm rose to his feet, his Colt leveled on Kilmer's gut.

"Drop it," Longarm said quietly, "or you'll never find that mother lode, Kilmer."

"You ain't cocked your weapon," the man replied desperately.

"This is a double-action. I don't need to cock it. Reckon I'll just have to give you a demonstration."

The knife fell to the ground.

Longarm picked up the bowie, hefted it thoughtfully, then tossed it into the darkness. He shook his head and peered through the dimness at the man who had asked him to stay the night, so he could enjoy for a while the companionship of a fellow human being. "You are a fraud, old man," Longarm said. "A deceitful, disreputable old fraud, at that. I suspicion those Possum Boys were just giving you what you deserved. What did you do, attack one of the girls?"

The man took an unsteady step backward. "Gawdamighty, Marshal! Don't shoot! I dropped my knife! I'm an unarmed man!"

"My dander's up, Kilmer! Pulling this here trigger would do me a world of good!"

"I was just thinkin' of you leavin' and takin' them fine cigars with you! And me bein' alone again. Ain't no tellin' how long it'd be afore I'd get a chance like that again. Mister, you gotta believe me! I do crave tobacco."

"What else do you crave, old man?"

"Well, them Poser boys, they took my supplies and shot my mule just to watch it kick. So I don't have no pack animal. I . . . I needed your horse too."

"I see."

"I done the wrong thing, Marshal! I see that now. Ain't no excuse for such behavior, and that's a fact. Makes me no better than them others that beat on me. But you are a lawman. I saw your badge. You can't kill an unarmed man!"

"No, I can't," Longarm admitted. "But I want to sleep. I got a long ride ahead of me tomorrow."

"Why, just tie me up, Marshal. That ain't no problem, and I sure wouldn't blame you none."

"You wouldn't?"

"No, sir. I just wouldn't."

"And that's a fact, is it?"

"Yes, it is."

"You got any rawhide?"

"Inside my hut."

"Go get it."

As Kilmer went after the rawhide, Longarm uncoiled the rope stashed under his saddle and looped it over the branch of a gnarled pinyon clinging to the side of the cliff that hung over the campsite. When the old man emerged from his hut with the rawhide and saw the rope dangling from the pinyon, he froze abruptly.

"My God, Marshal!" he cried.

"I ain't going to hang you, you old reprobate. But you're going to know you been caught with your fist in a bear trap. Now march over here!"

Not long after, Longarm was back in his soogan, but he had moved it some distance from the prospector's hut, close to the spring pouring from the rock cleft. The sound of the icy water trickling down the rock face masked somewhat the unpleasant sounds the old prospector was making as he hung from Longarm's rope. Longarm had bound his ankles and tied his hands behind his back with the rawhide; then he had tied the rope around the man's chest, under his armpits, hauled him up, and stuffed a piece of the prospector's own filthy underwear in his mouth to keep him from crying out.

Nevertheless, the prospector was still making a considerable fuss as he turned slowly in the night wind, the tips of his toes inches from the ground. Thoroughly exhausted, Longarm closed his eyes. The sound of the outraged old man faded, and soon Longarm was asleep.

Longarm reached Pine Valley close to sundown the next day. Pulling up on a ridge overlooking the valley, he gazed down at what he assumed was the Tatum place. The old prospector was right; it was difficult to miss the ranch. The yard in front of the main house was littered with the ruined torsos and broken wheels of old freight wagons. The barns were badly in need of repair, and a huge, untended mound of manure filled most of the corral that held Tatum's mules. The mules themselves were a scrawny, pathetic-looking bunch.

After Longarm had cut down the prospector that morning, he had asked the man for more information on Tatum. The now docile old man told him what he could. It wasn't much beyond what he had given Longarm the night before, but one interesting fact had been added: Tatum had bid for the contract to supply ties and ballast for the Rio Grande Western and had been upset to learn that Ty Flynn's outfit had outbid him. The prospector had been at the Tatum place at the time, bargaining for a new mule, the same one the Possum Boys had killed.

As Longarm watched the ranch, he saw two hulking men leave one of the barns—the one nearest the house —and trudge toward the ranch house. A second later two women left the barn and straggled after them. Looking closely at the two women, Longarm thought he saw one of them walking with her head down, while the other helped her along. Both of them seemed a bit unsteady on their feet. Before the two women reached the house, the door was flung open, the two men hurried inside, and a tall, husky woman appeared in the open doorway. She seemed to be shouting something at the women. At her appearance in the doorway, they had looked up and started to hurry toward the house. Now they began to run. A moment later they ducked past the woman, and the door slammed shut behind them.

Longarm frowned. Something about the scene troubled him. Not only was it the apparent distress of the two women; it was the fact that Kilmer had told him that the Tatum household consisted of Jefferson Tatum, his wife Amelia, and their two sons, Pike and Stringer. There had been no mention of sisters or wives.

Who were those two women, then?

Longarm nudged his black and let it pick its way down the slope toward the valley and Jefferson Tatum's ranch.

"Now just let me hear that again," said Tatum, shifting the shotgun to his other arm. "And speak out so a body can hear you."

Longarm chucked his Stetson back off his forehead and nodded agreeably. "I been sent by Mike O'Leary. He wants to know if you'll consider supplying him with ballast."

"That's what I thought you said," the man bellowed, obviously enjoying himself immensely. "What happened to Ty Flynn's outfit? Can't he cut the mustard?"

"All I know is what O'Leary told me. He knew I'd be passing through, and he asked me to see if you'd consider hauling the ballast."

"Passin' through, are you?"

"That's right."

"What's your business, mister?"

"I'll give you my name. Don't figure you have to know much more than that."

"What is it, then?"

The man's tall, big-bosomed wife was standing in the doorway behind him, peering over Tatum's shoulder at Longarm. Longarm could feel the woman's hard eyes on him.

"Name's Long. Custis Long."

"Well, you bring good news, Long," Tatum said agreeably, "so light and set a spell. Fact is, it's late enough. You could stay the night."

"Much obliged," said Longarm, swinging out of his saddle.

Tatum turned and shouted into the house, and one of his boys came boiling out past the two in the doorway to take Longarm's horse. This boy was taller than his father, but not any taller than his mother. He was dark, lean, with coal-black eyes and shiny black hair. The woman had a lot of Indian blood left in her, and so did this son—Ute blood, more than likely.

As Longarm entered the ranch house, he found it spare and well kept—surprisingly so, considering the state of the ranch buildings, fenceposts, and barns. The woman was a tenacious housekeeper, it seemed. Longarm nodded politely toward her as he stepped into the kitchen, laid his hat on the table, and sat down. The remaining son was standing in the outer kitchen doorway; his arms folded impassively over his broad chest. Behind him, huddled nervously in a shadowy corner, were the two girls Longarm had glimpsed from the ridge. No longer holding his shotgun, Tatum sat down opposite Longarm.

"Maw," Tatum said to his wife, "bring that jug. This here feller and I got some sociable drinkin' to do." He grinned at Longarm, revealing uneven, yellow teeth. "An' you ain't invited. You know damn well half-breeds can't hold their liquor like a white man."

The big woman said nothing as she turned about and reached under the sink for the brown and white jug. When she slapped it on the table between them, however, Longarm caught a gleam in her eyes—as they flicked over her husband—that caused a shiver to tremble up his spine. Tatum was running out his string with this woman of his, only he didn't have the sense to know it—or pay it any heed if he did.

At the moment, he appeared to be as happy as a pig in a root cellar as he tipped the jug up and took two gargantuan swallows. Cleaning off the neck with a single swipe of his dirty palm, he handed the jug across the table to Longarm. Longarm took it, tipped it quickly, and swallowed the liquid fire. It went off like nitroglycerin in his stomach and he felt his eyes watering, but he said nothing as he wiped his mouth and handed back the jug.

Tatum hunched forward, his eyes fixed on Longarm. "So Ty Flynn's havin' trouble, is he?"

Longarm shrugged. "All I know is what I told you."

Tatum leaned back and looked at Longarm speculatively. "What else does O'Leary need, besides ballast? I can get him all the stone he wants, and I can get him plenty of good-quality pine for telegraph poles and solid, dependable ties. My boys and I could handle the whole deal. Hell, he don't need them tinhorns, Ty and Tramp."

"You ain't afraid of those Indians?"

The man exploded in laughter. "No, mister. We sure as hell ain't! That's a good one, that is!" He turned then to his son standing behind him. "Ain't it, Pike?"

"You better not say too much, Pa," the boy said, his eyes narrowing as he peered at Longarm. "You don't rightly know who this feller is."

"He's a bearer of good tidings!" Tatum declared happily, reaching once more for the jug. "We got that O'Leary right where we wants him—and we're slammin' the door on Ty Flynn, leavin' him and that uppity partner of his out in the cold!"

"I guess you'll be wanting to haul supplies for O'Leary, then," Longarm said. He sat back in his chair. "That right?"

"Yes, sir, mister. I was countin' on that contract. But them two four-flushers outbid me. Didn't know they could, less'n they hired lots of scab labor to mine the ballast, and Chinamen to cut and haul the timbers." He leaned back. "Which they did."

"And you ain't afraid of losing your scalps to the Indians? They've sure been making a mess of Flynn's operation. I hear they've slowed Chapman down considerable."

"Of course," said Tatum. "Chapman can't grade without ballast and he can't lay tracks without ties. And Ty Flynn couldn't deliver. But me and my boys, we can!" He smiled then and, reaching back, took hold of his wife's wrist and pulled her closer to the table. "See here? This is my charm! The Utes won't hurt one of their own kind!" He glanced back up at her. "Ain't that right, Maw?"

Slowly but firmly, she disengaged herself from his grip and straightened her back. With a cold, withering glance at her husband, she said, "You know the Utes are not attacking Ty's men."

"Shush, Maw!" Pike cried. "You just let Pa handle this!"

The other son, Stringer, entered the kitchen at that point, paused in the doorway, and looked around inquiringly. Stringer wanted to know what was wrong. When he looked at Pike, his brother put a finger to his lips to warn him.

"Gettin' too crowded in here," Tatum announced. "Come on, Long. We'll go out onto the porch and let Maw rustle up supper. And it won't be long, will it, Injun?"

She shook her head sullenly.

Snatching up the jug, Tatum led Longarm from the kitchen. Already Longarm's senses were reeling somewhat from that lightning-in-a-jug he had just sampled. He hoped fervently that Ma Tatum did not waste much time in preparing supper. He did not see how he could stay on his feet with this old moonshiner matching him drink for drink.

Longarm's head was spinning dangerously throughout the supper, but it did not prevent him from appreciating Ma Tatum's magnificent repast. There were bright yellow squash, potato pie, beef-and-dumpling stew, great slabs of freshly made bread, and all of it washed down with gallons of black coffee. He was fit to burst and his head was almost steady on his shoulders once again by the time the two girls began clearing the table.

"I must say, Mrs. Tatum," Longarm said to the woman, "you sure do know how to warm a man's heart."

The woman was in the act of clearing off the table, and held a large bowl in her hand. She paused, and for a brief moment Longarm thought she was going to throw the remains of the hot stew in his face. Her eyes stared right through him, and in that instant Longarm realized that Ma Tatum did not mind one bit the way her husband treated her. Any other kind of treatment was a mistake; she undoubtedly regarded it as a form of weakness. Now, staring at him with contempt, she appeared to be trying to figure out Longarm's motive in complimenting her. It was impossible for her to believe his remark was sincere.

Longarm pushed back his chair quickly and got to his feet without bothering to excuse himself. He glanced down at Tatum. "A little more of that firewater, Tatum," he said, "and I'll just sleep like a baby."

"Good idea, Long," the man said.

Tatum snatched up the jug from its place under the sink and followed Longarm out onto the front porch.

Despite the way the universe rocked about him—or perhaps because of it—Longarm was in no danger of falling asleep. And that was just the way he wanted it.

They had placed him in a back room next to the kitchen and had fashioned a bed for him out of a considerable pile of burlap bags and flour sacks. Over the top of this he had spread his soogan. The bare wooden walls were damp, and bluebottle flies buzzed maddeningly about his face and neck. But it was his racing thoughts that bothered him the most. Getting a handle on them took some doing.

On the one hand, he had struck pay dirt. Tatum was obviously behind the attacks on Ty Flynn's freighters. His motive was simple: by slowing down and disrupting Flynn's operation, he put himself in line for the job. Longarm's hunch that this was so—coming at the moment he had heard that Tatum had attempted to outbid Ty Flynn for the contract to supply Chapman's work force—had been right on target. On the other hand, there was really no way he could prove a thing now. By the time Tatum learned that Longarm had lied, the tracks would have reached Eagle Pass, and his motive for further attacks would be gone. Defeated in his attempt to discredit Flynn and stop O'Leary, he would simply fold his tent and steal sullenly away—to some other disreputable scheme, Longarm had no doubt.

That meant Tatum would escape prosecution and conviction for his many crimes. The Possum Boys and the other "Indians" who rode with them were Tatum's henchmen, carrying out Tatum's orders. It galled Longarm to think of this miscreant getting clean away like that.

And he did not intend to allow it.

This led him once again to the consideration of his scheme involving the two girls. They were not part of the family. From the moment he had seen them from the ridge, he had realized what they were doing on this ranch. They were on hand to amuse Pike and Stringer. They were virtual slaves. That had been perfectly obvious throughout the meal. As a result of their frolic in the hay not long before the meal, one of them had a bruise on her chin, the other a deep, angry scratch down the right side of her neck. Both of them were scared witless.

They were the two prostitutes the Possum Boys had taken with them from Eagle. What mean quirk had prompted the brothers to leave them here with Tatum was no concern of Longarm's. What was his concern was whether or not these girls knew for sure who he was. He had never met either of them personally, but surely the Poser boys must have told them about Longarm, and his reason for pursuing them.

There was a good chance, therefore, that both girls knew who he was and why he was here, which was the reason he had given Tatum his correct name—and why he was lying awake now in this fly-infested back room, waiting. . . .

The girl was through the door so swiftly, it looked as if she had just materialized on his side of it. It was the older of the two girls, and the taller. She paused with her back against the door, peering down at him in the darkness; then she darted from the door and ducked down beside him, her face close to his. In the moonlight filtering through the small, dirt-encrusted window, he saw her strained, distraught face, the desperation in her eyes.

"Mr. Long!" she whispered urgently. "Mr. Long! Wake up!"

"I'm awake, girl," Longarm told her, raising himself at once onto his elbows. "Keep your voice down."

"Oh! You've been waiting!"

"You might say that. Which one are you? Cherry or Faith?"

"I'm Faith. You mean you know who we are?"

"Just as you seem to know who I am. Do you?"

She nodded quickly. "You're a lawman. Dick told me you were after him. He told me what you looked like. When you walked in with Tatum, I knew it was you."

"What happened? Did the Poser brothers dump you?"

She nodded, ducking her head in shame.

"Why?"

"It's shameful, Mr. Long."

"Tell me."

"We're . . . we're sick. Both of us. We didn't know we had it, but then Dick and then Lou—and after them, Jason Hardamen—got sick, so they knew it had to be us. Them Posers were real mad at us, and Hardamen said some awful things to me. It was Dick had the idea. They never liked Pike Tatum or Stringer, his brother, so they . . . sold us to Tatum for his boys. Said we'd make men of them. I don't think Tatum knew what they meant, not really."

"And of course you ain't let on yet to either of them . . . about your condition, I mean."

"We're afraid, Mr. Long. But pretty soon them boys is goin' to get sick, just like Dick and Lou. And then they'll just beat on us and beat on us!" She began to weep then, holding her face in her hands.

"If I take you and Cherry away from here, will you testify in court about what you know? I mean about the way Tatum has been working with the Posers and this fellow Hardamen?"

She nodded quickly. "Oh yes, Mr. Long! Just take us away from here. Please!"

"Now settle down, Faith. Let me find out just what you *do* know about Tatum and his connection with the Posers. Go on now. And keep your voice down."

Faith leaned closer to Longarm. In a breathless whisper she told him of Tatum's dealings with the Posers and the Hardamen gang, of which Tip Wills had been a member. In surprising detail she related the planning of the assault on the Chinese powder monkeys. She had even witnessed the men's transformation into "Indians," in one instance actually helping to gather the berries used to stain their faces.

When she had finished, Longarm could hardly believe his good fortune. Both girls would make excellent witnesses. If he could capture the Posers and what was left of the Hardamen gang, getting the goods on Tatum would be a fairly simple matter.

"What about Otto Pears?" Longarm asked.

"Who's he?"

"Didn't Tatum or any of the Posers mention him?"

"No, Mr. Long. Honest."

"And what about Jack Lynch?"

"I don't know who he is, either."

"Is that the truth, Faith?"

"Oh yes. Please believe me. I'm not lying. I wouldn't lie. All I want is for you to take us away from these Tatums—and that woman of his. That Indian."

"Can you and Cherry leave tonight?"

"Oh yes!"

"All right. Get Cherry and take as little as possible. I'll take you back to Eagle and expect you to testify later. Is that understood?"

She nodded quickly.

Longarm sat up. He had taken only his boots off. Swiftly he drew them on, stuck his hat on his head, and rolled up his soogan. "I'll be outside in the barn, saddling the horses."

"All right," she whispered.

He finished tying up his bedroll and turned. She was gone, as silently as she had entered.

Longarm was leading three saddled horses from their stalls when he heard the scuff of a boot in the barn's open doorway. He turned. In the light of the single lamp he had lit, he saw Tatum—dressed in a long white nightshirt, his shotgun in one hand—stride into the barn and fling Faith ahead of him. She stumbled, then sprawled forward, coming to rest at Longarm's feet.

Before Longarm could reach for his Colt, Tatum lifted the shotgun coolly. "I don't need to aim this ten-gauge, Long. It's loaded with nine buck to the barrel. Only thing is, you're standin' in front of some pretty costly horseflesh." Tatum waggled the shotgun impatiently. "Move away from them horses. Now!"

As Longarm began to edge sideways, Tatum swore bitterly, his eyes on Faith.

"And take that little sneak along with you," the man said. "Might as well take care of two birds with one load."

"Leave her be, Tatum," Longarm said. "She just wanted to go back to civilization, and I promised to take her."

"You think I didn't hear you two in that back room? You think I don't know now why that son of a bitch Dick Poser left them two sluts here? I saw her sneakin' off to see you right from the first, mister. Thing was, I was hoping for some of that stuff myself, seein' as how my boys were so all-fired pleased with it." He shook his head in wonderment. "Damn good thing I got the itch tonight and went to find her. Yessir, the Good Lord looks after his servants. She's a turncoat and a diseased slut, and you're a lawman. I don't like neither." He directed his furious gaze at the girl. "Now get up, damn it, woman! And stand over there near that lawman you're so anxious to help!"

Faith picked herself up. She glanced wearily, hopelessly at Longarm, unconsciously brushing a damp lock of hair off her forehead. She was fully dressed in torn skirt, torn bodice, and high-button shoes—a wan, forlorn figure. Longarm reached out to her and she stumbled, weeping softly, into his arms. As he pulled her close and comforted her, he let his right hand steal under his frock coat.

"Ain't that touching," Tatum said. "The lawman and the whore."

His eyes narrowed as he steadied the shotgun on them.

At that moment—just as Longarm's hand closed about the grips of his Colt—a pale figure rushed at Tatum from out of the night. The light from the lantern on the wall behind Longarm caught Cherry's wild, desperate face—and her upraised, rapidly descending arm with the knife blade gleaming in her hand. Longarm heard Tatum's gasp and saw him stagger forward into the barn, a look of awesome pain and astonishment etched on his face.

Behind him, standing stock-still in the barn doorway, was Cherry, fully clothed, wearing a pale print dress as ragged as Faith's. She was holding both hands up to her face as she watched Tatum stagger away from her. She seemed about ready to scream.

Before she could, Tatum turned woodenly to face her. The handle of a huge kitchen knife protruded from his back between his shoulder blades. Tatum's shotgun roared. The top of Cherry vanished as swiftly as if she had been a lit candle snuffed out by a cold wind.

Tatum had loosed only one barrel. He turned back to Longarm and Faith. Longarm, his Colt out now, flung Faith to the floor of the barn and fired pointblank at Tatum. He fired twice. Each bullet hit the man in the chest, driving cloth into flesh as two black, then bright dots appeared level with each other, centered three inches apart. The impact of both slugs driving in almost simultaneously lifted Tatum off his feet and hurled him backward. He landed sprawling on the rough barn floor, driving the knife blade still deeper into his back, the shotgun clattering to the floor beside him.

On her knees, wild-eyed, Faith stared at the dead man and what was left of Cherry. Longarm holstered his Colt and dragged her to her feet.

"Mount up!" he told her. "Before the others get here!"

Faith looked at him blankly. He turned her about

roughly and shoved her toward the nearest horse and helped her mount up. By the time he had thrust the reins up into her hands, she appeared to have recovered sufficiently. Longarm flung himself aboard his black and led the way out of the barn.

As they swept into the yard, Longarm saw Pike, Tatum's oldest son, racing from the house toward him, a rifle in his hand. Pike pulled up and leveled his rifle at Longarm.

"Hold it right there, mister!" he cried. "Where's my pa?"

Longarm did not hold up. Drawing his Colt, he galloped straight for the boy.

Pike fired. The round whispered over Longarm's head. He bent low over his mount's neck and spurred the horse on. A well-trained animal, it veered slightly to avoid the boy, but Pike, in his singleminded attempt to get a clear shot, stepped directly in front of the black. Before he could fire again, the black's forelegs thumped into him. The horse stumbled slightly, regained its balance, and swept on. Glancing back, Longarm saw Pike's broken, sprawled body lying facedown in the moonlit yard.

From the house came a shot. As Longarm glanced in that direction, he heard Faith—galloping close behind him—cry out in shock and pain. He fired once, swiftly, at Stringer standing in the open doorway. A second shot brought the boy to his knees. As Stringer pitched forward, Longarm caught a glimpse of the boy's mother bending over him.

Longarm was aware that Faith's horse was no longer pounding along behind him. He pulled up and rode back. The horse was standing beside Faith's crumpled figure. Dismounting swiftly, he lifted her head and shoulders.

"I'm hit," she told him.

"Where?"

"In my side. It don't hurt so bad. Please take me with you. Don't leave me here!"

Longarm lifted the girl swiftly in his arms, placed her across his horse's neck, then swung up behind her. As he spurred his horse from the compound, he glanced back at the ranch house in time to see Ma Tatum walking slowly across the yard toward her other son, who was still sprawled facedown in the dust.

Chapter 8

On his way back to Eagle with the wounded girl, Longarm caught sight of a lone woman trundling a wheelbarrow load of dirt to a small sluice outside an abandoned mine's entrance. She was working steadily, head down, intent on her labor. A large, black, flopbrimmed hat was on her head, and the skirts of her dark dress brushed the ground as she trudged behind her barrow. Towering over her and set starkly against the wall of sheer rock behind it were the broken, weathered remnants of a stamp mill, portions of its roof gone completely and great, gaping holes in its sides. On the other side of a narrow gully, atop a small rise, he saw a small cabin. From where he sat his horse, he was able to catch the bright gleam of a curtain in one of the windows.

At once Longarm turned his horse toward the mine entrance. The nearly unconscious Faith groaned slightly as the horse picked its way down the talus-littered slope. Longarm leaned forward and stood slightly in the stirrups as he lifted Faith gently to reduce the pounding she was taking.

Faith turned her head slightly. "It's all right, Longarm. I'm just fine."

He did not argue with her, but he knew she was not

fine. She was in considerable pain. The round had passed through her side, leaving a gaping wound he had been able to staunch only with great difficulty. Yet she had uttered not a sound as he worked on her. Indeed, throughout this morning's ride, her grit had humbled him. She leaned her head back against his chest. He glanced at her and saw the tears leaking down her sallow, sweat-stained cheek.

When Longarm's horse reached the stream that cut below the mine and began to pick its way across, the woman caught the clink of iron on stone. Letting down the wheelbarrow, she turned completely around and shaded her eyes. As Longarm guided the black up the slope toward her, he saw that she was a woman of perhaps fifty, with a strong, raw-boned face. Watching him approach, her large, dark eyes were narrowed with suspicion, her mouth a grim line.

By the time Longarm had ridden to within ten yards of her, her face had softened somewhat as she saw Faith's drawn face and realized that the girl had been wounded. Longarm pulled up in front of her. The woman glanced with some concern up into the girl's face.

"What is it, child?" she asked. "You in a bad way?"

"She's been shot," Longarm told the woman. "You got a place where she can rest? We've been riding since last night."

The woman looked at Longarm through narrowed eyes. "You the one shot her? A lover's quarrel, maybe?"

"No, ma'am," Longarm said. "But it's a long story, and I'd sure appreciate having someone like yourself take a look at her."

The woman turned and started toward her cabin. "Follow me, then," she said. "But you sure better have a good reason for hurting that poor girl."

"Don't mind her, Longarm," Faith whispered. "I'll explain it to her."

"Just so she's got a place to lay you down, Faith," he said, as he nudged his horse after the woman, "I don't care what she believes."

The woman's name was Augusta Fields. She was working the mine alone, as Longarm had surmised when he rode up. She had little to say to him beyond this as she busied herself tending to Faith's wound. Longarm kept out of her way, sitting on a battered wooden chair in front of the cabin while Augusta Fields stripped Faith of her soiled dress, bathed her, and fed her.

It was late that afternoon when the woman emerged from the cabin and looked down at Longarm. He was smoking one of his last cheroots. He took the cheroot from his mouth and looked questioningly up at her.

"She going to be all right?" he asked.

"She's young, but she ain't so strong. And it looks like she lost a lot of blood. She's sleeping now, and that's a good sign. But I ain't too optimistic."

Longarm nodded and went back to his cheroot.

"She told me what happened. I guess I had you figured all wrong."

"Don't think anything of it, ma'am. And I sure do appreciate you helping this girl. I was beginning to think she wasn't going to make it."

"Where were you taking her?"

"Back to Eagle."

"She wouldn't have." The woman turned and started back into the cabin. "There's coffee on," she told him. "And I've got some beans and flapjacks heatin' on the stove. Come in when you've a mind to."

Longarm moved the black's picket pin, hunted up a bucket, which he filled with water from the stream and placed down next to the animal, and then went into the cabin. The woman had cleaned the place so that it almost sparkled. His meal was waiting for him on a well-scrubbed plank table, an oversized mug of black coffee steaming beside the plate. The flapjacks were piled high and there was even some syrup.

As Longarm sat down on the bench chair, he looked around for Faith. But she was not in sight. Then he saw the bedsheet folded over a line, creating a partition in the rear of the cabin, and realized that Faith was asleep behind it.

Augusta sat down at the table across from him and leaned her elbows on the table to watch him eat. She seemed to enjoy it. After a few moments, she straightened and fixed him with her eyes.

"You're a lawman, huh?"

"That's right, ma'am."

"My friends used to call me Gus."

"Don't they still do that?"

"My friends are all dead. Like my husband. What he left me was this mine, and that's all. So I'm working it and making do."

"My friends call me Longarm."

She nodded. "That's what Faith called you. She's a sporting girl, ain't she?"

"She worked at Jane Clyman's parlor house in Eagle."

"Jane Clyman! A terrible woman."

Longarm shrugged. "Not anymore, she ain't." And then he told Augusta what ill luck had befallen Jane Clyman as she waited in the street below for her man to rejoin her.

Augusta shook her head. "A terrible woman. I know all about her. You seem to have handled her rather well. She was not a credit to our profession, and that's a fact."

Longarm looked sharply at her. "*Our* profession, ma'am?"

The woman smiled. "For many years, Longarm, I ran a sporting house in Leadville. It was there that I met my husband, Tad. I staked him, and he struck it rich. And for a time that's what we were—very rich."

Her eyes began to glow as she remembered. "Trips to Europe, a mansion, stables, fancy carriages. For a while it was my wildest fantasies come true." She smiled sadly. "It was surprising how soon we got used to all that money." She shrugged. "And then the mine played out."

"So you came back here alone."

"I tried to return to my profession, but it was difficult to get the right girls, and my locations were always poor, it seemed. Besides, you know, it can be a very depressing business at times. There were too many women like Jane Clyman for my taste."

"It is a sorry business, no matter who runs the parlor," Longarm agreed quietly.

She waited until he finished his coffee before saying anything more. She seemed anxious to explain herself. "I went into the sporting life because it was the only business a woman was allowed to own. It was business, pure and simple. I had to live, didn't I? I had no education, and I had no man. My face has character now; it was just plain ugly then. What was I to do? It was a way in those days for a woman to make money, and I made it. I operated the best houses in town. Why, Longarm, I had as clients some of the most important men in the West."

"I wasn't thinking of you. I was thinking of the girls, ma'am—like Faith in there."

"I never took a girl into my house who was a virgin or inexperienced. That was a rule I never broke. Most of the girls that found their way to my house had already run away from their husbands—or else they had become involved with a man and then been abandoned. It was the street and starvation for most of them—or my house. No innocent young girl was ever enticed into the profession by me. Hell, some of my girls married the customers. And my girls made good wives, from all I've been able to gather. They understood a man's needs and knew how to pleasure him, and they were faithful to their husbands."

"You make your house sound like a school for wives."

She smiled. "Maybe that's what it was, Longarm. It made me a good and loving wife to Tad. I never cheated on him. He was a good man and I loved him."

"And he never brought up your past?"

"Never. Like I said, he was a good man. He was also a gentleman."

Longarm glanced at the sheet that separated Faith from the rest of the cabin. "If that girl in there makes it, I sure wouldn't like to see her go back into the profession. She's been through enough."

Frowning with concern, Augusta glanced toward where Faith lay and nodded. "I agree. She certainly has."

"She's sick too."

"She told me that, as well." She shook her head. "The girls who worked for me made good money. But . . . they seemed unable to keep it. Some saved, but most did not. They were ignorant, crude, ill-educated, and that's a fact. They died early. Bungled abortions, too much bottle, disease, suicide . . . I had one girl who committed suicide when her steady man started to see the other girls in my house. He had been a virgin, you see, and the poor little scatterbrain thought for sure that made him special. She drank all the laudanum she could get her hands on one night . . ."

The woman sighed and got up to clear off Longarm's table.

Longarm took out his last cheroot, intending to light up outside. "How soon will you know for sure if Faith's going to make it?"

"She's got a fever. An infection from that wound, most likely. By tomorrow morning we should know."

"Then I'll stay over the night."

"All right, Longarm."

Longarm stepped outside the cabin and slumped wearily into the chair. He was exhausted. He had gotten no sleep the night before, and this day's ride had drained him. But he was relieved that he had found this strange woman to care for Faith. He lit up his cheroot and leaned back, remembering how odd she had looked when he first spotted her trundling that wheelbarrow toward the sluice, her long skirts dragging on the ground.

Longarm turned over in his soogan, instantly awake. "Who's that?"

"Shhh," Augusta said. "You'll wake up Faith. She's sleeping more quietly now."

"Oh." Longarm relaxed and lay his head back down on the straw-filled pillow.

The woman had brought in planks from the mine entrance and laid them down on the cabin's dirt floor. Over the planks, Longarm had unrolled his bedroll. He had turned in at sundown and gone almost immediately to sleep.

He was aware that the woman was still standing over him, and he realized also that she had bathed and scented herself. He had bathed himself by the stream before retiring for the night. She had provided him with the soap. In fact, it had been her idea. The cabin was as black as pitch, but even so, as his eyes peered up through the darkness at her, he gradually became aware of her tall, naked form. In the close darkness it appeared to waver slightly as his eyes struggled to see her. Her black pubic patch seemed to disappear and reappear in the midst of her shimmering paleness.

And then she was kneeling beside him.

"I am older than you, Longarm. But I am clean and free of disease. And I still know how to please a man."

"I'm sure you do, ma'am."

"Call me Gus. Please. I told you earlier you could do that."

"All right . . . Gus."

"That's better."

She brushed her finger swiftly over his face, and a moment later she was kissing him, softly at first, her head moving only slightly, her lips parting his with a gentleness that was close to a caress. Then she lifted her face away, turned her head, and rested her cheek against his cheek.

"Was that the kiss of an old woman, Longarm?"

"No, Gus," Longarm managed, astonished. "It was not."

Swiftly, yet lightly, she opened the flap of his soogan and slid in beside him. As he felt the warmth of her long limbs beside his, he realized how well she had kept herself. Undoubtedly the work on the mine had kept her in shape. Her breasts were still full, almost buoyant, as she held herself against him. He felt the embers of desire within him leaping to life.

Her lips found his a second time. Again there was the gentleness, the delicious, practiced restraint. She teased him with the tip of her tongue. It was only for an instant. He moved closer to her, enclosing her shoulders in his arms, moving onto her. She pulled her mouth away from his and began to nibble his earlobe.

"Slow down, Longarm," she whispered. "There's no hurry!"

He chuckled, then moved his lips down her angular chin and began kissing her neck. Her heard her soft murmurs of pleasure, and moved his lips still farther down until he found her breasts. He could not believe their warmth. They became full under his questing mouth, thrusting. Her nipples hardened. He toyed with them expertly, nipping at them lightly with his teeth, flicking them with his tongue. She had tried to play upon him, to drive him to distraction by her deliberate lovemaking. But he was in charge now; she had ignited him completely. His lips moved down to her belly.

He felt her being caught up as well. What had been

for her at the beginning simply an exercise in craft was now something more, much more.

He kissed her belly, then moved back to her breasts, crouching over her now, his erection pulsing eagerly beneath him. He heard her moan. He chuckled and she sank her teeth into his shoulder, biting almost hard enough to draw blood. He leaned quickly over her breasts and took one in his mouth, roughly. Groaning again, she spread herself to receive him, her legs raised high, her hips rolling and rising under him as he plunged deep into her. He was astonished and pleased to find her as tight as a clenched fist.

"Slow," she whispered huskily, her head back, both arms flung about his neck. "That's it. Oh, so nice and slow. Yes . . . !"

Twice when he felt her nearing climax he slowed to a stop, plunging fully into her hot depths, holding her tightly and pressing in as deeply as he could go without motion. Each time, her breathing eased and her moans died away until he began thrusting again. At last she began to cry and tremble from head to foot. He knew she was ready now. He stepped up his tempo, and soon forgot her as he soared himself, bringing her with him to a final, dazed explosion that left them both limp and motionless.

After they regained their breath, Longarm rolled off her and she ran her fingers through his damp hair. "How soon before the encore?" she whispered huskily.

"My God," he said, chuckling.

"I am insatiable, Longarm."

"I reckon so—if that means you can't get enough."

She laughed softly, her voice rich and warm—as if all her years had been wiped away in that flood of passion. "Yes. That's what it means. Do you blame me? How often will such an opportunity come again to an old woman?"

"You sure don't feel old, and that's the truth of it."

"Lovemaking does have a way of stopping time,"

she murmured, closing her eyes and breathing deeply. "Sometimes even rolling it back some."

Longarm rested his head upon one of her breasts, and she put her arm around him and held him against her warmth. The smell of her lulled him. He felt his senses spinning away into delicious tides of sleep.

And then he became aware of her hands moving expertly over his limbs, exploring every secret part of him. She had shifted so that he was on his back under her, while she leaned her face over his, the moist tip of her tongue tracing his eyelids and ears, then trailing mischievously down his cheek before it insinuated itself into his parted lips. Her warm hands had already brought him nearly erect, and now, as her tongue darted wantonly into his mouth, his erection peaked.

In that instant she was astride him, plunging down upon his shaft. He heard her gasp, then whimper as she came, shuddering. Longarm clapped his big hands over her buttocks then, and kept her on top of him. She uttered a tiny little cry and arched herself back over his quivering, upthrusting body. His momentum increased. She hung on, delighted. At last she came to life again. Half-shouting through gritted teeth, she let go her third orgasm, while Longarm simply continued his wild plunging. Her juices were flowing freely now, running down onto his belly and down his thighs, but his calloused hands held her tightly down upon him.

Groans began breaking from deep within her throat. She was riding him now with eyes squeezed shut, her hair a wild gray cloud about her head. Longarm reached for her breasts. Grabbing them both, he hung onto her as she rocked with demented abandon above him. Her groans were even deeper and more full-throated than before. Longarm felt himself surging, moving swiftly beyond the point of control.

"Now!" she cried. "Oh, *now,* Longarm . . . !"

He felt her body tensing. She began to come then, in a long, shuddering climax as he arched up under her.

His hands clung to her breasts fiercely. He found himself hanging for just an instant as his own violent spasm wrenched him. At last he was spending himself deep within her, exploding, gushing furiously. . . .

She sank down upon his chest and enclosed him in her strong arms while she hugged him close, not wanting to let him go, willing his erection to remain forever within her. But he realized achingly that there was no way she could do that now. He was strong and he was reasonably young and he was healthy, but he was not eternal.

After breakfast the next morning, Longarm was returning from seeing to his horse when he saw Gus leave the cabin and start across the rough ground toward him. As she approached, he could not help noticing once again the glow on her cheeks and the clean sparkle in her dark eyes. *Hell, you feel pretty damn good yourself, old son,* he told himself as Gus stopped in front of him, a pleased smile on her face.

"I was right, Longarm," she said. "Faith's fever broke during the night. She's as cool as a summer morning now, and hungry as a hog. She'll be all right, I'm thinking."

"How soon can she ride?"

"I can't say for sure. Not for a while anyway. She can stay here with me, Longarm. I won't mind. Like you said, she's sick. Wouldn't be good for her to go amongst men until she's got that taken care of. Soon's I scrape up some cash, I'll take her to Eagle and find her a doctor. Not that that'll do any good," she added bitterly.

"She'll be company for you, anyway," Longarm suggested.

Gus smiled. "Yes, she'll be that."

"Guess I'll be riding on, then." He smiled warmly down at the woman. "And much obliged for the hospitality."

"It was no chore," she said. Then her face grew serious. "Remember what you asked me during breakfast, Longarm?"

"About the Posers?"

"About the Poser brothers and how far Butte Canyon was."

Longarm nodded. "What about it, Gus?"

"Nothing, except you're the second man in as many days who's asked me the same thing."

"Someone else came by here looking for those two?"

"That's right."

"You wouldn't want to describe him, would you?"

In a few well-chosen phrases, she described Wally Stanton perfectly, right down to the fact that he had a tendency to talk more than was necessary. She had liked the dude, however, and had found no offense in him; and when she had warned him about the Posers, he had thanked her, tipped his hat to her, and ridden on—somewhat grimly, she decided, as she thought back on it.

"Glad you told me, Gus," he said to her, frowning with concern. "And then again, maybe I'm not. I'm going to be worried about that fool dude now until I learn he hasn't got his blamed ass shot off." He shook his head in exasperation.

"Guess you'll be moving right out," she said.

"Yes, Gus, I will," he told her, not without reluctance.

"Well, I got some fresh jerky and rolls for your saddlebags, so you just hold on while I go get 'em."

As she turned and hurried back to the cabin, Longarm turned about and went to fetch his black.

It was close to sundown when Longarm rode cautiously into Butte Canyon, his wary eyes searching every inch of the rock on each side. He passed through the entrance without trouble and kept going, the cool shadows beneath the cliff walls providing a welcome respite from the sun.

When the canyon walls began to widen, he dismounted and led his horse, keeping close to the canyon wall. Gus had known the canyon well enough to tell him where the Posers' ranch was. Longarm led his horse across an open stretch that was still being hammered by the fierce, late-afternoon sun. Lizards scuttled for cover, small streaks of green on the hard-packed ground. He surprised a jackrabbit, and it went sailing over the flat in great, high bounces.

Rounding a shoulder of rock, he caught sight of three buildings—a house, a bunkhouse, and a barn—across the flat on the other side of the canyon. It was the Posers' ranch, of that Longarm had no doubt. He could barely make out the corrals and the few horses grazing in a patch of green behind the barn. The stream that had cut the canyon crossed the flat just in front of the ranch yard. For anyone to approach the ranch, he would have to cross that desolate, open space and ford the stream, all the while in plain sight of the ranch's occupants.

Pulling his horse back with him behind the rock shoulder, he started up a game trail that led well in among the rocks, and started looking for a place to camp until night. He could not possibly approach the ranch before then. Even with the darkness as a cloak, he would have a hard row to hoe if he didn't time his approach so he was across the stream and well in among the buildings before the moon rose.

The quarter-moon was whitening the sky beyond the mountains, though it was not yet visible itself, when Longarm finally ducked behind the corner of the bunkhouse. It had been dark for some time, fortunately; the canyon's walls had seen to that. His horse was back where he had camped, and he carried his Winchester.

As he had raced across the flat in the darkness, he

had been on the lookout for any sign of movement about the ranch buildings. The fact that he had seen none had done little to quiet his anxiety concerning Stanton; if the fellow had reached this place ahead of him, where was any sign of his presence? Was he hiding somewhere in the rocks above the ranch, waiting to make his lone assault? Longarm had lost his sign on hard, stony ground a full mile before he reached the canyon. He had seen no sign since then, and this worried him. He had hoped to overtake Stanton so they could join forces in this assault.

Peering around the bunkhouse's corner, he found himself close enough to the house to reach it with a thrown rock. The bunkhouse he had already checked. It was empty. The oil lamps inside the small, two-room frame building were burning, and the light coming from the two front windows made rectangular yellow patches on the ground outside. As Longarm watched, a shadow moved across one of the windows.

The door to the house swung open suddenly. Light flooded down across two wooden steps and out into the yard. A man Longarm did not recognize appeared in the door and emptied a slops jar. The sound of the wet contents slapping the ground came to Longarm clearly —along with the stench. The fellow went back inside and closed the door.

Longarm allowed himself to relax. Those inside the house suspected nothing, or they would not have let any one of them expose himself like that. Longarm waited a while longer, then moved swiftly toward the house, flattened himself against the front wall, and listened.

He heard the lazy hum of voices inside and tried to figure how many there were. He gave it up as an impossible task, relying solely on the sound of their voices, and peered carefully into the room from which most of the voices were coming. He caught a glimpse of the Poser brothers playing cards with three others, one of whom was the fellow who had just dumped the slops jar. As the men played, another fellow emerged from the adjoining room. He was stretching lazily, and as Longarm watched, he pulled his suspenders up over his shoulders and sauntered over to the table to watch the card game. There was an open whiskey bottle on the table, and the players were giving it a steady play, Longarm noticed.

He left the window and crouched down in the darkness. Six men, it looked like; but there could be others in the room that fellow had just emerged from. That room was probably the bedroom. Still, he had seen six men. Some of them, Longarm guessed, were the Hardamens he had heard about.

Six men. Too many for him to tackle while they were all bright and sassy; and there was little likelihood he could bluff them into coming out with their hands up. No, he would just have to wait until they had exhausted that bottle and their senses, then turned in for the night. Meanwhile, Longarm realized, it would be a good idea for him to circle the house and look for a rear door. A look-see into that other room should tell him for sure how many he was up against.

Moving with the silence of a shadow, Longarm made his way along the side of the house, past the privy, and around the corner to the rear. He found two more windows, but no back door. That meant he would have to enter through the front door, since the rear windows, warped by weather and covered with ancient grime, were more than likely stuck solid.

Wiping off the dirt carefully and peering in through one of the rear windows, Longarm found himself looking not into the room adjoining the front room, but into a small tack room, with an array of harnesses and bridles hanging from pegs on the wall. The door to this room was ajar, and through the slim crack he could see the cots in the next room, and the open doorway that led into the room where the card game was in progress. A lantern hung on a wall outside the tack room. It was a three-room house, then. As Longarm's eyes grew accustomed to the gloom and clutter of the tack room, he found his attention drawn to something oddly misshapen that seemed to have been flung in one corner. The yellow band of light from the open door slashed down the length of it.

Longarm groaned and almost dropped his rifle. His stomach turning, he pressed his face still closer to the windowpane. He was certain now. On the floor beside the pale, misshapen thing was a hat—a straw boater. Now, though his mind fought against believing what his eyes conjured out of the darkness, Longarm saw what was left of Wally Stanton. That which had appeared to be a pale, shattered bowl thrown carelessly down upon a pile of rags was what was left of one side of Stanton's face. The long, rumpled pile of flour sacks now became Stanton's sprawled, naked body. Long, raw strips traversed the length of his body. And the light filtering into the room seemed almost to brighten as Longarm stared in horror at the dark, bloody mess— the gaping hole between his legs—where once Stanton's genitals had hung.

Longarm pushed himself away from the window, turned around, and slid to the ground, his back against the cabin. His stomach gave him a few queasy moments as the night spun sickeningly about him. There was an acid taste in his mouth, and his heart was thudding hard against his ribs. He had the weird conviction that its pounding could surely be heard from within the house.

Stanton was dead. No. Worse than that. He might still be alive. Slumped in that back room—dimly aware of the movements of those around him, conscious of excruciating pain and hanging dimly on the edge of consciousness—he might be waiting, praying, for someone, *anyone*, to release him from his agony. Longarm closed his eyes and saw once again the figure slumped behind him in the house. It appeared that great ribbons of his flesh had been ripped from his body, starting from his shoulders and extending down almost as far as his thighs. There was a hole where his nose should have been, and his mouth appeared misshapen.

Was he alive, then? Surely no man could live through such punishment.

With an inward groan, Longarm realized he must find out. There was no way he was going to sit out here in this cool night and wait for those monsters to drink themselves to sleep now. Longarm had to know if Stanton was alive; and if the man was, he had to do what he could to help him.

Now!

He stood up and looked through the window once again. He tried to see if Stanton's chest was moving at all. But the light was simply not strong enough for Longarm to tell one way or the other. He reached up and tried to lift the sash. As he had surmised earlier, it held fast. Dirt had encrusted its edges and now held it solidly. Longarm doubted if anyone had ever tried to open the window since the house had been built. But again he tried to raise it.

His desperate rage gave him a strength that surprised him, and the sash gave just a little. It was not much, but it proved that the sash could be moved. He closed his eyes, took a firm grip on the top of the sash, and pushed. It gave perhaps half an inch. Encouraged, Longarm tried again. The sash edged up another half-inch.

Longarm stepped back, thrust his rifle barrel in under the sash, and pressed down. The sash moved enough to enable him to reach in and grab the bottom of the sash with both hands and lift it. Blood pounded in his temples and the night reeled as he exerted every last ounce of strength he had and slowly, steadily, remorselessly, lifted the sash higher and higher until at last it was wide enough for him to boost himself over the windowsill and pull his rifle in after him.

Aware that the cold night air would find its way through the open doors and into the front room where the gang was playing cards, Longarm silently pulled the door shut. Then he moved closer to Stanton. He leaned his ear against the man's beribboned chest and heard the soft, barely audible drum of his heart.

Longarm winced. Seeing now at closer range what damage had been done to the man—in addition to his castration—the thought that this man was still alive and suffering was almost more than he could bear. He felt the tears running down his cheeks as he gently took Stanton's shoulders and shook him.

"Wally!" he whispered hoarsely. "It's Longarm! Can you hear me?"

The man's head nodded almost imperceptibly. Longarm would not have believed it if Stanton's right arm had not moved slightly as well.

"Lie still!" Longarm told him. "Don't try to move. I'll kill these bastards, then I'll get help."

"No," Longarm heard from Stanton. It was not Stanton's voice, only a distant imitation. And then it dawned on Longarm why it sounded as raspy and hoarse as it did. The man must have torn his throat to pieces screaming. No man could remain silent under this kind of treatment. "No!" Stanton said again, his voice a bit fainter. "Don't get help . . . ! Kill me, please . . . !"

"No, Wally, you . . ."

"Please . . . ! Longarm . . . friend . . ."

Longarm did not trust his own voice, so he nodded.

Stanton's hand reached up. With astonishing strength, he grasped Longarm's shirt front and pulled the lawman closer to his face. "Lynch was here . . . attack . . . Eagle Pass with the Posers and Hardamen . . . stop them, Longarm!"

Again, Longarm nodded.

Stanton appeared to sigh. The ragged, toothless hole that was his mouth went slack and the man appeared to collapse inward. Longarm leaned quickly closer.

"Stanton?" he whispered.

The man's eyes flickered open. Longarm saw tears in them. "Daisy . . . dead. Went back and found her dead . . . doctor drunk. He took the money I gave him and drank it . . . left Daisy to die. Not fair. Not justice . . . at all."

"No," Longarm said, aware of the unreality of the conversation. "It isn't."

"Get . . . the Posers for me . . . Longarm . . . *my* justice . . . !"

"Sure, Wally," Longarm said. "Lie quiet now."

What was left of Stanton's head nodded almost imperceptibly, and then he quietly closed his eyes. Longarm leaned close again. The man's faintly beating heart had stopped. A kind of coldness—like a chill wind—seemed to envelop Longarm. He shivered fitfully and drew back.

Then he reached down carefully and closed each eye. As he did so, he thanked God. He had not wanted to send a bullet crashing into Wally Stanton's brain, even though he had promised. . . .

Straightening slowly, carefully, Longarm turned to the door leading from this small back room. He had closed it, but not tightly. He pushed it open a tiny crack and looked through the narrow opening into the bed-room. A cot was next to the door, the blanket on it rumpled. There was also a booted foot clearly visible. It was pointed straight up and partially covered by the disordered blankets. Pressing his ear against the door, Longarm could hear the sleeper's fitful snoring.

Longarm pushed the door open and slipped into the room and looked down at the bearded face of the man sleeping the sleep of the just on his back, his mouth open, his yellow teeth gleaming, his gray, ragged mustache moving with each snorting exhalation. Looking closely at the man's hands as they rested on the blanket, Longarm saw the bloodstains. Stanton's blood was caked on the man's knuckles and visible under his long fingernails. It looked as if he must have torn at Stanton's body like some ravening beast, after which, exhausted, he had stumbled to this cot and slept. The true horror of it was that this man could lie back—with Stanton's screams fresh in his ears and Stanton's blood staining his fingers—and sleep so peacefully.

Longarm tipped his head slightly in the direction of the open doorway. The men in the next room were still playing cards. He heard the fellow who was not playing moving heavily about, his comments harsh, the players returning his cracks with comments or oaths just as brutal. Occasionally they would give off bursts of harsh, barking laughter; they sounded to Longarm like a pack of rapacious coyotes, animals the Indians believed had no souls, only appetites.

Longarm tensed. The sixth man was approaching the doorway. Moving soundlessly, Longarm flattened himself against the wall beside the door, his Colt out and pressed against his vest. The fellow entering the room, paused with his hand on the door and turned to make a retort to one of the players.

"If I find that bottle, you unlucky son of a bitch, it's mine!"

He turned and pushed the door all the way open and entered. So intent was he on finding his bottle that he looked neither to the right nor to the left as he advanced into the room and started for his cot. Longarm waited until the man had passed him, then reached out and softly swung the door back. He was careful not to close it entirely. The tall fellow heard the door's creak and began to turn. Before he could swing all the way around, Longarm brought the barrel of his Colt down on the crown of the outlaw's head.

The sound the barrel made as it crunched into the

man's skull was unmistakable. As the fellow thudded heavily to the floor, Longarm saw the sleeping man come awake. The outlaw's eyes widened as he saw Longarm crouching over the slumped figure at his feet. He opened his mouth to cry out. Longarm aimed his Colt and fired in one motion. Part of the man's face disappeared, the soiled pillow under his head turning suddenly a dark crimson.

Startled voices erupted from the next room. Longarm heard a table overturning and the sound of a kerosene lamp shattering as it crashed to the floor. Holstering his Colt, he snatched up his rifle from the cot where he had left it and strode to the door just as a burly fellow with wild red hair slammed it wide open. Levering a cartridge into the Winchester's chamber, Longarm fired into the man's gut without bringing the rifle up. Punching through the man's stomach, the round's impact flung him back against an outlaw crowding behind him.

While the two men stumbled back through the doorway, Longarm saw the sudden wall of flame following the stream of spilled kerosene across the floor. The outlaw Longarm had just shot dropped screaming into the flames. The other one regained his balance, threw up his own weapon, a big Peacemaker, and punched a shot at Longarm. The round sucked past Longarm's cheek. He surged into the flaming room, levering and firing twice at the man with the Peacemaker. The impact of both slugs flung the man back over the upended table. The Poser brothers and their remaining companion were scrambling for the door. Longarm swung his rifle and fired through the flames at them. The Posers flung the door open and darted out into the night as Longarm cut down the third one from the rear.

Longarm ducked through the flames and started through the door after the Posers. But a rough hand clamped heavily down onto his shoulder and flung him spinning back into the blazing room. It was the outlaw

Longarm had slugged with his gun barrel. A great gob of blood stood like a shining blister on the top of his head, and one side of his face was lost behind a bloody mask. His eyes demented, he swung at Longarm, his big fist crunching into the side of the lawman's head. Longarm staggered back into the wall. The back of his head struck the pine boards. Momentarily stunned, he saw the big outlaw looming over him, the raging flames at his back.

The man kicked Longarm under the ribs. Longarm flopped over. Again the man's boot lashed out, lifting Longarm inches off the floor. Longarm, head down, his right hand snaking under his coat, waited. Then, as the outlaw reached down to grab him, Longarm shifted slightly and fired up at him with his Colt. The blast burned his own flesh and the round plowed through the socket of the outlaw's right eye. It appeared to suck the man's entire face after it as the socket became a gaping hole. The man straightened, turned blindly around, then collapsed into the flames.

Longarm holstered his Colt and lunged across the smoking floor to his fallen Winchester and flung himself toward the still-open door. The moment he reached it, a volley of rifle fire slammed at him from out of the darkness. He felt his hat quiver as a bullet snicked its brim. Another round splintered the doorjamb as he ducked back and slammed the door.

Turning, he found himself facing a devouring wall of flame. In the midst of the inferno, he saw two bodies struggling like damned souls caught in hell's fire. Without pausing, he ducked through the flames and into the bed-room. He saw the man he had surprised on his cot crawling on his hands and knees toward the back room. Longarm, his eyes burning from the thick smoke, kicked the man out of his way, dropped his rifle ahead of him out the window, then flung himself out into the night, carrying glass and pieces of broken sash with him.

He landed heavily, rolled over, snatched up his rifle, and kept rolling until he was in darkness, well out of the glow from the burning building. Then, keeping low, he raced through the darkness and cut around the corner, keeping the privy between himself and the barn. He pulled up then, his eyes searching the moonlit yard for any sign of the Posers. Abruptly, Longarm heard a fusillade from within the barn. He ducked low, until he realized he was not the Posers' target. Two horsemen broke from the barn. Longarm dropped to one knee and brought his Winchester up. He got off two quick shots before the riders disappeared into the darkness of the canyon.

Longarm raced for the barn, hoping he would not find what he suspected. Bursting inside, he saw what the Posers had been shooting at. There was not a horse left alive. Sickened, Longarm left the barn. Someone inside the flaming cabin was screaming. Longarm trotted back to the cabin. The screams were coming from the rear. He moved past the privy and cut around the corner. The heat was not so intense at the cabin's rear, and he saw the one he had shot in the face trying to pull himself out through the rear window. He was not the one who was screaming, however. Blindly, silently, like some giant worm trying to wriggle out from under a campfire, the man struggled to pull himself over the windowsill. The fire was in the room behind him now, enormous tongues licking up the walls. The man groaned and pushed and succeeded in dragging himself a few inches farther out over the sill. Then the flames rushed for the open window, licking at his backside.

The man raised his head and screamed.

Longarm unholstered his Colt, aimed carefully, and fired into the man's face a second time. The round caught him high on the forehead and hurled him back into the roaring inferno. The flames danced higher, slicing hungrily through the roof. Sparks and flaming embers began to shower down around Longarm. The screaming inside the cabin grew more terrible, then died completely.

Longarm holstered his Colt and, shouldering his rifle wearily, turned his back on the flaming cabin that was now Stanton's funeral pyre.

Chapter 9

Longarm found the black where he had left him, and mounted up in the darkness. On a hunch, he moved back out through the canyon in the darkness and kept going south. He rode slowly, steadily, anxious to conserve his mount. The sun was inching up over the mountains in the east, sending golden shafts of light across the flat, when he cut sign.

Pulling the black in, Longarm studied the still-fresh prints of two horses. The tracks were not much more than two hours old. Longarm raised his eyes to follow them as far as they could be seen along the flat. They disappeared finally in the morning's shimmering haze, but they were headed unmistakably back the way Longarm had come.

He didn't like it.

He lifted his horse to a lope. Inside half an hour he left the flat and began to climb, the tracks of the two riders still sharp and clear on the ground ahead of him. The higher he got and the rockier the ground became, the more his anxiety increased. On the harsh, clattering ground the hoofprints he was tracking soon disappeared for long stretches. But Longarm pressed on—a dim, unhappy picture in his mind of what he must expect if he did not overtake the two men soon.

After a mile or so, the rockiness petered out into hills of soft red earth, and he cut their sign once more. He cursed, almost wishing he had lost them. He knew now, for sure, which way they were heading. Noticing something, he swung off his horse and inspected closely the two men's tracks. One horse had thrown a left hind shoe; the other had bars fitted on both hind shoes. The horse with the thrown shoe might slow them down. It was a forlorn hope, little more than that.

He mounted up again and pressed on, aware that his black was laboring but unwilling now to give in to the horse's weariness.

A little before noon he topped a high bluff overlooking Augusta's abandoned mine. He searched the trail leading past it and saw it empty of horsemen, and felt a mighty shudder of relief pass through him as he saw, almost directly below him, the tiny, black-skirted figure of Gus as she leaned over the sluice, her wheelbarrow alongside her.

And then he saw the tiny, crumpled bundle of cloth near the mine entrance. The high, hot wind was tugging at a single ribbon. It flashed blue in the bright white light. Faith. Glancing back at Gus, he saw that she had not moved an inch from the moment he topped this ridge.

He swung his horse around and sent the animal charging down the trail to the mine below.

Hope stirred in him as the sound of his black's pounding hooves seemed to bring Gus back to life. She lifted her head at his approach, then lost her grip on the sluice and fell backward to the ground. Dismounting, Longarm knelt swiftly beside the woman. She opened her eyes and looked up at him.

"Waited for you to get here . . . knew you'd come. Bury us on that bluff . . . so I can watch this damn hole in the ground. . . ." She smiled wanly. ". . . Maybe put a curse on it. . . ."

He couldn't see any wounds. He reached around behind to lift her and found a mess of sticky, broken ribs and torn tissue. She had been shot in the back. More than once. It was the tight, black bodice she insisted on wearing in this searing heat that was holding her together. He pulled his bloody hand back.

"The Poser brothers?" he asked, knowing full well what her answer would be.

She nodded. "They was mad as hornets . . . said I sent you and that dude after them." She smiled. "They was right, of course I did that . . . gladly."

"Why, Gus?"

"They been a miserable cross for me to bear since I come out here, Longarm." She began to cough, closing her eyes as she did so. Her face lost what color it had. Then her eyes flashed open. "Used me, they did—whenever they felt the need. Animals. Not like you . . . us, Longarm." She smiled dimly at the memory, and then went on, her eyes revealing the pain she felt at recounting it: "They shot poor Faith too. She's up by the mine, I think. She came at them with a knife after she saw what they done to me."

Longarm nodded. "How long ago?"

She closed her eyes. "Hours . . . minutes . . . lost track, Longarm. Find them . . . for me and Faith. . . ."

Her head sagged forward. She began to cough weakly, a thin trickle of blood coming from one corner of her mouth. And then the coughing subsided . . . and stopped. Longarm stood up and looked down at the old woman.

Yes, she was old, all right. Every one of her fifty years was visible on her dead face, now that the bright spirit he had seen flashing so indomitably in her dark eyes had been snuffed out. He was glad she had come to him in the night. As she had told him, lovemaking had a way of stopping time. And so it had—for both of them.

He left her and headed toward the mine entrance and Faith's crumpled body, where he hoped to find a shovel.

He saw no sense in haste now. The Poser brothers were well ahead of him, and Longarm's horse was nearly spent. Furthermore, the reason for his haste that morning no longer existed. He had failed to overtake them before they reached Gus and her mine. This knowledge burned a hole deep in his core, but as soon as he found a shovel he could use, he kept himself busy enough not to dwell on it.

Taking his time, he selected a spot high on the ridge that overlooked the mine and the massive, shouldering flanks of the mountains behind it, the Divide visible in the far distance as a series of white peaks. By the time Longarm finished burying the two women, placing large flat rocks just under the surface to discourage coyotes, it was late in the afternoon.

He spent the time until dark fashioning a wooden marker for the two women. Inside the mine entrance he found a good, solid piece of rough maple that had served as the door to a tool cabinet. It would not last forever, but it would stand for a good long time. Lighting a fire on the ridge, he heated the end of a crowbar and burnt into the wood the legend, *Gus & Faith*. He didn't bother with the date. Then he pounded the marker into the soft ground at the head of their graves.

He stood back and surveyed his handiwork, his hat in his hand. He studied the two names and realized the marker would tell quite a different story to passersby than it did to him. But he was sure Gus would not mind. He wished he could have put more on the marker, something more fitting. He had come across a poem once by an Englishman, which spoke of his grief for the death of a woman he had known. It referred to the dead woman as having no motion anymore, no force, and that now she rolled with the earth's motion, part of its rocks and stones and trees. Longarm wished he could have remembered the words for sure.

He clapped his hat back on, swung the shovel onto his shoulder, and walked back down the trail through the dusk to Gus's cabin.

When Longarm arrived at Eagle Pass two days later in the middle of a hot, blistering afternoon, he realized that the storm which had been gathering had at last broken. Construction on the Rio Grande Western had been halted; a huge camp, disordered with restless men and great piles of supplies, was sprawled across the low hills approaching the pass. And for the past half-hour, Longarm had been hearing the rifle fire echoing from deep within the pass.

A small crowd of workers gathered to watch him as he rode in. He asked one of them where he could find Chapman, and was directed to a large tent off to the right on a slight rise. As he rode up to it and dismounted, Chapman stepped out of the tent. Behind him, to his great surprise, Longarm saw Molly and her father.

"Where you been, Longarm?" Chapman asked. "Li Wang said you got up, shaved, and lit out."

"I did that," Longarm said, dismounting and tipping his hat politely to Molly and then to her father. "But I'm back now. Fill me in."

Chapman nodded grimly, turned, and led Longarm into his tent. There were enough canvas chairs for the four of them. Sitting down wearily, Longarm took a deep breath, tipped his hat back off his forehead, and smiled at Molly.

"You're looking fine, Molly," he told her.

"You look tired, Longarm. Very tired," she replied, her voice worried.

"I hope you can help us, Marshal," said a worried Mike O'Leary. "Otto's got us between a rock and a hard place. That man of his, Lynch, has taken the pass from us. And he's holding it. Brazen as you please. Outrageous."

Longarm looked at Chapman. "Why not tell me what you can, from the beginning."

Chapman nodded and proceeded to do just that. His men had been laying track within sight of the pass, while his graders were already working through it, blasting rock and laying ballast. They were jubilant, since the workers had all been aware of the race they were in, and they thought they had won it.

Jack Lynch and his hardcases had struck at night. They moved into the pass, stationing themselves at various points—behind rocks, high in the cliffs, every vantage spot they could find—and when the workers streamed back toward the pass the next morning, they were stopped in their tracks by warning shots. The few hardy souls who insisted on keeping on to the pass were fired upon and a few were actually wounded. That cured the rest, and Chapman wired back to O'Leary for instructions.

O'Leary broke in then: "I wired him to go in there and get them bastards! This an outrage!"

"Father!" Molly cried, her hand to her mouth. "Please!"

O'Leary caught himself dutifully and glanced at his daughter. "Now, you've heard worse than that from me, Molly," he complained. "And if you don't like the way I express my honest outrage, you can leave this tent."

"I won't leave this tent," she said impudently, "and you can't make me."

For a moment the two looked into each other's eyes with fierce combativeness. O'Leary was the first one to look away. Before the will of his daughter he was, as everyone knew, helpless. She was as incorrigible as he was—only maybe a little better at it, since he had had such an excellent teacher.

The two even looked alike, Longarm commented to

himself. And well they might. The same large brown eyes, small-boned face, strong chin, and straight forehead. Father and daughter. Longarm could still not get over the fact that O'Leary had let Molly serve as payroll guard. But then again, it had most probably been Molly's idea to begin with—while her father pleaded and warned her, all to no avail. Molly saw Longarm looking intently at her, and smiled dazzlingly back at him.

O'Leary also looked at Longarm. "It *is* an outrage, Longarm. Otto Pears is behind it with that murderer Lynch and his so-called rangers at his back. I am sure of it now. They are the ones who have been raiding Ty Flynn's freighters."

"What did you do, Chapman?" Longarm asked the small, intense foreman. Chapman had endured O'Leary's interruption stoically, but Longarm sensed the man's irritation.

"I did as I was told," Chapman snapped. "I asked for volunteers, and we attacked Lynch's men. We did not do very well, I am afraid, and succeeded only in getting two of my best men wounded."

"I came out then," said O'Leary. "I just got here not long before you arrived, Longarm. At the moment we are discussing a plan of action."

"I suggest you wire Colonel Mackenzie," Longarm said. "Let him handle this."

"We have already done that," said Molly. "But he is off somewhere north of here. In the field. We have heard no word from him."

"We can't count on him," snapped O'Leary. "Pears' men are laying tracks at this very moment. Soon they will be at the pass and will be able to claim it. My plan is to stop Pears by stopping his railroad."

Longarm stood up. "I don't think that would be a very good notion. This fellow Lynch will have thought of that. He'll be ready, and you'll only get more of your workers shot."

"But, Longarm!" Molly protested. "We've got to do something."

Longarm glanced at Chapman. "Soon's I get some food and a fresh horse, I'd like to ride up to the pass, look over the terrain some. The way I see it, the best thing for us would be to take back the pass. Without any further bloodshed."

"And just how in Sam Hill do you plan to work *that* miracle?" Chapman demanded, his dark eyes glowing with sudden amusement.

"Yes," Molly said breathlessly. "Tell us."

"Hell," said Longarm, taking out his last cheroot. "I won't know that till I ride out there, now will I?"

An hour later, aboard a fresh mount, Longarm rode out of the camp toward Eagle Pass. Beside him rode Chapman and Ben Ogilvy. The tall, slim engineer was resplendent in his sheepskin jacket and fawn Stetson, its brim turned down. He seemed eager for action, unlike the cautious Chapman. Ogilvy had shown up with O'Leary and his daughter. Unlike Chapman, he had yet to see blood flow in this ridiculous little war.

They passed small pockets of men scrunched down in hollows and behind rocks, all of them armed to the teeth and most of them either angry or frightened foolish. Twice the three men were challenged, and Longarm did not feel easy as the nervous men leveled their motley weapons on him as Chapman explained their mission patiently or, furious and upset, chided them for their impertinence.

They kept on past the last outposts, following the newly laid tracks until they came to the bunkhouses-on-wheels and other railroad cars, all of them showing signs of having been hastily abandoned. And then they were riding over gentle sand hills, which in turn gave way to a narrow flat. The pass was just in front of them, an immense V slicing through a forbidding escarpment that shouldered itself with massive intimidation out of the ground—as insurmountable as the Great Wall of China. It was true, Longarm noted wearily; there was no other way through this particular mountainous terrain.

When Longarm caught the gleam of sunlight on metal among the rocks flanking the pass, he pulled up. The two others halted also. Ogilvy looked questioningly at Longarm.

"You see any of them?"

"Not a one."

"Well then, why are we stopping?"

Longarm smiled at the engineer. "You can ride on, if you want."

The man sat back in his saddle and frowned nervously. "No sense in that," he said. "I'll stick with you fellows."

Longarm looked at Chapman. "I caught sunlight on gun barrels just ahead. This about as far as you got with your men?"

"No. They were hiding further back in the pass. When they chased us back, I guess they took up new positions. Well, what do you think?"

The tall lawman considered for a moment. Then he spoke. "You two stay here. I'm going to dismount and work my way closer on foot."

"There's no need for that," Ogilvy protested. "We can go with you."

"No, you can't," Longarm said, dismounting. "I won't let you. Stay here with Chapman and watch the horses. And watch out that those men in the rocks don't sneak up on you and take them away from you."

Before Ogilvy could respond to that warning, Longarm had taken his Winchester and slipped away into the rocks alongside the right-of-way. Head down, he slunk swiftly closer to the pass, moving parallel to the nearly completed grades Chapman's men had built. They had been within sight of the pass, all right. It was no wonder that Otto Pears had decided he had to take this desperate action.

He slipped out from behind a clump of rocks and went down a small slope, then into a dry gully. He kept going, feeling the wall of rock looming higher and higher over him as he moved swiftly closer to it. Aware that he was perhaps moving too swiftly for his own good, he ducked abruptly behind a huge boulder squatting in the soft blow sand.

The movement most likely saved his life. There was an angry hum, like a large hornet speeding past his cheek; and then, at almost the same time, there came the sharp *spang* of a slug ricocheting off a rock face behind him and the bark of the rifle from the pass. Peering cautiously around the rock, Longarm's gaze swept over the entrance to the pass and the large rocks flanking it.

Of course he could see nothing.

Another slug whanged off the rock just above his head. Longarm ducked back behind his cover and considered the situation. He had allowed himself to go too far in the open. His best play was to move to his left in among what appeared to be a field of juniper and rocks. He still had a ways to go if he wanted to get a closer view of the pass, and that approach appeared to offer the most cover as he kept good and low.

He left the cover of the rock on the run, crossed the gully with two strides, then flung himself up the embankment. Bullets started chopping into the ground all around him as the men at the pass began firing swiftly. Mixed in with the scream and whine and thud of slugs striking ground and rocks nearby, Longarm heard the distant cries of the men at the pass shouting encouragement to each other.

And then he was on his belly in among the juniper and rocks. He belly-crawled swiftly, using his elbows and knees, his rifle held in both hands in front of him, his head down. Soon the shooting from the pass became random until, for want of a target, it stopped completely.

He crept still closer to the pass and found his way blocked by another gully, this one cutting across his path at a right angle. But the gully was a narrow one, and he saw that it was only a short dash before he would be in the cover of a hill on the other side. He paused a moment to wipe the sweat from his eyes, then gathered himself, took a deep breath, and plunged down the slope, across the gully, and on up the other slope. He kept going until he reached the crest, then leaned against a waist-high boulder to catch his breath.

As soon as he was ready to move again, he left the boulder and, still crouching, continued up the hillside, occasionally slipping and sliding on the loose, gravelly ground. Keeping himself crouched down, his rifle ready in front of him, he came to an island of rock and juniper, stepped cautiously around it—and came face to face with a bearded gunman in the act of loading his sixgun. The fellow snapped the loading gate shut, brought his gun up at Longarm, and squeezed the trigger.

His hammer came down on an empty chamber. He swore and leaped toward the rockside for cover. Longarm's rifle tracked him briefly and bucked against his shoulder. The man fell hard. Moving swiftly to his side, Longarm lifted him onto his back with the toe of his boot and saw that he was already dead.

He left him and started racing toward the pass, heading for a high patch of rocks dead ahead. He was well in among them when he glanced back and saw two of Lynch's men examining their dead companion. Longarm turned back around and threaded his way through the forest of rocks until he was in the shadow of the pass.

Those defending the pass were behind him now. The pass itself offered more cover than had the open ground before it. Taking advantage of the shadowed rocks and the occasional thick vegetation that crowded the walls, he moved on into the pass. He kept going until he found a game trail leading to an elevation that overlooked the swift stream cutting through the pass. He climbed the narrow trail swiftly, came to a ledge, went down on his stomach, and inched to the edge.

Looking over, he saw Lynch's camp on the far side of the stream. Longarm had asked Chapman where those of his men who had been working in the pass had set up their camp and had been given this location, a park bounded on two sides by the willows and cottonwoods shading it. As Longarm had guessed, Lynch and his so-called rangers had taken it over. Longarm peered closely at the men moving about the encampment, hoping to catch a glimpse of the Poser brothers. He remembered their appearance from their near-hanging well enough. It suddenly struck him that he did not yet know which one of the bastards was Lou and which one was Dick. It didn't matter much, he reflected grimly. Just so long as he got them both.

A fellow Longarm thought might be Lynch, a tall man in a bowler hat with two or three other men hanging close about him, emerged from a tent to meet someone approaching the campsite. The newcomer was still on the near side of the stream, out of sight beneath Longarm. Abruptly, this new fellow broke from some pine and splashed across the shallow stream and came to a halt in front of the man in the bowler. The newcomer seemed excited; and as he talked, he pointed once in the direction of the pass's entrance. Yes. The tall one was Lynch, all right, and at the moment he was getting a report about that poor, surprised bastard Longarm had shot outside the pass.

Soon a large crowd of angry men had gathered around Lynch. Longarm felt a mite uneasy as he watched the men streaming from the rocks and trees about the encampment. Jack Lynch had more men than a dog has fleas. Longarm was glad that he hadn't come this far in order to take them all in single-handed. A conversation he had had with Chapman before setting out had given him a better motive for scouting this far into the pass.

Longarm turned his head and looked up at the wall of rock towering over Lynch's encampment. He had to strain his neck to catch a glimpse of the blue sky far above. He looked again, more carefully now, at the way the rock leaned out. Chapman's description of it had been apt. The construction foreman had likened the wall to a great, massive, leaning fist of stone—waiting to fall.

It had waited centuries, of course, without falling; but as Longarm studied the enormous crown of white rock, he knew that what he was considering had a good chance of turning the tables. The rock was wrinkled with massive ridges and bristling with pine. On its topmost ridge a huge cottonwood was perched. From where Longarm was lying, it looked like a tiny toothpick flecked with green.

If by chance—or more likely, through the handiwork of man—that great stone fist were dislodged and sent thundering down upon those below, it would create terrible havoc. Lives would be lost in abundance, but more important, at least in the eyes of the railway tycoons, the pass would no longer remain as an ideal route through these mountains. Longarm studied the formation a while longer. It was more than likely, he realized, that Lynch had stationed men atop that frowning ridge.

Well, he concluded, the only way to find that out for sure was to go up there and see what happened. But first things first: he had to get back out of this pass and rejoin Chapman and Ogilvy.

Then ask for volunteers.

Longarm found Chapman and Ogilvy where he had left them. They looked impatient at having to wait so long, but not so impatient that they were about to press on into the pass to find out what might have happened to him. There were quick, relieved smiles on their faces as the towering deputy marshal trotted wearily toward them from out of the gully.

"It'll work," Longarm said as he pulled up in front of Chapman. "But it'll take some doing."

"Good," Chapman replied, nodding grimly. "I only hope O'Leary will go for it."

"If he won't, Molly will," cracked Ogilvy.

The three men mounted up and rode back the way they had come. They had not gone far when a single, wistful shot echoed among the rocks far behind them. The range was too great for them to hear the bullet strike and all it did was nudge the three riders into a lope, which was most likely what the rifleman had intended in the first place.

"I'll want your best powder monkeys," Longarm said to Chapman, above the pounding of hooves. "With maybe Li Wang in charge. I like him."

"He's the best," Chapman agreed.

Longarm nodded. That took care of who would plant the dynamite. He would prefer to choose those men who would go with him to take the crest and guard the Chinese himself. And he would let Ogilvy sell the idea to O'Leary.

Ogilvy pulled his horse closer to Longarm's. He leaned close. "I'm going with you!" he cried.

"Where?" Longarm demanded.

The man smiled eagerly. "That ridge overlooking the pass! You'll need men to take it and hold it, won't you?"

Longarm nodded wearily. The man was entirely too eager for the action. But there was no way he could deny him participation in the assault.

"Is it a deal?" the man persisted.

Longarm nodded. "You'll lead one of the parties."

He did not like the expression of boyish enthusiasm

that crossed the engineer's face. He looked quickly away and urged his horse faster and kept himself ahead of the two for the rest of the ride back to their camp.

Before the three men set out for the pass, Chapman and Ogilvy, in answer to Longarm's questions, described the ridge hanging over the pass. At once Longarm outlined his plan. It was simple, but dangerous. Longarm would plant dynamite below the ridge and then approach Lynch with a simple proposition: give up or get buried.

Longarm watched O'Leary as Chapman explained the plan. O'Leary's original surprise was giving way to some enthusiasm. Chapman finished; O'Leary looked at Longarm.

"You think you can do it?"

"We won't know until we try."

"It is so dangerous, Longarm!" protested Molly.

"We can handle it," said Ogilvy, with embarrassing bravado. "After all, we have the element of surprise. Lynch thinks we're beat. He has no idea we would try such a daring scheme."

Longarm ignored Ogilvy and looked at O'Leary. "Chapman is going to choose the powder monkeys, and then I'd like him to help me choose those who are going with Ogilvy and myself to take the ridge and protect the Chinese while they're planting the dynamite."

"There's just one thing, Longarm," O'Leary said.

"What's that?"

"This is just a bluff, isn't it? If that pass gets blocked, it won't do either Pears or me any good."

Longarm nodded. "It's just a bluff, O'Leary. Until they call it. I'm hoping they won't. You better hope the same thing." He smiled thinly. "And there's one more thing."

"What's that?"

"If push comes to shove, I'm going to suggest that you and Otto Pears meet on neutral ground and come to some kind of an agreement. There's been too much bloodshed because of you two, already."

O'Leary began to bluster, but Molly cut him off. "I think that's only fair, Longarm," she told him. "An excellent idea. I'm sure my father will cooperate." She looked sternly at Mike O'Leary. "Isn't that right?"

The man shrugged unhappily. "Anything to help, of course. You're right, this business *has* gone too far already. I'll be glad to cooperate."

Longarm watched O'Leary carefully as he spoke. It seemed to him that the older man was not entirely in agreement with what he had just said to mollify his daughter; but that didn't matter. He had given his word and there were plenty of witnesses.

Despite the moonlight, it was so dark that Longarm—and the five men behind him on the slope—kept cracking their shins on the rocks. But it was a minor annoyance and did not slow their progress up the cliffside. And so far the men had been as silent as snakes as they wormed their way the last hundred yards to the crown of the ridge. Far below Longarm's men, Li Wang and his ten powder monkeys were waiting. They had been instructed to climb no higher until Longarm's party had cleared the ridge of Lynch's men.

Longarm pulled himself over a flat rock, then reached up and fitted his right hand into a deep crack splitting the surface of the rock facing him. His rifle was slung across his back with an improvised sling made from a strip of rawhide, giving him the use of both hands. It was a precaution he was glad he had taken. Now, with both hands fitted into the crack, he pulled himself noiselessly up over the lip of the ridge and found himself in a ragged bunching of grama grass that covered the crest. He saw no movement before him in the moonlit darkness, but kept himself flat and continued to ease himself through the grass.

After crawling a couple of yards, he looked back and

saw two, then three men pulling themselves over the ridge's crest. He waited for the men to reach him. The fellow who had stuck right behind him, a man he had designated second-in-command, was named Jake. In a moment Jake was breathing softly beside him.

"See anything yet?" Jake asked Longarm.

Longarm shook his head.

"They're up here, though," Jake said.

Longarm nodded; that fact had long since been established. Longarm had sent two riders around the mountain's flank with orders for them to climb to a spot higher than this ridge on the opposite wall. The men had done so, and had returned to report that Lynch was keeping four men on the ridge. Since the range was too long, the two horsemen made no effort to cut Lynch's men down from the other flank. There was no alternative. As Longarm had suspected all along, they would just have to go up and take the ridge from the men Lynch had stationed on it.

So where were they?

The five men were now lined up on the ridge, side by side, facing forward, with Longarm in the lead. Longarm started forward. He came to clean rock, naked of vegetation or any other cover, raised himself up off the ground, and continued on, staying as low as he could manage, his rifle now held out in front of him.

There was a clump of stunted pine just in front of him, their branches tipped with silver in the moonlight. Longarm led the way around it. On the ground before him were two dark, recumbent forms. Beyond them, two men were standing. They were about twenty feet distant and seemed to be talking quietly, their gaze directed down at the moonlit stream winding through the pass far below them.

Longarm went down on one knee and waved the rest of his men toward the two sleeping forms. By this time he was wondering where Ogilvy and his party were, since he had given them a head start when he sent them up the other side of the ridge. He was about to give up on them and move toward the two men who were standing up when he saw Ogilvy's men materializing out of the darkness on the far side.

Longarm waited tensely. He hoped Ogilvy would be able to move in on the standing men as silently as Longarm's men were closing in on the sleepers. If this ridge could be taken without firing a shot, it would make things a whole hell of a lot smoother. One of the sleeping men stirred, then sat up. He cried out as one of Longarm's men loomed out of the darkness over him. His companion woke up instantly, his hand reaching in under his blanket. The two standing men whirled about, drawing their weapons as they did so.

But all of them were too late.

The fellow who had cried out was dealt a murderous blow on the back of his head from a rifle stock. The one reaching for his revolver had it kicked out of his hand, after which one vicious punch to his jaw knocked him senseless. At the same instant, Ogilvy and his men poked their weapons into the backs of the two others, both of whom saw the wisdom of dropping their guns and slowly raising their hands.

The ridge had been taken without a shot being fired.

"Tie them and gag them, the whole bunch," Longarm instructed, as he went back to the spot where he had climbed onto the ridge. Peering over into the darkness, he felt for a couple of tiny pebbles and tossed them down the steep slope. Then he waited. Before too long he saw the silent bobbing of heads, the flash of pale hands, as Li Wang and the other Chinese continued on up to the ridge.

As daybreak lightened the sky and revealed the morning mists hanging in the pass, Longarm glanced up at the ridge from his position behind a nest of boulders in front of the pass. Behind him stood O'Leary and Chapman.

"There they are," said Chapman, almost reverently.

He meant the Chinese powder monkeys, suspended in their wicker baskets. They had been dangling against the face of the ridge since an hour before dawn, and in that time they had been able to plant quite a few charges in the cracks that scarred the rock. Quite a few, but not nearly enough. Now they were waiting for Longarm's signal to begin drilling in under the overhanging shelf. Had they started drilling during the night, they would have alerted Lynch's men before Longarm could have deployed his own forces.

But the Chinese had not wasted their time during the predawn hour. Longarm saw that the seven baskets were deployed evenly along the face of the rock at what appeared to be the fault line of the overhang.

Longarm looked at Chapman. "Ready?"

"Go ahead," Chapman said.

Longarm levered a fresh cartridge into his firing chamber, aimed his Winchester at the heavens, and pumped four quick shots into the sky.

Even as the shots echoed among the rocks about them, and a second later between the walls of the pass, the Chinese began their drilling, sounding like a chorus of iron-billed woodpeckers.

Longarm and Chapman went back to their horses and mounted up. Chapman handed him his handkerchief. Swiftly, Longarm knotted the white handkerchief to the end of his rifle barrel, then, with a nod to Chapman, began to ride toward the pass.

Rifle fire began to crackle about the pass's entrance, but Longarm and Chapman paid it no heed as they rode slowly forward. After getting to within a couple of hundred yards of the pass, two men stepped out from behind some rocks and grinned up at them.

"We got them bottled up in there pretty good now!" one of them cried.

Longarm smiled, saluted them, and rode on.

In the shadow of the pass, Longarm and Chapman

pulled up. "Lynch!" Longarm called. "Jack Lynch! Sam Chapman's out here and he wants to palaver! You're trapped good and proper, so you better talk!"

Longarm saw Chapman's small but erect body stiffen as one of Lynch's men stepped out from behind a tall finger of rock just inside the pass's entrance. There was a rifle in his hand, and he held it trained on the two men as he walked toward them.

A few feet from their horses, he stopped. "We got guns trained on you two. So don't make any sudden moves!"

"We want to see Lynch," Chapman snapped.

"I don't give a goddamn what you want, mister. You're my prisoners now, so you better do what I say, both of you."

Longarm smiled at the man. "Tell Lynch there's two men here who want to talk to him. Tell him if he don't want to talk, he should look up at that chunk of mountain hanging over his head. It won't be hanging there much longer."

The fellow with the rifle glanced nervously up at the cliff wall as Longarm's words sank in. He could not have failed to notice the activity on the rock face; the steady drilling of the powder monkeys sounded faint but incessant.

"What the hell are you bastards up to, anyway?" the fellow with the rifle demanded.

Sam Chapman had reached the end of his patience. He squared his small but powerful shoulders and fixed the man in front of him with his dark eyes. They were like gun barrels. "Listen to me, you hireling. Fetch your chief and fetch him right now, or I will get down off this horse and stuff that rifle up your ass, pull the trigger, and blow your brains out!"

At that moment another man came running from inside the pass. He came up beside the man who was detaining them. "Lynch says let them in!" he ordered.

"Was just goin' to," the man said sullenly, stepping back and waving Longarm and Chapman past him.

Lynch did not ask Longarm or Chapman to dismount, nor did either man request it. Longarm rested his Winchester across his lap and let Chapman do the talking. It didn't take Chapman long to make clear to Lynch the purpose of those Chinese powder monkeys dangling over his head at the moment.

Lynch was a broad-shouldered, round-faced individual with jutting eyebrows and a surly mouth. He was dressed in a checked frock coat, tight fawn trousers, and felt boots—every article of clothing stained or covered by a fine patina of alkali dust. The ex-Pinkerton agent looked as if he had stepped out for a Sunday stroll and been kidnapped.

As soon as Chapman finished, Lynch took a solid, spread-legged stance, folded his arms, and peered insolently up at the little foreman. "You expect me to believe O'Leary would let you block this pass?" the man demanded. "It's a bluff, pure and simple."

"It's not a bluff," Chapman snapped back. "I guess O'Leary figures if he can't use this pass, he sure as hell doesn't want anyone else to use it. Leastways, not that fat bucket of swill, Otto Pears."

From the tent behind Lynch, Otto Pears lurched out, his corpulent face brick-red with outrage. "I heard that, Chapman!" the man cried, his voice high, resembling somewhat the squeal of a stuck pig. "You keep talking like that and I'll see you never get a job in this country again!"

Chapman laughed, a deep, rich baritone that belied his small stature. Then he winked at Longarm. "I knew that would bring you out, Pears," he said. "Saw that big paint of yours back there. Well, it's you I've come to see, then. Now you tell me. Do you want me to blow down that mountain on your backs?"

Pears pulled himself together as he stopped alongside

Jack Lynch. "Mike's serious, is he?" he asked, mopping his raw face and glancing nervously up at the drilling Chinese high above.

"He's serious. Why shouldn't he be? What's he got to lose?"

Pears glanced nervously at the silent Longarm, then back at Chapman. "Well, damn it, maybe we should talk, then."

Chapman chuckled and indicated Longarm with a nod of his head. "That's just what the marshal here figured. Glad you're open to the idea."

"Is Mike?" Pears asked.

"Yes, he is," Longarm broke in.

"I wouldn't be in such a hurry, Otto," Lynch cautioned. "They ain't got us yet. I'll send some of my boys up there and cut them heathen down."

"There's eight armed men up there just waiting for your boys to show, Lynch," said Longarm. "Send them up if you want, but I'm betting they'll come down a mite faster than they went up."

As he spoke, Longarm became aware that the furious drilling high above them had stopped. Glancing up, he saw the baskets and their tiny occupants being hauled back up the rock face. The charges were now set. At a prearranged signal from Longarm's rifle—another four quick shots—the dynamite would be set off by Ogilvy.

Longarm glanced significantly at Chapman, then up at the rock face. Chapman glanced up quickly, then looked back at Pears. "The charges are set, Pears. O'Leary's outside the pass, waiting to talk. What'll it be?"

Pears nodded wearily. "All right," he said. "Let me get my horse." He left Lynch and started through the crowd of gunmen to where he'd left his mount.

By this time at least ten of Lynch's men had gathered about them, listening intently to what was going on. Longarm had not yet seen either of the Posers, and was about ready to believe they had not joined up with

Lynch after all, when he glimpsed one of them peering cautiously at him from behind what appeared to be the cooktent. It was the smaller of the two, his face chinless, his eyes shadowy slits in his face.

Longarm knew he could take after this one and hope to get the other one later. He should be nearby. Longarm also knew that he was outnumbered considerably, and that until he knew where the other Poser was, he was more likely to get a bullet in the back than either brother.

Longarm glanced back down at Lynch. "Listen close, Lynch," he said. "You got two brothers working for you—the Posers. That right?"

Lynch shrugged. "Sure. They joined up with me. So what?"

"Just this. When we come back with Otto Pears, I want you to have both men waiting for me. Otherwise I'm going to haul you in on a federal warrant for harboring two escaped criminals, men convicted of conspiracy to commit grand larceny." Longarm smiled thinly. "Since they murdered two people during their escape from custody, they are also wanted for murder. I want them both, Lynch. Or you."

Lynch glared angrily up at Longarm. "Federal warrant? Say, who the hell *are* you, mister?"

"Deputy U.S. Marshal Custis Long. Some call me Longarm. You're an ex-Pinkerton; maybe you've heard the name before."

"Yeah," said Lynch, his bluster gone the moment he heard Longarm's name. "Maybe I have."

Pears, aboard his big paint, rode through the ranks of sullen men, past Lynch, and looked at Chapman. "Lead the way," he told the foreman. "Just make sure them trigger-happy yokels you got working for you don't shoot first and ask questions later."

"Sure," Chapman agreed cheerily. "But stick close, Otto. A big target like you will really whet their appetites."

His face flushing darkly at that irreverent crack, Pears pulled in behind Chapman, and Longarm followed behind them both.

As he rode from the camp, Longarm glanced back and saw Lynch already issuing frantic orders to his cronies. Longarm smiled grimly and turned back around in his saddle. Jack Lynch would not have an easy time cornering the Possum Boys. He might even get his head shot off in the effort. But that didn't bother Longarm all that much. Hell, it took a rat to catch a rat—and in this particular case, to catch two rats.

Chapter 10

O'Leary and Pears greeted each other cautiously as Pears dismounted. Both men appeared somewhat subdued—as if each had been caught with his hand in the cookie jar. But when they started talking seriously, they became uncomfortable discussing their business in front of Longarm, Chapman, and the many others crowding around curiously, and took refuge in the privacy of Chapman's tent. Even Molly was excluded from their deliberations.

She came over to stand nervously beside Longarm, while Chapman mounted up and rode off to check on the men he had still guarding Eagle Pass. Longarm was acutely aware of Molly's presence as she stood close beside him.

"It's awful hot out here under the sun," she said to him. "Let's go over there under that tree and wait."

Longarm saw no way he could find fault with that suggestion, and soon the two of them were sitting in the cool shade of a cottonwood, their backs resting against its trunk.

"Do you think it is going to be all right?" Molly asked.

"If either of them has any sense."

"That doesn't sound very hopeful, Longarm."

Longarm chuckled. "Then we'll just have to wait and see. Seems to me we've got Pears between a rock and a hard place. He can't get out of that pass now—at least his men can't—and we've got that mountainside ready to drop on them. This way—and he must see this, Molly—he can't win. Mike won't let him have the pass, and if we set off that charge, he won't have it, either. Not for a good long while anyway."

"Yes. I admit, that *is* perfectly logical. I can see you have quite neatly turned the tables on Otto Pears and that man Lynch. But will Pears admit it, and give in?"

"I don't know."

Molly sighed and leaned her head wearily back against the tree trunk. After a while she said, "Longarm, where's that man Stanton? Didn't you and he go after those two prisoners that escaped?"

"Stanton's dead."

"Oh. I'm sorry. He was such a strange man. We called him the philosopher, he read so much. But he was always willing to lend me a book. He had some funny ideas, and a lot of us couldn't abide him because of the big words he used. Still, he *was* a gentleman."

"Yes, he was a gentleman. And he did read a lot. He talked a lot, too. He was a strange one, all right, with some very curious notions. But he saved my life more than once. I got to like him—more than I realized, I guess."

"How did it happen, Longarm?"

"I don't want to tell you. Let's just say he ran into the Poser brothers alone and they were too much for him."

"The *Poser* brothers? *That's* who those two turned out to be?"

"Yes."

"I've heard of them." She shivered slightly. "That means they were part of the gang that tried to rob the train."

"That's right."

"I'm glad Ogilvy found them when he did, then."

She looked at Longarm. "And it's too bad you didn't let them hang those two."

"Maybe."

"And did they get away?"

"Not yet."

"I don't understand."

"They're part of Jack Lynch's army now—trapped in the pass with Lynch and the others. Earlier, together with the Hardamen gang, they were the ones who were shooting up Ty Flynn's freighters, in an effort to discredit Flynn."

"But why?"

"Ever hear of Jefferson Tatum?"

"Yes, he lost the bid to Ty Flynn's outfit. His prices were way out of line. You should see what he was charging for ties and telegraph poles. And he wanted twice what Ty quoted for quarrying and hauling the ballast."

"Well, Tatum had hired the Poser brothers and the Hardamen gang to dress up like Indians and raise hell with Ty's operation. I guess he figured that would make your father turn to him for supplies. If not this year, then next."

She shook her head. "And was Tatum behind the attempt to rob the train?"

"Looks like it. He appeared to be someone who could use the money, and with your work crews ready to strike if they didn't get paid, that would sure as hell add to your father's woes. One more reason for turning to Tatum for supplies."

"I never liked him. I hope you have proof we can use in court. I think Father should press charges."

"He won't need to," Longarm said, wishing he had a cheroot left.

"Oh?" Molly said, looking sidelong at him. "He won't?"

"No need for me to say anything more, Molly."

"I gather Tatum won't be submitting any more bids."

"That's one way to put it."

"And meanwhile, the Poser brothers have sold themselves to another pirate crew—Otto Pears and his number-one henchman, Jack Lynch."

"Yes, but I've got the Posers and Lynch pretty well sewed up now. Soon as your father and Pears settle this Eagle Pass business, I'll get my hands on those Posers."

"And you'll see to it that they get justice. *Your* justice. Is that it, Longarm?"

"You remember what Wally Stanton shouted at your dinner party, I see."

"Yes."

"I'm still studying on that, Molly. It ain't as simple a decision as I thought it was."

Molly shook her head wearily. "I know, Longarm. Nothing is as simple as it used to be. I'm getting pretty sick of all this about now. Does Colorado really need another railroad when you consider what it is costing, in lives alone?"

"These new mining towns springing up need the railroads to haul their ore."

"Yes, I've heard that often enough. And it *is* true, I guess. But it is taking so much out of Father. . . . And what you've just told me. . . !"

Longarm smoothed his mustache with his forefinger, knowing that there was little he could say to comfort Molly—or himself, for that matter. This railroad *was* sure as hell costing a lot.

Abruptly, shouting from the tent alerted them both. Molly turned around, her face showing the alarm she felt.

"It's Father! He's shouting something!" she told Longarm, getting hurriedly to her feet and starting back to the tent.

She was soon running, Longarm keeping up with her

simply by lengthening his stride. They were almost to the tent when O'Leary burst from it. At sight of Longarm, he headed directly for him.

"Just the man I want!" he cried.

"What is it?" Longarm asked.

"You will be my second!"

"Father!" Molly cried. "What on earth do you mean?"

Otto Pears strode purposefully from the tent. "He means, Molly," the round man said icily, "that he has accepted my challenge. We are going to settle this matter like gentlemen. With a duel!"

Molly turned for help to Longarm. "Oh my God, Longarm! Will you listen to this? I don't *believe* it!"

"Well?" demanded O'Leary of Longarm. "Will you consent to be my second?"

"I think you are both acting like two damn fools," Longarm told them. "But if you want me to act as your second, Mike, maybe you'd better tell me what you expect me to do—send out invitations, or just maybe talk you out of it."

Pears spoke up. "You will inspect my weapon, Marshal. And *my* second will look over Michael's. If, that is, I can find anyone about who will do so. At this moment I am not altogether convinced that I am surrounded by cadres of well-wishers."

Longarm was trying to be amused by all this, but he felt, nevertheless, a growing undercurrent of dismay. He had seen a few duels in his time, formal and informal, and what he had witnessed on those occasions was sometimes comical, but too often tragic. Molly, on the other hand, looked as if she were about to swallow her fury and promptly choke on it. She did not see any of this as humorous. To her it was simply a complete abdication of the senses. And maybe that was just what it was. Only that didn't really make any difference. The two men were bound and determined to go through with it.

Good sense never did seem to have much to do with how most people lived or died, Longarm thought wearily. He cleared his throat. "Maybe you might better let me be your second, Pears," he said. "And Molly can act as her father's second."

"As you wish," O'Leary said, turning to his daughter.

"Father!" she cried. "Are you *serious?*"

"I have no choice," O'Leary said bitterly. "Otto has challenged me. Enough blood has already been spilt because of us. It's time to put an end to it, don't you agree?"

Molly looked long and hard into her father's eyes, saw finally that the man was indeed serious, then, with a cry, flung herself into his arms.

Those workers not on guard at the pass were lined up on both sides of the two men, well out of the line of fire. Ty Flynn and his sidekick, recently arrived with a load of ballast, had seen to that. Longarm had inspected O'Leary's Navy Colt, and Molly, with grim and surprising competence, had looked over Otto Pears' Smith & Wesson. Both revolvers were single-action.

The two men were standing now with their backs to each other, waiting for Longarm's signal. There was to be nothing fancy about it—no romantic folderol, such as a dropped handkerchief. At a nod from Longarm, O'Leary and Pears were to walk off fifteen paces, turn, aim—and fire at will. One shot and one shot only was to be allowed each duelist. Both men had wanted the distance to be the standard ten paces, but Longarm —determined to do what he could to temper this madness—had insisted on fifteen.

"Are you ready?" Longarm called.

Both men said they were.

Longarm straightened, then nodded his head sharply. Molly was standing beside Longarm. She watched the two men for an instant, then turned her back to them and buried her face in Longarm's chest. He held her tightly as the two men continued their slow, steady pacing.

They finished at approximately the same time. The crowd of onlookers hushed suddenly as O'Leary and Pears turned about and aimed carefully at each other. Longarm braced himself. He could feel Molly tensing. O'Leary fired first, and it seemed to Longarm that his gunhand wavered a second before he squeezed the trigger. The shot echoed flatly as the slung whined harmlessly off a rock wall behind Pears. A clean miss.

Longarm held Molly tighter. "It's not over yet," he whispered.

Pears licked his full lips and squinted carefully as he aimed. His gun barrel too seemed to waver a split-second before he fired. The slug tore up the ground at O'Leary's feet.

Both men had missed.

A roar went up from the crowd as Molly flung herself around to see both her father and Pears still on their feet, unscathed. The roar became a sudden, raucous cheer, however, as O'Leary and Pears, obviously furious at their failure to settle matters once and for all, flung their weapons aside and rushed for each other. The two men met solidly, like two bull baffaloes in springtime, and began to roll in the dirt, fists flailing.

"Now that ties it!" Longarm muttered angrily.

Pushing Molly to one side, he raced over to the two men, reached down, and angrily hauled first O'Leary and then Pears to his feet. When O'Leary tried to reach Pears with a fist, Longarm gave the older man a solid shove and sent him spinning to the ground.

"That's enough, you two!" he scolded them.

As Molly rushed up to help her father to his feet, Longarm turned to Pears.

"Do you know why O'Leary missed you, Pears?" Longarm demanded.

The man, wiping a smudge of dirt off his face, shook his head sullenly. "No, damn it! How the hell would I know that? He's just a lousy shot, is all."

"No more than you are. He missed for the same reason you missed."

"Why?"

"Because neither of you *wanted* to kill the other. Unfortunately, you don't seem to have the killer instinct. Besides, you two old farts are also old friends. Ain't that true? Didn't you once prospect together?"

"Sure," O'Leary said, wiping himself off wearily. "What's that prove? We ain't prospecting now."

"No, but you're still friends."

"Friends!" exploded Pears. "Why, you must be out of your mind, Marshal."

"I watched you two. Both of you deliberately missed. You can try to deny it if you're of a mind to, but I know what I saw."

Pears took a deep breath and seemed to be preparing himself to make a rejoinder, but then he relaxed and looked away. O'Leary, also, made no effort to deny Longarm's assertion. Instead, he shrugged and avoided looking at Pears.

"Now you two have caused enough trouble. You couldn't end it with a bullet. So I'm ending it," Longarm said with a tone of finality.

"You?" both men said at once.

"That's right. Me."

"How?" O'Leary asked suspiciously. "What the hell's on your mind, Longarm? Don't think I'm going to let this pirate have that pass."

"Sure you are."

"Now you just see here . . . !"

"Listen here, Marshal," Pears broke in. "This is our problem. We'll solve it. We don't need you butting in." He smiled. "Of course, I do think you're right. One solution would be to let me have the pass. Would you see to it personally that the explosives are removed from under that overhang?"

"I would."

O'Leary's face went purple. Even Molly stared at him in stunned surprise.

"Well, thank you, Marshal," said Pears, straightening himself and looking nervously about him. He was obviously having difficulty in believing his good fortune. "I think you're being very fair."

"You can have the pass, Pears—and so can O'Leary. You two are going to join forces. *Together* you're going through Eagle Pass, or you ain't going through at all. I'll close it." He smiled coldly. "I'll just make a little mistake. I'll give the signal and half of that mountain will come tumbling down. Like Humpty Dumpty."

"What do you mean, both of them?" Molly asked.

By this time Ty Flynn and quite a few other men had gathered around. They were listening avidly.

"I think these two old reptiles should join up."

"Join up!" cried O'Leary.

"You heard me," Longarm said, turning to the owner of the Rio Grande Western. "You both need the pass. So use it. Instead of *one* more line, Colorado will have *two* more lines." Longarm glanced at Otto Pears. "Where's your southern terminus, Pears?"

"Chama, New Mexico."

"And your eastern terminus, O'Leary?"

"Leadville."

Longarm looked back at Pears. "There you go. Two different railroads sharing the same pass, but covering different routes and sharing others. And maybe saving a lot of money in the process. You could call your line the Rio Grande, Denver."

"No," said O'Leary, a sly smile beginning to light his smudged and weary face. "The Rio Grande, Denver & Rocky Mountain."

Pears looked at O'Leary. "I'd have to change all my

stationery," he said. "But maybe it would be cheaper than keeping up this nonsense, at that."

"All right, you two—shake," Longarm said, feeling suddenly weary and very drained. "And I don't expect to get any more trouble from you old reprobates from here on in."

As the two men reached out and shook hands, a great, lusty cheer broke from the men surrounding them. Molly turned to Longarm, tears of relief streaming down her cheeks.

"Thank you," she whispered, rising up onto her tiptoes and kissing him. "Thank you, Longarm."

Riding back into Eagle Pass an hour later with Chapman and a relieved, even enthusiastic, Otto Pears, Longarm was still thinking with pleasure of Molly's impulsive kiss when Chapman pulled his horse up suddenly and glanced at him.

"I don't like it, Longarm."

Longarm halted also, as did Pears. "Don't like what?"

Chapman pointed up at the great, leaning shelf of rock. "Where're my powder monkeys? They should be in their baskets right now, pulling out the charges. They couldn't have finished this soon."

"When did you send word to Li Wang?"

"About half an hour ago."

"Longarm!" Pears said. "Look there!"

Longarm followed Pears' pointing finger and saw Jack Lynch scrambling through the rocks toward them. The fellow was minus his hat, and he was having trouble with his right foot. He appeared to have sprained it. When Lynch saw them, he started to shout and point up at the rock face.

"Jesus!" said Longarm. "The Posers! They're up there—on that ledge! Get yourself out of here, Chapman! You too, Pears! Move it! Now!"

As Chapman pulled his horse around, he grabbed

the reins of Pears' horse and pulled him along after him. In a moment the two had lifted their horses to a gallop as they raced back toward the pass entrance. Longarm spurred his black toward Lynch.

Lynch was pathetic as he scrambled over the rock-strewn floor of the pass to meet Longarm. He was pitching forward onto his face, it seemed, as often as he was on his feet. As Longarm galloped closer, he saw the cruel welt running down the right side of Lynch's face.

"Give me your hand!" Longarm called to the man, as he neared him.

The fellow stood on his feet shakily, and reached out with his right hand. Longarm galloped up, reached down, grabbed the man's wrist, and swung him up behind on the cantle. "Hang on!" Longarm cried.

"We ain't got time!" the man cried in Longarm's ear. "I tell you, we ain't got time!"

"Sure we have!" Longarm called back over his shoulder. "If this horse holds up!"

The horse held up for a good hundred yards. And then the world shifted on its axis. Longarm was glancing back at the overhang when it appeared to spread out miraculously, blotting out the sky and all the rest of the towering wall on either side of it. Then came the blast. It was as if someone had clapped hands over his ears. Longarm felt himself being flung violently forward. He clung with his knees to the stumbling horse, but was having a difficult time drawing a breath.

Only dimly was he aware of the horse's frightened whinnying, or the fact that he was roweling furiously in a desperate effort to give the horse wings. A bend in the pass offered some protection, and he leaned the horse in that direction. Before he reached it, however, a great dark cloud of debris enveloped him. He heard the clatter of pebbles and then rocks as they rained down upon him. He felt something heavy strike his back. He tried to stay in the saddle, but his hands had lost their ability to hang on—and the horse too was slipping sideways, going down in a crunching, neck-twisting loop. Longarm felt himself strike the ground, then flip over.

A rock slammed into his shoulder, infuriating him. He scrambled up on all fours and dove for the bend in the rock wall ahead of him, the same one he had tried to reach before he lost his horse. He was only dimly aware of plowing through an incredible hailstorm of rocks and pitiless shards, and then throwing himself down under a narrow overhang. As he crawled deep in under the ledge, he felt the ground begin to shake ponderously. For a moment the noise appeared to have blasted his eardrums into bits. He opened his mouth to relieve the pain as the wall behind him shuddered convulsively. It felt as if a race of giants were dancing on the floor of the pass.

Dust—thick, choking—swept in over him. He wondered dimly about the horse and Lynch, then closed his eyes tightly to keep out the stinging grit and tried to pull into himself. He knew only seconds had passed since the explosion, and yet it seemed that he had been cowering in this crevice forever.

Abruptly, it was over. The silence was miraculous. The dust still hung low over the ground, but it was settling. Longarm peered through slitted eyes at the landscape around him. What he saw appalled him. Great, newly chiseled blocks of granite sat in a jumbled heap along the floor of the pass in front of him. The trail he had been following into the pass was covered up to five or six feet by debris. And there was no sign at all of his horse—or of Jack Lynch.

With some difficulty, Longarm worked his way out of the narrow cleft into which he had flung himself. He saw at once that if he had remained where the horse had gone down, he would have been finished. Great boulders, like enormous fists, had been flung across the trail. From the positions of the boulders, Longarm could see that had he not been protected by the bulging rock wall just over his head, they would have crushed him as completely and as finally as they had Lynch and the black gelding. Clambering painfully over them to get away from the cliff face, he reached a spot that gave him a clear view of the interior of the pass.

He was awed by what he saw. Longarm had never been directly under the overhanging ledge. Had he been, there would have been no possibility of survival. The avalanche of rock had come down upon the narrowest section of the pass and appeared to have filled it to a depth of a hundred feet, even more in some spots. Working his way farther into the pass, Longarm glanced up at the cliff where the ledge had hung and saw what remained: a great, shiny, concave scar that extended up the face of the cliff as far as the eye could see. The rock had an unnaturally pale cast to it, almost like bone left to bleach on the prairie.

Longarm tried not to think of Lynch's men. Many of them must have been trapped under the titanic shower. Indeed, they would probably never know the actual toll, now that Lynch himself had been killed.

Slapping the dust and rock particles from his Stetson, Longarm fitted it onto his head and, turning gingerly among the loose and quite sharp chunks of stone, proceeded to make his way out of the pass. It was not until he saw Chapman and Ty Flynn clambering over the debris to meet him and raised his hand to wave back at them that he realized how much his shoulder hurt and recalled the spinning chunk of rock that had bounced off it earlier.

Later that night, he discovered that his body was a mass of bruises. Actually, it was Molly who discovered them, and did what she could to soothe his hurt. She did fine.

Chapter 11

By noon of the next day, the cause of the blast had been established beyond any doubt. As Longarm had realized the moment he saw Lynch calling out to them and pointing up at the rock face, the Poser brothers were responsible. Ironically, it was Lynch who had asked the Posers to help him take back the ridge.

It was Ogilvy who provided the facts. He and Li Wang had been checking the fuses when the Posers and three others, with Lynch in the lead, stormed the ledge and took it back. Escaping up the mountainside, Li Wang and Ogilvy stayed out of sight—but not earshot—during all that followed.

The four men guarding the prisoners that Longarm and Ogilvy had taken earlier were clubbed down from behind and their prisoners released—and then, despite Lynch's pleas, the Posers hurled them from the brow of the ridge.

During this argument, Lynch was clubbed down and kicked back down the mountainside. His disagreement with the Posers had evidently been fundamental: while Lynch had simply wanted to take back the ledge and neutralize it as a factor in the struggle for the pass, the Posers were intend on blowing the charge and burying the pass when Longarm returned to Lynch's camp with

203

Pears. The Posers evidently had no faith in Lynch's promise that he did not intend to turn them over to the marshal when Pears returned. It was a short, ugly debate, all of which Ogilvy heard.

When Longarm was sighted entering the pass with Chapman and Pears, there were disagreements aplenty on how to set off the charge. For a while, Ogilvy had figured they would botch it. But they had the luck of the devil. They found and lit the main fuse, abandoned the securely bound Chinese powder monkeys on the ridge, then hightailed it down the mountainside. Li Wang raced out onto the ridge in an attempt to free his fellow countrymen, despite Ogilvy's pleas. A moment later the mountain seemed to shift under Ogilvy's feet. He was slammed flat against the mountainside, and the great, overhanging brow of rock disintegrated beneath him and disappeared into the maw of the pass.

Ogilvy was the sole survivor of those men he had led up onto the ridge with Longarm. He expressed some pleasure when he saw that Longarm and his party had escaped; but aside from that, after telling his story, he was inconsolable and wandered apart from the others with only Molly to comfort him as he tried to live with what he had experienced. It was, after all, a pretty gruesome ending to what, for him, had seemed a fine and exciting adventure when first he had set out with Longarm to storm that ridge.

Longarm set out after the Posers first thing the next day, heading for the nearest settlement on the other side of Eagle Pass, a mining town called McCoy. Unable to use the pass, he had a difficult time crossing the mountains and did not reach the small mining community until sundown the next day. He found that he was nevertheless only a day, perhaps less, behind the two brothers.

They and two of Lynch's men had stormed into a saloon the evening before, with guns blazing. They had slugged the bartender and backed eleven terrified citizens into a corner as hostages. One old man, whose right hand they had blown off, was sent out to the gathering crowd to collect the ransom. All that the Posers and their two confederates wanted was whatever was contained in the local bank's vault.

The weary banker who told Longarm what had happened that night finished his glass of beer and indicated a fellow sitting by himself in the back, a bottle of whiskey and a glass before him on the table. He had an unopened deck of cards beside him, and was evidently waiting for someone to join him in a poker game.

"See that fellow?" the banker said.

The banker's name was Fred. "Yes, I see him clear enough, Fred. What about him?"

Fred leaned forward, his beefy, indoors face still registering awe. "That fellow rode in while we was all trying to figure what to do. We couldn't let them animals kill all them citizens—and we knew they was capable of just such an outrage—and we couldn't turn over the townspeople's savings to them, either."

"You were on the horns of a dilemma," Longarm said dryly, lifting his glass of Maryland rye to his lips. "What's this got to do with that gambler back there?"

"Why, he heard us going on and made a crazy suggestion—after he stopped coughin', that is. He said he'd go in after them citizens with the bank's funds, but he wouldn't let them animals in there have the money."

Longarm glanced again at the lone gambler. He had a long, sallow face with a drooping mustache and haunted eyes. Even as Longarm glanced at him, the man swiftly brought out a dingy handkerchief from his frock coat pocket and coughed painfully into it. A consumptive, Longarm realized. In the mountains for his health, more than likely.

Fred shook his head. "It was a most amazing suggestion. And all he wanted was a percentage of the bank's funds—assuming he succeeded in foiling them four animals, that is."

"How much of a percentage?"

"It was out of the question, what he wanted." Fred began to sweat, just thinking of the amount. "But we finally convinced him to take a more realistic amount."

"You did, did you?"

"Yes. And he was right cooperative. A hundred dollars, we offered. He swore at us and smiled. I honestly don't believe, Marshal, that he expected to leave that saloon alive."

"But he did."

Fred nodded eagerly. "He called out to the men inside holding the hostages, and told them he was coming in with the money, but that he was coming in armed. He said he didn't trust them. They trusted him and let him in. He opened the gladstone on the counter and showed them the bills, kept his gun on them, and told them to free the hostages."

"And as soon as the hostages were safely outside, he began to fire."

Fred blinked. "Why, yes. That's precisely what happened."

"But the Posers got away."

"Yes, the two you described to me. But their cronies were fatally wounded."

"And that gambler sitting back there escaped without a scratch."

"He's a right peculiar cuss, you got to admit."

"Like you said, maybe he didn't care all that much if he left this saloon alive or not. And for that he charged you a hundred dollars."

Fred's face went suddenly red. He swallowed unhappily. "Actually, the fellow insisted on two hundred when we approached him afterward. He was . . . cleaning his gun, and we decided . . ."

"Not to argue," Longarm finished.

Fred nodded. He took out a handkerchief and

mopped his brow. "After all, Marshal, he did us a great service."

"Yes, he did. Excuse me, Fred. I reckon I'll go over and pay this fellow my respects, if you don't mind."

"Not at all, Marshal. And thank you for the drink."

Longarm nodded agreeably to the lone whiskey drinker as he approached his table. "Mind if I join you?"

"If you're buying and appreciate good whiskey."

"I'll buy and I do purely appreciate good whiskey. Maryland rye suit you?"

The man smiled, his thin face becoming almost grotesque as he did so. Longarm had never seen a man whose face so resembled that of a bleached skull. The thick, dark hair and lush John L. Sullivan mustache only seemed to emphasize the man's ivory pallor, the deep, shadowy sockets out of which his death-haunted eyes stared.

Longarm waved the bartender over and asked him to bring him the bottle Longarm had been sampling with Fred, and fresh glasses. When the barkeep brought the Maryland rye, the gambler gave him back the bottle of whiskey from which he had been drinking.

"Why don't you drink this foul rotgut yourself," he told the barkeep. "It ain't fit for a Christian."

The barkeep started to protest, then thought better of it, and left.

The gambler reached for the bottle of rye. "This is by far the cheapest town in all of Colorado. And that's saying a lot." He downed the full shotglass with one quick motion.

Longarm poured himself a drink. "I understand you chased the Posers."

"You after them?"

"That's right."

"You're a lawman, ain't you?"

"That's right. Deputy U.S. Marshal Long."

"I'm John Henry Holliday. Some call me Doc. I'm a

dentist, but don't count on it. I lost my pliers some time ago."

As Holliday poured himself another drink, Longarm smiled. "You can have that bottle, Doc. On me."

"Thanks, Long. I will sure appreciate it. This stuff won't cure what I got, and that's a fact, but it sure as hell makes dying a whole lot more pleasurable. What's the occasion?"

"Just to thank you for whittling that gang down some. And for any help you might be able to give me."

"Whittling that gang some was a pleasure. Livened up my evening and secured me a stake for some honest gambling. Them Posers are a mean pair, all right. Some call 'em the Possum Boys, and I can see why. Pale, chinless faces, scraggly mustaches—and they smelled something fierce. Even this permanent cold I got couldn't protect me from that rancid smell. They looked to me like they belong in a hole somewheres."

"I aim to see to that," Longarm said evenly.

"Personal matter, is it?"

"It wasn't."

"But now it is, huh?" Doc smiled and poured himself another drink, just a little slower this time. "I understand some good citizens in Redcliff got their hands on them two without knowing who they were. They were ready to give them both a hemp necktie when some fool lawman saved their asses."

"Watch who you're calling a fool, Doc," Longarm said with a rueful smile, as he reached for the whiskey.

"You're the one, huh?"

Longarm poured and nodded.

"I figured it was you. Just thought I'd needle you some. I get bored pretty easy at times."

"What can you tell me about them?"

"Well, one of the hostages heard the Posers talking about a place in Utah. Seems like that might be where they were headed. They've probably wore out their welcome here in Colorado."

"What place?"

He reached for the rye. "Need a little more of this. Helps to jog my memory and steady my hands." He poured with a very steady hand, sipped the whiskey, and looked at Longarm. "Moab. Seems like one of them Posers has got himself a girl there."

Longarm frowned. "Only way they can get through those mountains is to follow the Dolores past Gateway."

He did not want to let those two get into Utah. For two reasons. He would lose them for sure in that country. And he would have some difficulty accounting to the chief for his moves if he went that far afield. His mission had been to find out if the Ute Indians were responsible for the attacks on Mike O'Leary's subcontractor and on the workers building the Rio Grande Western. That mission had been accomplished. Both he and Colonel Mackenzie had established that the Indians were innocent. Longarm should now be on his way back to Denver. Billy Vail was undoubtedly wondering at that very moment where the hell he was—or at least why he hadn't telegraphed.

Longarm got to his feet. "Thanks, Doc," he said. "A pleasure meeting you. Hope your luck stays with you."

"Hell, Long! I lost my luck when I got this cough." He smiled then, and held up his freshly filled glass. "But it picked up some when you sat down. Much obliged."

Longarm nodded to the strange, haunted figure and left the table to pay the barkeep for the bottle. Glancing back once more as he left the saloon, Longarm saw Doc Holliday bent over a handkerchief held tightly in his clenched fist, his body caught up in a paroxysm of coughing, while his other hand was still reaching out for the bottle of rye whiskey.

Longarm saw the dust cloud and pulled up on the ridge. Not too long afterward, he saw the column of mounted bluecoats moving onto a flat on the other side of a low series of hills southwest of him. Squinting through the harsh midday sunlight, he thought he could see the slight figure of Colonel Mackenzie leading the column.

And then he was sure.

He hauled out his rifle, levered a cartridge into the firing chamber, and pumped a shot into the cloudless sky. As the rifle's crack rolled its way over the uneven ground toward the column, Longarm turned his big dun mare and angled down the sandy slope. He saw the colonel turn in his saddle and fling up his right arm to halt his men. A moment later the colonel was galloping across the sandy hills toward Longarm, two aides strung out well behind him.

Remembering what he had been told concerning the colonel's old war wounds, Longarm was sorry that his need for assistance had prompted him to call upon the aging officer. Longarm pushed his dun to a fast lope so as to reduce the distance the colonel would have to travel. It was a white-faced, grim Colonel Mackenzie who finally brought his mount to a sliding halt alongside Longarm.

"We meet again, Longarm," he said, squinting through the dust.

"It's my pleasure, Colonel," Longarm replied. "Did you put down that uprising on the Wyoming border?"

The man laughed shortly, bitterly, while his two lieutenants came to a sabre-rattling, jingling halt just behind him, raising another cloud of eye-stinging alkali. "An old Indian with a single-barreled shotgun, two braves with bows and arrows, and two young'uns, neither one more than eight years old. They took two beeves and a hog. That was the Indian uprising the United States Government sent my men and me to quell." He laughed shortly, disdainfully. "And now I understand we've got a small war on our hands over Eagle Pass. I'm on my way to settle that now. What can you tell me, Longarm?"

"It's over."

"The War for Eagle Pass is over, Marshal?" he said ironically. "Could I have the details?"

Longarm settled back on his saddle and related the events of the past few days as efficiently as he could. Mackenzie was amused at Longarm's account of the duel. But he was shaking his head unhappily when Longarm told him of the blast that had rendered the pass impassable, for the coming weeks at least.

"And so now you are after those Poser brothers?"

"I think they're heading for Utah. Have you caught any sign of them?"

"Yes, I have. Earlier this morning they crested a hill a few miles north of us, took one look, and charged down the other side. I sent one of my aides to watch them. I knew they were bandits of one kind or another. Their reaction to sighting us proved that. I was curious to see which way they might head after stumbling on us like that." Mackenzie leaned around in his saddle, wincing painfully as he did so. "Lieutenant Michaels! What can you tell the marshal about those two men you tracked for a while this morning?"

The shavetail urged his horse alongside Longarm, moistened his lips nervously, and tried to decide whether or not he should salute Longarm. He could not have been more than twenty, and as yet needed to have only a passing acquaintance with his razor.

"Get on with it, Lieutenant," the colonel prompted, not unkindly.

"They were going west when they stumbled on us —toward Utah, I'd say. Once they realized we were not following them, they crested the ridge again and headed for the Dolores River. They did not seem to be in a hurry."

"When was this, Lieutenant?"

"About nine."

"Thank you, Lieutenant."

The shavetail smiled quickly and returned his horse

skillfully to its former position at the rear of his commanding officer. He almost saluted.

"I need some help, Colonel," Longarm said.

"Of course."

"This here dun's about finished. I lost a pretty good animal in Eagle Pass. A big, powerful black. I am not getting any closer to those two—and I'm not going to on this dun. I'd like two of your best mounts, Colonel. I'll sign for them all nice and legal. The government will pay you what they're worth, I'm sure."

"No problem about that, Longarm," the colonel assured him. "We are, after all, still working for the same government. I'll let you pick them out. Two, you say?"

"That's right. I'm going to be doing some hard riding if I want to overtake those two before they reach Utah."

"I am at your service, Longarm," the colonel said, turning his horse to ride with Longarm back to his command.

There were only about three hours of good daylight left when Longarm caught sight of his quarry. He was cresting a hill that rimmed a vast, rolling plain, through which the Dolores River flowed toward a distant, sawtoothed range. The mountains formed a solid barrier with only one break where the river sliced through it. Five, maybe six miles distant, two horsemen—tiny black specks—were heading for that pass. It was the Posers, all right; there were two of them, they were heading in the right direction, and they were pushing their mounts ruthlessly through the blistering afternoon. Low foothills followed alongside the benchland, until after what Longarm judged to be seven or eight miles, at which point they merged with it.

Dismounting swiftly, Longarm transferred his saddle from the big chestnut he was riding to the horse he had been leading, a blood bay that stood even taller than the chestnut. Mounting the bay, Longarm leaned over and patted the chestnut affectionately on his neck, then watched him trot off toward a bright splash of grama flourishing in the shade of a cottonwood. Longarm had ridden the chestnut full out since leaving Mackenzie's troop, and its great heart had gotten Longarm within sight of his quarry. But though the chestnut might still have the heart, he no longer had the stamina.

Longarm slapped the rump of the bay and started off with a bound, angling carefully off the ridge toward the hills below. Sweeping down into the low sand hills, Longarm felt the wind tugging on his hatbrim. But he did not let up. He had no intention of sparing his mount —not until he had turned the Posers' flank and was riding at them out of the hills in front of them. He wanted to corner them while they were still on that benchland, well before they were in sight of the pass.

And it didn't matter what this might do to his horse.

Longarm had given the matter considerable thought. There was no way he could besiege the two gunmen. One of them would always be able to work his way around behind Longarm. And bushwhacking them was out of the question, since he might well get only one of them, or worse, succeed only in warning them of his presence. Accordingly, he had settled on a sudden frontal attack—one that would take one of them out of the action immediately, and the other soon after. An exercise in gunplay it would have to be. No chance for either of them to hide or room for them to run.

Now, with the sun a bloodshot eye resting on the peaks behind him, Longarm sat his trembling, lathered mount and waited for the Posers to get closer. They were above him on the benchland, riding almost directly toward him. They could not see him and he could not see them, but he could hear the steady drumbeat of their horses' hooves and the drone of their conversation. As they got closer, he caught the sharp bark of their idiot laughter and found himself remembering the two of them playing cards in that cabin—with Wally Stanton's mutilated corpse in the back room.

It was a particularly loud bark of merriment that ignited Longarm. He hauled the bay suddenly and hard to the right. Swatting him on the rump, he raked the animal with his spurs. Driven by pain and fear, the bay bounded into a dead run on its first leap and raced toward, and then up the steep embankment to the benchland beyond.

Longarm's Colt was in his hand as he burst over the crest. Before the bay's hind hooves had come down for its first stride on the bench, Longarm had fired at the nearest of the startled Posers. He missed. Still racing toward the two men, Longarm fired a second time, holding his gun so close to the horse's head that the animal shied away from the detonation, almost tripping himself up. But this shot, aimed again at the nearest Poser, was pulled off just as the man's horse reared, throwing its head up. The bullet caught the horse under the jaw and the animal kept on going up and over backwards, whinnying with pain. The outlaw almost succeeded in leaping clear, but one leg was caught under the thrashing backbone of the horse as it slammed down onto the ground.

Longarm jumped his mount over the thrashing animal, firing down at the prone rider as he did so. The bullet punched into the outlaw's exposed shoulder and Longarm saw him fling his head back in pain. The man was caught securely under the dying horse and was wounded seriously. He would not go far, Longarm concluded as he took after the second Poser, who had broken in panic before Longarm's furious charge and was now galloping back toward a grove of cottonwood, at least a half-mile distant.

But that last plunging drive up the embankment, followed by the leap over the downed horse, had taken all the strength the bay had left. The animal stumbled drunkenly and almost went down. Longarm hauled on the reins and kept the animal on its feet and with a fierce, loud cry, startled the bay into one more burst of speed. It had nothing left but heart now, but that seemed to be enough.

Longarm was gaining only slightly on the remaining Poser brother, who was already halfway to the cottonwoods. Longarm shouted again to urge the horse on across the darkening flat, squeezing the last ounce of speed from the animal. Its headlong run was getting ragged and wobbly. Longarm could hear it rasping for air. With knees and reins, Longarm lifted the bay over a gentle rise; but on the far side the horse stumbled, and this time Longarm could not drag its head up. Its front feet went out from under it, and it stuck its head out straight and crunched down jaw-first into the ground. As it flopped over on its side, Longarm went headlong over the bay's neck, rolled once, regained his feet, and darted back to the thrashing animal.

Snaking his rifle out of the exposed sling, he whirled and knelt on one knee, intent only on hitting Poser's horse at this distance. He tracked the fleeing Poser, lifted the rifle some to allow for the distance, and squeezed off a shot. It missed. He levered a fresh round into the chamber, kept himself grimly calm, and tracked the horse and rider a second time, just as carefully. Squeezing off his second shot, he jumped to his feet and watched as the horse pitched forward, catapulting Poser over its head. A second later Longarm saw Poser scramble to his feet and, carrying a rifle, limp painfully into the cottonwoods.

Longarm raced after him into the swiftly gathering darkness.

It was almost pitch-dark by the time Longarm flung himself down behind the dead horse and proceeded to pour a steady fire into the thin stand of cottonwood. After a moment of this, he got to his feet and, still levering furiously, raced the remaining yards to the trees, his rapid fire cutting a swath before him.

Plunging into the inky darkness of the cottonwood stand, he heard a scream of rage as a deafening gunshot roared to his left. The round smacked into a tree trunk just over his head. Longarm flung himself in the direction from which the shot had come, bringing up his rifle. Levering, he squeezed the trigger. The hammer came down on an empty chamber. Without pause, Longarm flipped the rifle in his hand. As a second shot roared up at him from the ground, he clubbed down at the barely visible form crouched in the tangle of underbrush.

He felt the stock strike flesh and bone, and heard the cry that came with it. And then, with nothing but a shattered rifle in his hand, he flung himself onto the figure below him. A .45 went off in the struggle, and Longarm felt exploding powder burn his cheek and the hot breeze the slug made as it went past. Slamming down with the barrel, he heard the crash of metal on metal, and the revolver fired again.

"Oh, Jesus! I'm hit!" Poser cried.

Longarm reached down with both hands and hauled the fellow onto his feet, then flung him furiously to one side. As the man began to crawl swiftly away into the trees on his hands and knees, Longarm booted him powerfully in the ass and sent him slamming sideways into a tree. He lunged after him, picked him up a second time, and again flung him to the ground. This time the back of his head struck a solid tree trunk. The man slumped to the ground and began flopping like an oversized worm someone had stomped on.

His face streaked with sweat, fighting for breath, Longarm looked vacantly down at the slowly twisting body at his feet. A black sea of total exhaustion washed over him. Every muscle in his body seemed to be made of soaking-wet cotton. Collapsing to one knee, he reached a hand out to grab a tree trunk. The roaring in his ears faded. The still-twisting figure on the dark ground became clearer to him. He saw the pinched, gray face and the narrow eyes, watching him the way a cornered animal watches, in desperation and hope, as it looks for a direction in which to dart.

"What's your name, Poser?" Longarm managed between gulps of air. "Which one are you?"

"Dick."

"You're my prisoner, Dick."

The man's tongue licked out. "I know."

Longarm reached across his stomach and pulled out his Colt and leveled it at the man. "Get up!"

"I can't!" Dick Poser bleated. "My ankle's twisted fearful from when the horse came down on it. And I'm hit!"

"Where?"

"In the side. I'm bleedin' somethin' awful!"

"I said get up." Longarm got to his feet, his Colt still trained on the man. "Get up or I'll kill you where you lie."

"You can't do that! That would be murder. You just said I was your prisoner."

"Are you going to get up?"

The man hesitated only a second, then reached out for a handhold on a tree beside him and pulled himself to his feet.

"That's better."

Longarm frisked him quickly. The man was bleeding, all right, but the wound in his side did not appear to be a serious one. With the barrel of his revolver, Longarm prodded the outlaw around and then sent him stumbling painfully out of the cottonwoods. Poser managed to stay on his feet all the way.

"Keep going," Longarm told him. "It's a long walk back to your brother."

With a groan, the man limped painfully around the dead horse and started back across the dark flat.

"Did you get him, Dick?" Lou Poser cried anxiously

as his brother loomed closer out of the night. "The son of a bitch shot me and left me here!"

"He's right behind me, Lou. We're his prisoners."

"Oh no, we ain't! Here!"

Longarm caught the dull sheen of moonlight on metal as Lou flung a handgun up to his brother. Dick snatched the revolver out of the air and whirled. Longarm was already aiming, however, and his shot came first. Longarm's slug spun Dick Poser; then the outlaw dropped to his knees, his head sagging forward. Longarm heard the man drop the revolver to the ground.

"That was smart," said Longarm to Lou Poser, as he walked closer and leveled his Colt on him. "You maybe just got your brother killed."

"Hey, Dick!" his brother cried. "You all right?"

"I'm just fine, you stupid bastard," Dick said tightly, his head still down. "I'm bleedin' like a stuck pig!"

Longarm frisked Lou Poser, saw that he was still securely jammed under the dead horse's back, then walked over to see what further damage he had inflicted on the other one. Longarm's slug had caught him high on the meaty part of his right shoulder. It was not a fatal wound, though it was bleeding quite a bit. Dick Poser's face had a wan, pasty look in the moonlight.

"You're a lucky man," Longarm told him, reaching down and picking up the revolver the man's brother had thrown him. As he stuck the weapon into his belt, he said, "I want your help in getting Lou out from under that horse."

"Leave the stupid asshole under there," the man hissed virulently.

"You heard me."

"I'm wounded!"

"I'll kill you right now if you don't help me."

Dick Poser hesitated a moment, then got painfully to his feet and limped slowly back with Longarm to his trapped brother.

It took a while, but working patiently with the

wounded Dick Poser, Longarm managed to lift the dead animal just enough for Lou to pull himself out from under it. An inspection revealed that Lou had broken his right leg beneath the knee. It was swollen painfully and Longarm could feel the two broken ends of the bone through Lou's trouser leg. Lou's earlier wound in his forearm had stopped bleeding, it appeared. But it was painful and Lou complained about it incessantly through clenched teeth.

With his brother free of the horse, Dick slumped wearily down alongside him. He looked feverish in the moonlight, his eyes wild. Lou, groaning softly, lay quietly beside him. They felt very sorry for themselves, and whenever they thought of it, they cursed Longarm with a steady, deadly intensity.

To hear them discuss their predicament between themselves, Longarm was the sole source of all their woes. They had done nothing to deserve their present punishment; they were the innocent victims of a monstrous lawman. And, of course, they believed every word they told each other. They felt no remorse for the ruined lives, the sad litter of dead bodies they had left in their wake, from the moment Longarm had saved them both from a lynch mob.

"All right," Longarm said wearily. "Get up."

Neither man made any motion to get up onto his feet.

"You must be out of your head, Marshal," Lou said. "My brother and me, we can't hardly move. And you saw my leg. We been hurt bad."

"You're goin' to have to go and get help for us, Marshal," Dick Poser said flatly. "There's a doctor in the town up ahead."

"I said get up," Longarm repeated.

"Up your ass, Marshal," Lou said.

Lou was perhaps a year younger than his brother, with a chin even more receding, with eyes just as furtive, and a sloping, uneven-looking forehead, as if it had been shaped carelessly when he was taken out of the oven. Lou grinned up at Longarm, despite his painful wounds.

Longarm took out his Colt, aimed carefully down at Lou, and fired. The bullet creased the man's forehead, slamming Lou back into the ground with brutal force. He cried out in terror and pain, his eyes starting out of his head. His brother sat up violently, his face contorted.

"My God, Marshal!" he cried. "You've killed him!"

"Not that time," Longarm told him. "Maybe the next one."

"I'll help him up! For the love of Jesus! I'll help him up!"

"Good," said Longarm. "You do that."

"But why? What do you want from us? We can't walk to that town! And we got no horses!"

"You're not going that far—just back to those cottonwoods, and don't ask me why until we get there."

It took them a long time. The moon had set and the cottonwoods were only a dark smudge against the night sky when they reached them. Lou had fallen numerous times, despite his brother's attempt to keep him hopping alongside him. The falls had not done the broken leg much good. Often, both of them sprawled forward onto the ground together, moaning and crying out, cursing Longarm, finally pleading with him to quit driving them before him through the darkness. At last they told him to shoot them, that they couldn't go on any further. Each time, Longarm simply waited, aware of their genuine exhaustion and the severity of their wounds and subsequent loss of blood. Then he started shooting at them. The shots, blazing at them out of the night, terrified them sufficiently to get them moving again.

It had been a hellish journey for both men, and at

the end of it, as they reached at the cottonwoods, Longarm saw tears of relief on their gaunt faces.

"What you doin', you bastard?" Dick asked Longarm. "Ain't you goin' to get help for us?"

"No."

"Ain't that why you drove us here? So we could keep out of the sun in the cottonwoods while you went for help?"

"That hadn't crossed my mind."

Longarm had taken the ropes from his horse and from Dick's. The two men were lying under what was, for him, the most likely tree. He walked under the overhanging branch and tossed the rope over it, feeding it expertly, then reaching up to catch the knotted end. He had already fashioned the noose. Then he threw over the second rope.

And by that time, both men knew why Longarm had driven them across the benchland to this grove of cottonwoods.

Chapter 12

Longarm glanced once more at the telegram he had found waiting for him not long before in his hotel mailbox.

> TO DEPUTY U S MARSHAL LONG REDCLIFF STOP WHERE ARE YOU QUESTION MARK COLONEL MACKENZIE REPORTS NO UTES LEFT IN COLORADO STOP SHALL I SEND WALLACE AFTER YOU QUESTION MARK VAIL

Chuckling, Longarm turned to the young telegrapher and sent a reply he hoped would satisfy his anxious chief. Then he paid the fellow and stepped out of the small office and started back to his hotel.

His route took him past what had been Wally Stanton's saloon, The Miner's Hole. He had stopped into the place late yesterday to give the lady manager the bad news about her ex-boss. Her name was Sally, and she had taken the news badly, as had all the other girls and the ancient bartender Stanton had hired before riding out after the Possum Boys. As a result of that sad visit, he had not thought he would soon want to enter the place again, but to his surprise, it appeared that a party was going on inside.

The sounds were so merry, the shouts so full of good cheer, that even the occasional tinkle of shattering glass seemed to add to the merriment. He pushed his way through the batwings. It was a pleasant enough place to begin with, though now more than a mite crowded. Longarm was feeling peaceable, however, and didn't mind the outsized hilarity. But it did puzzle him.

Could these people be celebrating the news of Wally Stanton's death? The thought made his peaceable thoughts turn to ice. A miner tore away from the bar, his .44 in his hand, and bolted from the place, yelling. A moment later Longarm heard the crazed miner pumping shots into the sky. He shook his head and elbowed his way through the crowd, ordered his Maryland rye, then fought his way back through the ranks at the bar and found himself a quiet table in the corner.

Almost at once, a grizzled prospector sighted the empty chair opposite him and sat down in it. He had a full bottle of rum clutched in one hand. Slapping it down on the table, he reached across it with a calloused hand. Longarm shook it vigorously.

"Name's Pete!" the fellow cried above the hubbub. "On my way out to strike it rich!"

"That so?"

"Yup! I got me a stake—thanks to Wally!"

Longarm frowned. "Wally? Wally who?"

"Why, Wally Stanton. That's who! Ain't you heard, mister?"

"I'm a stranger in town. Just rode in late yesterday. Maybe you'd be kind enough to fill me in?"

"Why, sure! Wally's dead. Sally got the news yesterday. So she went in and opened the safe, like Wally told her to do when he left her in charge. That Wally was somethin', he was. He'd left some envelopes to be opened if word of his death was to reach her, and so Sally went ahead and opened them!"

Longarm had forgotten about his drink. He leaned forward. "What was in the envelopes, Pete?"

"Money! Money for each girl in here, and for Sally and for the bartender. And in Sally's envelope was the deed to this place and to a couple of mines Wally had grubstaked. And then there was one more envelope!"

"What was in that?"

"*More* money! For grubstakin' us prospectors, with Sally in charge of it!"

"So that's why the celebration today."

The man nodded vigorously. "Hell! You ought to see the crowd at the hardware supply store, and the feed store, and the livery! Us prospectors'll be off in the hills come sundown. I got a place in mind, let me tell you!"

Longarm leaned back, smiling broadly. "Good luck, Pete."

The fellow uncorked his bottle, put it to his lips, and tipped his head back. His Adam's apple did a jig for a moment; then he slapped the bottle back down onto the table. As he was wiping off his mouth with the back of his hand, someone called to him from the door. Pete waved to him and jumped up.

"So long!" he cried to Longarm. "That's my partner."

Snatching up his bottle, he ran for the batwings. Longarm was laughing as the man vanished through the door. Sally spotted him at the table, left the bar, and hurried over to the table to sit with him.

"You heard?" she asked. "I mean what Wally did with his money?"

Longarm nodded. "I heard. He was a strange one, all right."

She nodded. "Strange, yes. But *nice* strange. He left me a note. Wally said he was going to see justice done. Did he, Longarm? Is that how he died? You didn't say much about that yesterday, but I want to know."

"Did he see justice done?"

"Yes."

"He didn't *see* it, Sally. But it *was* done, I promise you."

Sally leaned back. She was a round, pleasant-faced woman who could no longer count on her face and figure to make her fortune. She seemed satisfied with Longarm's reply, but before she could question him further, Longarm said goodbye to her and pushed himself through the happy crush of miners and out the door. He felt a deep warmth within him and knew it was not only from the rye.

"Longarm!"

The tall lawman turned. Molly was leaving her father and Ben Ogilvy on the run. He smiled warmly at her as he waited for her to reach him.

"Ben said you were back!" she cried, throwing herself into his arms. "Weren't you going to let me know too?"

"I've been a mite busy, Molly," Longarm explained, somewhat overwhelmed by the warmth of Molly's greeting, especially with her father and Ben Ogilvy looking on. But Longarm had learned that Molly was one girl who did what she liked—and got away with it. "Matter of fact, I was thinking of you just a few minutes ago."

"No you weren't. But thanks for lying."

"And how is Ben—and your father?"

"Ben is fine. And father has just swung a loan to get him through the winter. He and Otto are partners again, at least until they get that pass cleared. My, aren't you the gentleman! All manners and polite questions." She grinned mischievously. "Aren't you going to invite me up to your room?"

Longarm looked nervously over at the spot on the sidewalk where Molly's father and Ben Ogilvy had been a moment before—and saw that both men were gone. He smiled quickly down at Molly.

"I don't have any etchings, ma'am," he told her, as

they started along the sidewalk, "but I've got some pretty scars you could run your fingers along."

"You've got more than that, Longarm. And it's not just my fingers I'm going to use!"

They said no more as they hurried along the crowded sidewalk. A lot had happened since last he had enjoyed the company of this sunny Irish lass—and much of it not very nice to think on. Maybe that was why such lusty women as Molly O'Leary were sent here, Longarm mused, to help wash out the ugliness and pain that lodged sometimes—like a pesky arrowhead—in a man's soul. But whatever the reason of it, Longarm was purely grateful.

As he closed the door to his room a few moments later and turned to glance down at Molly, he saw the happy glow on her face and knew that Molly was grateful too.

SPECIAL PREVIEW

Here are the opening scenes
from

LONGARM ON THE OLD MISSION TRAIL

twenty-fifth novel in the bold
LONGARM series from Jove

Chapter 1

Longarm knew he was in trouble the minute he went in to see his boss, Marshal Billy Vail. He didn't know why. The banjo clock on the wall said he was only twenty minutes late this morning, but old Billy was drumming on his desk and scowling down at his green blotter like it had just done something awful. Longarm took a seat and lit a cheroot while he waited for the deluge. But when Billy finally spoke, his tone was pure sweet reason.

"My clerk out front is typing up your vouchers and travel orders. We're loaning you to the Interior Department and you're on your way to California."

Longarm blew a thoughtful smoke ring and said, "I sure wish you wouldn't do that to me, Billy. I promised the widow Brown I'd take her to the opera tonight. She's rented a box for the season and—"

"I know about you and the widow Brown's box," Marshal Vail cut in. "You're getting on the twelve-fifteen anyway. You wouldn't enjoy that fool opera, old son. My wife made me take her the other night and it was purely tedious. The program said some Eye-talian wrote it for the opening of the Suez Canal. But there was nothing about the canal in the story. It was about some colored lady named Ida who lived in Egypt back in the Good Book time. It was sung in Eye-talian, and you know how they fancy everything up. This Ida had a boyfriend called Ramsbottom and he was supposed to be a prince. But he sure didn't have much political pull. They nailed him and old Ida on a miscegenation charge and made it stick. My wife and all the other gals cried when the judge sentenced Ramsbottom and Ida, but I was just disgusted. After singing all night about how fond he was of Ida, Ramsbottom didn't fight worth a damn when the Egyptian lawmen closed in."

"Gals like to cry at the opera," Longarm said. "Why can't I catch a later train? What's so infernal important out California way?"

Billy sighed deeply. "Hell, it's not an important case. Just some rascals stealing cows from the Indian agency out there. The reason I am sending you, as soon as possible, has to do with another case altogether. You remember when you arrested State Senator Loving, about six weeks ago?"

Longarm nodded, smiling slightly at the memory.

Vail saw the smile and continued, "I don't remember telling you to throw him down the State House steps, or to put handcuffs on him in the process. I mean it was only a warrant for attempted bribery, but I might have known you'd get testy when he said you couldn't pester such an important cuss."

Longarm chuckled. "I reckon he knows, now, that a federal agent can arrest anyone he has papers on. I invited him to come quiet, but he acted sort of bratty. Folks sure laughed when I split his pants as we rolled around together. But what has that old case to do with the one out in California?"

The pudgy chief marshal shifted uncomfortably as he said, "Senator Loving beat the rap. The grand jury, in its infinite wisdom, did not see fit to try him in an election year."

"Yeah, he mentioned something about controlling a mess of votes while I was pounding some sense into him," Longarm said with a disgusted grimace. "Are you saying you want me out of town because the senator's out gunning for me, Billy? I ain't afraid of the son of a bitch."

"I know you ain't. That's why I feel that Denver will be a lot more peaceable if the two of you don't meet up until the senator's had time to cool down some. He specifically asked for you as he was leaving the federal courthouse yesterday afternoon. But I figure he'll have other fish to fry in a few weeks, what with the election coming up and his other enemies accusing him of everything but smallpox."

"Hell," Longarm snorted, "if you just want me to hide out a few weeks, I have some vacation time coming and a lady up on Sherman Avenue who says she wants to improve me. I could just stay out of sight and—"

"At the opera?" Vail cut in, raising his bushy black eyebrows. "This case out on the Coast will not only keep you off the streets of Denver for a spell. It's the sort of case you're good at."

"Catching cow thieves, Billy? Hell, anybody can catch a cow thief."

Vail shook his head and said, "Not these rascals. They're sort of slick and spooky, and the local lawmen out there are stumped. Do you remember those highgraders stealing gold out there a while back?"

Longarm nodded. "Sure. Federal gold was sort of vanishing off guarded ore cars on its way to the San Francisco Mint."

"These cow thieves are pulling a similar game," Vail said. "Do I have your undivided attention?"

"No. I promised I'd take the lady to the opera tonight and there's a train leaving in the morning, but go ahead."

Vail said, "The Indian bureau has been buying beef to feed the Modoc, in Northern California. The Modoc just signed up for rations and such after playing tag with the army until a couple of years ago."

"I know about the Modoc War, Billy."

"Right. Anyway, the BIA gets the beef cheap down near Pueblo de Los Angeles, herds it up the Old Mission Trail to Frisco Bay, and ships it from there by steamboat, as needed."

"Where are the cow thieves hitting the herds, on the long drive up the coast?" Longarm asked, his interest piqued in spite of his annoyance.

"That's the spooky part," Vail said. "Nobody's been attacking the contract drovers. They form the herd down by the Los Angeles River, move 'em out, and nothing much happens along the way. But when they tally the herd at the north end of the drive, they end up with a third or more of the cows missing."

Longarm pursed his lips and whistled. "That's a lot of beef if we're talking about the usual trail herd, Billy."

"It is and we are. The last herd that sort of evaporated on the hoof left Los Angeles with three thousand head counted and trail-branded. A month later, when they ran 'em in the tally chutes at San Francisco, they had less than two thousand."

Longarm frowned and asked, "Didn't they tally on the trail, for Pete's sake?"

"Sure they did," Vail said. "It's hard to get more'n a rough count on the hoof when you bed 'em down for the night. But the drovers knew they were leaking cows along the way, they just haven't been able to figure out how. The spooky part is that not a cow has been stolen at night, when you'd expect it. The BIA has its own investigators riding with the contract drovers. So they tally before each day's drive."

Longarm took a thoughtful drag of cigar smoke before he said, "Let's back up and study these contract riders. The easiest way for cows to wind up missing in broad daylight is with a little help from their friends."

The marshal shook his head and said, "Interior is

ahead of you on that. They fired the first trail boss who limped in with all that government beef missing. They fired the second one too. They've checked the credentials of everyone they've contracted with, ever since. They even tried to drive one herd north with army personnel, but the cavalry spilled the herd just trying to cross the San Fernando Valley, so they had to go back to hiring cowboys. Which is getting to be a bitch, by the way. The good old boys around Pueblo de Los Angeles don't cotton much to being called cow thieves, so a lot of 'em have refused to work for the BIA. They say the job is jinxed. Some fool Mex tells everyone who'll listen that the ghost of some Mexican bandit is still haunting the coast ranges."

Longarm shrugged and asked, "What about *real* bandits? That's rough country and a hell of a long drive. Has anybody bothered to *look* for those stolen cows? You did say they were trail-marked, didn't you?"

"Sure. The government agent buys scrub Indian beef at a good price from the hardscrabble rancheros in the Los Angeles Basin. Then each one gets a big old ID branded on it as they run 'em into the holding yards. As to looking for them, the county and state lawmen all the way up the trail know the brand. They've looked over the herds of every outfit the trail passes anywhere near. None of the local rancheros seem to be expanding their herds at the expense of the U.S. taxpayer. Before you ask if I think the local lawmen are crooks, I already considered it. I'll buy a crooked sheriff here and a corrupt state brand inspector there. But the Old Mission Trail is over four hundred miles long, and if every lawman along it is a crook, we are in trouble."

"Two out of three men with a badge seem to be reasonably honest," Longarm agreed. "You can't pin down just which counties along the trail we're talking about, can you, Billy?"

"All of 'em. The cows just dribble away, all along the line. Hell, I wouldn't need to send my best hand if we could localize the problem. But nobody can. A cow vanished here, a cow vanishes there, until after a while a hell of a lot are gone. I figure some of it's normal wastage. You always lose a stray or two a day on a long drive. But when you get there with a *thousand* missing, some son of a bitch has *got* 'em! So I want you to go out there and make them stop. Do you figure your best move would be a straight investigation, or would you feel more comforted if you worked undercover?"

Longarm considered this for a moment, then said, "Well, everybody knows the BIA has its own officials riding with the herd, so the thieves will likely be watching them. I'll just see if I can sign on as a trail hand and play her by ear."

"I figured you would. I'll notify Interior that you're coming."

"I wish you wouldn't, Billy. I work best on my own and there's something fishy about the whole deal."

Vail looked surprised. "Jesus, do you suspicion somebody from the Indian bureau might be in on it?"

Longarm said, "Don't know. If they are, I'll stand a better chance of catching them if they don't know I'm watching them. Like I said, I'll just mosey out and wrangle myself a job. When is the next drive forming up?"

"About a week. The sooner you get there, the better."

"Maybe. Forget the case for a minute. Since you are an unsuspected opera fan, Billy, maybe you can fill me in on something the widow Brown was jawing about this morning as we parted fondly. She said this opera I was to escort her to was White Tie. What in thunder do you reckon she meant?"

Vail laughed loudly. "Hell, that's easy, old son. If she's got herself a season box, it means she listens to her music fancy. The folks sitting up in the boxes wear clawhammer coats and boiled shirts with little white ties, like the waiters at the Pullman House Hotel."

Longarm looked thunderstruck. "Sweet Jesus, where in hell would I get me a dude outfit like that, Billy?"

"I reckon she expects you to rent one," Vail said, shrugging his round shoulders. "She said she aimed to improve you, remember?"

Longarm stubbed out his cheroot grimly. "She sure did, but I didn't suspicion she meant she wanted me to dress like her butler. You did say there's a noonday train leaving, didn't you?"

"I did. I take it you aim to get an early start on them cow thieves?"

Longarm stood up and adjusted his gunbelt grimly, as he nodded and replied, "Yep. Duty calls, and what the hell, you told me what the opera was about, anyway. I could likely sit through a couple of hours of Italian screeching to please a lady, but not in any infernal boiled shirt."

Longarm was a deputy U.S. marshal, not a member of the Secret Service, and he didn't like to lie. Even if he had, some defense attorney could cloud up a case with a mess of dumb charges about entrapment. So Longarm had to walk a narrow line as he got off the train a few days later in Pueblo de Los Angeles.

He wasn't wearing false whiskers and he used his right name when he checked into the Angel's Rest Hotel on Olvera Street, near the main plaza and around the corner from the old Church of Our Lady, the Queen of the Angels. But he had shucked his frock coat and the fool tie the Justice Department made him wear, and the luggage he had toted over from the depot included a fifty-dollar double-rigged stock saddle he had borrowed from a public-spirited citizen riding for the Diamond K near Denver. The government-issue McClellan he usually worked with was inclined to hint at army or federal connections. A well-broken-in manila rope and a used pair of gunbarrel chaps tied to the stock saddle spelled out High Plains Cowhand to the curious who knew how to read such things. Longarm didn't intend to ask right out for a job with the contract drovers who were due to leave in a few days with the government herd. Folks would be less suspicious of a hand who had to be recruited almost against his will. Longarm knew already that the outfit hired to make the next drive was short-handed, and he figured that if he played his cards right, he wouldn't have to go to them; they'd come to him.

He paid a week's rent in advance for the room he hired, but he wouldn't be there. If any nosy cuss discussed him with the rummy-looking room clerk, they'd pick up on the fact that the tall stranger's original plans didn't seem to include riding off with just anybody at a moment's notice. Longarm locked his gear in the room, stuck an inconspicuous matchstick in the doorjamb to see if anyone visited his borrowed cow outfit while he was gone, and went back downstairs. The lobby was a small adobe cavern, but as usual, a couple of seedy old gents were camped in chairs, reading yesterday's papers by the light of a potted palm. Longarm handed his room key to the clerk and said, just loudly enough to be overheard, "I'll be back sort of late. What time do you lock the front door?"

"We don't," the clerk replied. "Everything is up to date in Los Angeles, now that us white folks are running it. We're open twenty-four hours a day. But if you get back all that late with a lady under your arm, we'll expect you to pay for a double occupancy. We don't make moral judgments, but you cowboys have to understand that we are not in business for our health. That room rents for fifty cents a head. So don't go trying to sneak no heads by us, hear?"

Longarm chuckled and said, "I did hear tell there's a little action over on Hill Street."

The clerk warned him, "Don't you *dare* come back

with one of them greaser gals from Bunker Hill! We don't rent rooms to Mexicans, Chinamen or colored folks, male or otherwise."

"Don't get your bowels in an uproar. I ain't looking for a woman right now. I'm looking for a job. I hear tell there's some oil sign here in the basin, and I worked one summer drilling oil, so—"

"*Oil?*" The clerk laughed incredulously. "There ain't no oil wells in California, cowboy."

One of the old loafers lowered his paper to opine, "He must mean them tar seeps out on the Hancock spread, Pete."

"Hell, them ain't oil wells," the clerk scoffed. "They're tar pits. They sell a few barrels of the goop down at San Pedro, now and again. The tar's all right for ship's bottoms, but it stinks too bad for burning and such. They ain't hiring out on the Hancock spread, young feller. Why don't you try over to the railroad yards? I hear tell Cracker McBride is hiring trail hands for a drive north. Just ask around the yards and they'll direct you to him."

Longarm shook his head and replied fervently, "I thank you for the thought, but I have done all the trail herding the Good Lord ever meant to pile one poor boy's plate."

"I noticed the grass-rope saddle. I understand old Cracker McBride pays pretty good, if you're a top hand."

Longarm raised his blue eyes heavenward and milked a forlorn sigh for all it was worth. "I've rid high and I've rid low. I've chased cows up the Chisholm and the Goodnight, and froze my ass on the Montana. I've rid for the Hash Knife and the Jingle Bob. I was ramrod on the Middle Fork when the Shoshone tried to eat all our beef one winter. I have been rolled, stomped and dragged by a vast collection of ten-dollar ponies the bosses expected me to work on. I tell you, boys, I have et my last trail dust and milled my last midnight stampede. There *has* to be an easier way to make a living."

The room clerk frowned suspiciously, but since Longarm had paid in advance, he decided it wouldn't be polite to ask the dumb cowboy if he had any visible means of support. The old man who'd filled him in on the oil industry of Southern California said, "I understand your pain and anguish, son. I used to be a cowhand, before I wised up. They do say there's a little color being dug over in Calico, a desert town not far from here."

The other old man put down his paper and broke in, "Now just hold on. The boy says he's looking for a *sensible* job! Gold mining is more work for less pay than herding cows!"

Longarm tried to look eager as well as dumb when he said, "Not if you strike it rich. How do I get to this Calico town?"

The room clerk rolled his eyes and said, "Jesus H. Christ, you must have worms or something. You ain't slept a night on your hired pillow and already you're talking about tear-assing out across the desert in the dry season! You'll fry your brains out, boy. If I were you, I'd give this growing city a chance. There's all sorts of jobs hereabouts. Los Angeles is growing like a weed."

"I reckon I'm just itchy-footed from the train ride," Longarm replied sheepishly. "I did promise I'd have me a good look at that ocean you folks have around here. How do I get to this here Pacific they keep talking about?"

"It's a mite late to start this afternoon, son," one of the older men said. "It's a day's ride out to Santa Monica along the Sunset Trail. If I was you, I'd hold off until morning."

The other oldtimer agreed. "It's a nice ride, this time of the year. But you wouldn't see much if you reached the ocean after sundown, and there ain't a durned thing to do in Santa Monica. It's just a stage station on the coast trail, and they charge captive-customer rates for beer."

Longarm took his Ingersoll watch out of a vest pocket and consulted it before he said, "I suspicion you're right. I'll just mosey over to the plaza or maybe find me a card house or whatever."

As he was leaving, one of them called after him, "Stay out of the La Paloma. The wheel over there is rigged beyond common courtesy."

The clerk and the loafers exchanged a chuckle as Longarm left. One of them said, "He might land a job in construction. He looks strong."

His companion opined, "Hell, can't you see he's a born cowboy? What'll you bet he winds up working for McBride's outfit?"

"Well, McBride pays pretty good," the other said, "and none of the local spreads would sign on a grass-rope hand if they could help it. But the boy says he don't want to work cows this season."

"Hell, they all say that, and it's true. Nobody *wants* to work cows. Not if they have any other trade, they don't. But that boy is over thirty if he's a day, and I've got him read to a T. He's been working cows since they was invented. Did you notice how busted up his stock saddle was when they brung it in?"

The old man looked a little wistful as he raised his paper to close the discussion. "I was like him once. A cowboy starts to think of the future as he leaves his twenties behind him. But that boy ain't ready to settle down just yet. He's dumb and restless. They make the best kind. All McBride has to do is mention San Francisco at the other end of the trail, and you'll see. He'll sign up."

The room clerk glanced at the register Longarm had signed. "I'll mention there's a top hand staying here, next time I see Cracker McBride. McBride has sent me business in the past, and one hand washes the other."

241

Chapter 2

It was just as suspicious for a grown man to be too dumb as it was for him to be too smart, so Longarm let the City of the Angels work at taking a new arrival to the cleaners. Marshal Vail had given him a hundred dollars to lose while setting up shop as an out-of-work drifter, so Longarm shot a couple of lines of pool with some hustlers who should have been ashamed of themselves. He shot a straight game to keep from looking like a total idiot. So, while he couldn't beat the usual pool shark, he'd only lost a few dollars by the time the sun went down and it just got too tedious to go on. He left and drifted over to the La Paloma Saloon that the oldtimer had warned him about. It was a ticky-tacky joint that reminded him of the Long Branch in Dodge, save for a big Wheel of Fortune against the back wall. A bored-looking gal in a red fandango dress was in charge of the wheel, but nobody was playing it. Word had likely gotten around. The gambling gal was seated on a bentwood chair, trying not to fall asleep. Longarm ignored her and the Wheel of Fortune, at first, and bellied up to the bar and asked for Maryland rye. As he'd expected, a man with enough in his jeans to order by brand drew a thoughtful look from the lady sitting by the wheel. It cost an extra cent a shot, too. But what the hell, he was on an expense account.

It was early yet. The only other customers were a couple of gents at the far end of the bar, near the doorway. They'd sized him up as he came in. He'd run their faces through his mental file of wanted posters and figured he wasn't after them, either.

They were dressed like cattlemen. The one who liked black duds had an interesting sidearm hanging low on his Border gun rig. It looked like an old Le Mat revolver. Longarm hadn't seen one for years. It was a French-made weapon that had never really caught on. The Le Mat was expensive and carried firepower to the point of ridiculousness. The big pistol couldn't make up its mind whether it was a revolver or a sawed-off shotgun. It weighed a ton and had two barrels, over and under. The top barrel fired .40-caliber slugs from a nine-chamber cylinder. The lower barrel fired a backup .66-caliber buckshot round. The shotgun part was single-shot, but how much lead did any one man need to throw in peacetime? The jasper in black either had a mess of enemies to worry about or, more likely, he just liked noise.

Longarm noticed that the gal by the Wheel of Fortune was giving him the eye, so he downed his drink, ordered another, and moseyed back to her, glass in hand. "Howdy, ma'am," he said. "What's that thing and how does it work?"

The girl stayed seated, but she smiled up at him as she said, "You can't tell me you haven't played Wheel of Fortune, cowboy."

He said, "I tried it at a carnival once. I got whipped disgraceful. I've heard it said that you folks can stop that wheel on any number, as long as it ain't the one I bet on."

The girl said, "This wheel is as honest as the day is long, cowboy. I will tell you true that the odds are against you. You look like a smart gent and anyone can see that there's more numbers you can lose on than there is one number you can win on. But I don't use a brake on my wheel; I don't have to. Do you want to pick a number, just for fun?"

Longarm vacillated as visibly as possible. "I don't know. I don't have much of my grubstake left, and I'm out of work too."

The girl stood up, letting him see how tight her dress was, and gave the wheel a spin. "Come on, I said we'd just try it for fun. Pick a number, cowboy. It won't cost you anything."

Longarm shrugged as he stared at the spinning wheel and said, "I'll pick seven, if it ain't costing me anything."

The wheel slowed down. The clacker atop the rig started hesitating as the nails set in the wheel between the painted numbers passed it. Lucky seven inched into place, looked like it was going to stop, and then moved on one space as the wheel stopped. The girl said, "You almost won. You want to try again?"

"For free?"

"Sure, why not? Business is slow and I like you."

Sure she does, Longarm thought, as the girl gave the wheel another whirl and he picked eleven. She was a pretty little thing, with too much henna in her hair and too many men's faces in her world-weary hazel eyes. He admired a good con artist's skill, but she wasn't as good as she thought she was. That was likely why the owner of the wheel had a gal working it. The wheel stopped on eleven and the brake was so obvious that it would have gotten a male gambler killed in Dodge or Cheyenne by now. She laughed and said, "Oh, you *won!* It's too bad you didn't have real money riding on eleven."

Longarm felt as foolish as hell, with the bartender and two grown men watching. But he reached in his pocket and took out a quarter. He put it on the beige counter in front of the wheel and said, "Well, maybe my luck is changing. Let's try six this time."

The girl shook her head and said, "Table stakes are a dollar a spin, cowboy. If you don't have real money, don't play. I'll spin it again for you, just to see if you'd have won, but put the two bits back in your pants. My boss would scold me if he caught me, but like I said, I like you and we're just doing this for fun."

She spun the wheel as Longarm thought: *Sure we are, you sly little bitch. That crack aimed at my manhood was slick as hell. I bet you charge extra for taking off your socks in bed, too.*

The wheel stopped on six. Longarm was surprised. Did he look *that* country? The girl said, "I don't know how you do it! Not many gents pick two out of three. It's a good thing we weren't playing for real money." Then she bent forward as if to whisper to him, but really to give him a look down her low-cut bodice as she added, "Or other things."

Longarm raised a hayseed's knowing eyebrow and grinned toothily as he asked, "Oh? Do you mean I might win, well, a pretty dolly, if I beat your wheel?"

She'd baited the hook and he'd nibbled, so she eased off with a light laugh and said, "Don't get your hopes up. You'd have to beat the bank before I'd be forced to bet anything like that. I've got a hundred silver dollars you'd have to win off me before we'd get to higher stakes."

He knew that she knew he had lower stakes in mind as he grinned and put a silver dollar down. "Powder River and let her buck," he said. "I feel lucky as hell about seven. I used to ride for the Lazy Sevens, up Colorado way."

The girl spun the wheel and managed to look worried when the number seven won. "Oh, dear," she said, adjusting her bodice to cover her cleavage as she covered his bet. He said, "Let it ride. But this time I'll try eleven again."

"I can see you know how to figure the odds," she said, as she spun the wheel again.

Naturally he lost, and naturally he'd only lost a dollar of his own, so naturally he put another down as she raked in the spoils and sighed, "I sure don't want to lose the boss's money and have to bet my all. Big men like you are sort of scary."

"I'll be gentle, honey," he reassured her. "Spin the wheel and hope it don't stop on six."

It was an interesting little charade, and Longarm was enjoying her act. But as the wheel was still spinning a voice behind him yelled, "Cowboy! Duck!" and all hell busted loose!

Longarm dropped to the floor and rolled, drawing his Colt .44 as the big smooth-bore Le Mat roared deafeningly in the confined space a split second after a smaller gun put a .45 slug in the spinning wheel above Longarm's head. He crabbed sideways along the floor to join the girl crouched behind the corner of the bar, as he stared into the smoke that filled the saloon from halfway down the bar to the entrance. The girl whispered, "Jesus Christ, you win! You didn't have to shoot my wheel!"

"I didn't," he answered, as the smoke started to thin and he could make figures out in the blue haze. The bartender had sensibly dropped out of sight behind the mahogany. The two men who'd been drinking together when he came in were still on their feet. Another man lay mangled on the floor, with his face in a spittoon and a Walker Conversion a foot from his clutching dead hand. The man in black was still holding his big Le Mat, and the awesome mass of steel was still smoking. Longarm saw that the thing wasn't pointed his way, so he got up, holding his own muzzle politely down, and asked, "What happened?"

"Beats hell out of me," the man in black replied. "This gent came in the door, took one look at you, and slapped leather. I didn't want him to shoot Trixie and she was lined up with you too close for comfort, so I shot him. I hope he ain't a friend of yours, stranger."

"Not hardly. I'm new in town. My handle is Custis Long. Let's see who this gent was."

The man in black said to call him Boomer. As Longarm rolled the bloody corpse over with his boot, the aptly named Boomer asked, "Anybody you know?"

Longarm lied. He had to. The man who'd tried to shoot him in the back was a well-known train robber that Longarm was surprised to see out of jail. "Jesus, I think I have seen him before. We tangled a year ago in Ellsworth. It was a friendly fistfight and I'm surprised he took it so serious. The dance-hall gal the discussion was about was sort of bowlegged, as I remember."

"You've an eye for the ladies, Long," Boomer observed as he started to reload the bottom chamber of his Le Mat. "It's lucky for you the galoot was too mad at you to consider us innocent bystanders."

Longarm put his own gun away as he said, "You are right as rain, and I would say I owe you more than a drink, Boomer. But a drink will have to do you. I'm bashful about kissing grown men."

A couple of men in blue uniforms came through the swinging doors. One of them sighed and said, "We heard there'd been a shooting in here and I can see we heard right. Is anybody here going to explain all the noise, or do we have to guess what happened?"

Longarm stared, frozen-faced. He knew he could flash his federal badge and make them listen to reason, but that meant giving his whole show away.

"I shot him," Boomer volunteered rather proudly. "We were just about to have a drink to celebrate. The cuss on the floor was trying to murder this cowhand when I stopped him."

"That was neighborly, I'm sure, but we try to discourage gunplay on Olvera Street, and I'm afraid you boys are all under arrest," one of the coppers said.

Boomer reached in his pocket and calmly took out a billfold. "I see no reason to pester the judge. I'm a government man. Long, here, didn't know it, but he managed to get on the wrong side of a wanted man. The cuss on the floor is a Texican gunslinger named Jennings. I've seen his face on the federal flyers they send to every office."

Longarm found it easy to look astounded as he asked Boomer, "Are you a lawman? No wonder you're so good with that cannon!"

Boomer looked a trifle smug as he patted his holstered Le Mat and answered, "I reckon I can handle most two-bit owlhoots after Uncle Sam's gold. I'm the boss guard here in L.A. for the BIA."

"You're an Indian agent, Boomer?"

"Not exactly. I work for a purchasing agent who buys for Uncle Sam. They pay cash on the barrelhead for Indian beef, so that means a mess of cash on hand at our office over by the railroad yards, and since cash on hand attracts thieves on the hoof—"

One of the coppers said, "Say no more about it. What we have us here is an open-and-shut case of whatever. Do you reckon this boy was out to rob the Interior Department?"

"Hell, no," Boomer snorted. "The cowboy here got in a fight with the rascal once, not knowing he had a rep as a badman. Jennings came in here for a drink or whatever, spotted a man who'd whipped him, and became ancient history. Why don't you get somebody to drag him over to the morgue? There may be a reward on him; I'll see when I get to the office."

The two coppers looked wistful. Longarm knew that most federal men shared reward money with the locals for good will. But when one of the coppers mentioned sharing to Boomer, the man in black laughed easily. "Hell, go shoot your own outlaws. I nailed the son of a bitch fair and square, and any money due on him is mine!" Then he nudged Longarm and said, "You come with us, old son. Let's go someplace quiet and talk about your future."

Longarm still owed him that drink, so he followed politely, but when they got outside he said, "I can thank you for such future as I may have, but I don't want a job as a guard, if that's what you have in mind."

Boomer laughed and said, "Hell, I can see you're a cowhand, not a gunslick. This here is Mr. Carver, by the way."

Longarm nodded at the silent man who'd stood by through it all without appearing to take much interest. As Boomer led them to another joint across the street, Carver said, "I'm with the BIA too. I'm the gent you see if you have any cows to sell us."

Longarm didn't comment. The three of them went in and took a corner table. Longarm put a coin on the table when the waitress came over, and he ordered drinks all around before saying with a frown, "Damn. I left a whole dollar back there and I never found out if I won or not."

Boomer laughed. "Nobody wins with Trixie. I found it sort of amusing to watch you try."

Carver said, "Forget your lost stake, Long. We might be able to put you on the trail of real money, if you're a top hand."

Longarm looked carefully dubious. "I don't know. I'm getting kind of old for chasing cows. I didn't know the Interior Department hired cowhands, anyway."

"We don't," Carver told him. "Not direct. But I just bought a mess of cows for the Modoc and some other Indians, and I'll be buying more in the next few days. We've hired a professional drover named McBride to herd 'em north for us. He's having a time getting a crew together. Interested?"

"Not hardly. Trail herding is the only chore I know more disgusting than stringing fences. What's wrong with this McBride jasper? There's generally something wrong with a trail boss who can't sign on enough kids to ride drag."

The two Californians exchanged glances and Carver waited until the girl had placed a bottle and some shot glasses on the table between them before replying, "We don't want green kids herding our Indian beef this time, Long. We want the cows to arrive at the far end of the trail."

Longarm poured as Boomer explained, "Our beef is getting strayed or stolen. This time we're sending some law along to watch for cow thieves. We'd feel better if we knew the herders knew their business, too. You may as well know we were looking for you when you wandered into the La Paloma. I was fixing to approach you when that rascal tried to shoot you." He paused meaningfully. "We know all about you, Long."

★★★★★
JOHN JAKES'
KENT FAMILY CHRONICLES

Stirring tales of epic adventure and soaring romance which tell the story of the proud, passionate men and women who built our nation.

☐ 05686-3	THE BASTARD (#1)	$2.75
☐ 05711-8	THE REBELS (#2)	$2.75
☐ 05712-6	THE SEEKERS (#3)	$2.75
☐ 05684-7	THE FURIES (#4)	$2.75
☐ 05685-5	THE TITANS (#5)	$2.75
☐ 05713-4	THE WARRIORS (#6)	$2.75
☐ 05714-2	THE LAWLESS (#7)	$2.75
☐ 05432-1	THE AMERICANS (#8)	$2.95

Available at your local bookstore or return this form to:

JOVE BOOK MAILING SERVICE
1050 Wall Street West
Lyndhurst, N.J. 07071

Please send me the titles indicated above. I am enclosing $_____ (price indicated plus 50¢ for postage and handling for the first book and 25¢ for each additional book). Send check or money order—no cash or C.O.D.'s please.

NAME_____

ADDRESS_____

CITY_____STATE/ZIP_____
Allow three weeks for delivery.

SK17

REX STOUT

MORE BESTSELLING PAPERBACKS BY ONE OF YOUR FAVORITE AUTHORS...

Adventures of Nero Wolfe

☐ 05085-7	BLACK ORCHIDS	$1.75
☐ 05119-5	NOT QUITE DEAD ENOUGH	$1.75
☐ 04865-8	OVER MY DEAD BODY	$1.75
☐ 05117-9	THE RED BOX	$1.75
☐ 05118-7	SOME BURIED CAESAR	$1.75
☐ 04866-6	TOO MANY COOKS	$1.75

Other Mysteries

☐ 05277-9	DOUBLE FOR DEATH	$1.75
☐ 05280-9	RED THREADS	$1.75
☐ 05281-7	THE SOUND OF MURDER	$1.75

Available at your local bookstore or return this form to:

JOVE BOOK MAILING SERVICE
1050 Wall Street West
Lyndhurst, N.J. 07071

Please send me the titles indicated above. I am enclosing $_____ (price indicated plus 50¢ for postage and handling for the first book and 25¢ for each additional book). Send check or money order—no cash or C.O.D.'s please.

NAME_____

ADDRESS_____

CITY_____ STATE/ZIP_____

Allow three weeks for delivery.

SK-18

IAN FLEMING

BOND DOES IT BETTER!

FIND OUT HOW IN:

- ☐ 05519-0 CASINO ROYALE $1.95
- ☐ 05516-6 DIAMONDS ARE FOREVER $1.95
- ☐ 05517-4 DOCTOR NO $1.95
- ☐ 05515-8 FROM RUSSIA, WITH LOVE $1.95
- ☐ 05514-X GOLDFINGER $1.95
- ☐ 05518-2 LIVE AND LET DIE $1.95

Available at your local bookstore or return this form to:

JOVE BOOK MAILING SERVICE
1050 Wall Street West
Lyndhurst, N.J. 07071

Please send me the titles indicated above. I am enclosing $_____ (price indicated plus 50¢ for postage and handling for the first book and 25¢ for each additional book). Send check or money order—no cash or C.O.D.'s please.

NAME _____

ADDRESS _____

CITY _____ STATE/ZIP _____
Allow three weeks for delivery.

SK20